The Spy in
Crinoline

Antonia Ford's
Civil War

To Jenn and Tyler,
Civil War buffs!

Karla Vernon

FIRESIDE FICTION
2006

FIRESIDE FICTION
AN IMPRINT OF HERITAGE BOOKS, INC.

Books, CDs, and more—Worldwide

For our listing of thousands of titles see our website
at
www.HeritageBooks.com

Published 2006 by
HERITAGE BOOKS, INC.
Publishing Division
65 East Main Street
Westminster, Maryland 21157-5026

International Standard Book Number: 0-7884-3642-2

Acknowledgments

Many thanks for the editing done by Nancy Tysdal, Royal Tysdal, Sarah Hamaker, Betsy Dill, Betty Morey, Heidi Graff, Don Hakenson, Pat Furgurson, and Charles Vernon.

Sincere appreciation goes to Capitol Christian Writers and Oakton Glen Book Club for your encouragement and support.

Thank you to Anita Ramos and Brian Conley, librarians in the Virginia Room at Fairfax City Regional Library, and finally, thanks to the Fairfax Museum.

Dedication

This book is dedicated to the memory of our "fallen brave" during the War Between the States. Almost as many American lives were lost during the Civil War as in all other wars combined. Of the 4,137,000 soldiers under arms in both armies, 622,000 died.

The muffled drum's sad roll has beat
The soldier's last tattoo;
No more on Life's parade shall meet
That brave and fallen few.

From "Bivouac of the Dead" by Theodore O'Hara

Table of Contents

Preface

This novel portrays the life of Antonia Ford. I have taken artistic license in Antonia's early years, although she attended the two schools mentioned. All of the battles that occurred in the book are documented events. Most of the letters and documents quoted are authentic. Most of the characters were real people who lived in the towns in which I have portrayed them during that time.

I have a personal interest in the Civil War as two of my great-great-grandfathers fought for the North. On September 8, 1862, their respective regiments, the 7th and 8th of the Maryland Brigade, merged, but I have no evidence that they knew each other.

My great-great-grandfather, William J. Clark, from Cecil County, Maryland, enlisted August 13, 1862 in the 8th Regiment Infantry, Company "A." The army discharged him on May 13, 1865 from Arlington Heights, Virginia, as a sergeant. He lived to be seventy-six.

My great-great-grandfather, William F. Miller, from Unionville, Maryland, enlisted August 18, 1862, in the 7th Regiment Infantry, Company "B," of the Maryland Infantry Volunteers. His discharge as a private occurred at Arlington Heights, Virginia, on May 31, 1865. He lived to be ninety-five.

Prologue

Carroll Prison, May 1863

The first rays of dawn flickered across my face through the barred windows and woke me from a fitful sleep. My toes twitched as a large rat scurried away with something dangling from its mouth. Too accustomed to this scenario to scream, I threw off the meager blanket and sat up. The rat, a mere twelve inches away from me, had a piece of the very dress I wore clenched in its teeth. As the rodent sniffled towards my supply of biscuits hanging in a bag on the wall, I jumped up and stomped my foot. The creature leisurely crept away into a small hole in the wall.

This eight by eight-foot cell had been my bedchamber for the last two months. The dank, musty smell permeated my senses, and I prayed to have the strength to endure another day. Once a robust, healthy twenty-four-year-old with a voluptuous physique, now, I resembled a sickly old woman. No longer did 120 pounds spread over my five-foot-seven frame, as I appeared skinny and felt a great deal weaker. My prized possession, my long mane of golden brown hair, now swung greasy and lank against my face, as I received water for washing only every two weeks. Before my imprisonment, I lived a life of relative luxury and ease, had attended college, and relished my loving parents and siblings, so the daily life of prison was obviously a horrible one for me to experience. At home, our servants took care of my every wish.

Having one sister, at least I was used to sharing a room. My present roommate, Abigail Williams, had been my cellmate almost as long as I have been here, and her story is all too common. She was shaking dust out of a cleaning rag from an upstairs window in her Vienna, Virginia, home, when a Union officer saw her and arrested her for signaling to the enemy. Her protestations of innocence were to no avail, and without even a trial, Northern soldiers imprisoned her in the Carroll Prison in Washington City, along with me and countless other unfortunates.

I, however, am not so innocent, although I pleaded so. My heart and fidelity belong to the Confederate cause. At various times during the war, both Union and Confederate forces held my town of Fairfax Courthouse, Virginia, which, to my dismay, is currently under Union control. My family surreptitiously provides as much information as possible about Federal movements to our contacts within the Rebel forces.

Situated on a steep hill, the Old Capitol Prison, at First and "A" Streets, had once been the U.S. Capitol building with legitimate offices inside. It now contains Confederate soldiers—prisoners of war. Adjoining it is Carroll House, which holds people, such as me, who Northern officials suspect of being sympathetic to the Southern cause. Occasionally a thief, pickpocket, or blockade-runner also is incarcerated here. Each house has two wings, so the center between them forms an exercise yard. Bars on the glassless windows, locks on the doors, and guards in the hallways create my prison.

I walked over to the small table beneath the window, poured some water from the stone jug into a tin cup, and drank the last of it. The other furniture consists of a wooden table and chair, two iron beds each holding a straw mattress, pillow, sheet, and a brown blanket. A brass candlestick and stump of a candle provide the only means of light, other than the meager rays of sunshine struggling in through the window. A looking glass and washstand complete the inventory. My cloak and bonnet hang on a nail protruding from the mildewed wall. Although there is a fireplace, there are no coal ashes to indicate a recent fire. Now that it is May, our jailers no longer supply coal to us, although the temperature is still chilly at night.

I have observed that guards treated the officers and civilians better than they treated the enlisted soldiers. Prison officials give preferential treatment to rich or influential prisoners by allowing amenities such as books, writing materials, and food from home in their cells. Affluent prisoners, like me, may have clothes, a daily paper, and baskets of provisions delivered. While my cell is sub-standard, I heard tales of far worse conditions from other women housed here. Guards took attendance twice a day, at nine o'clock.

At three o'clock each day, dinner arrived. It usually consisted of some kind of soup, such as beef and carrot. Other times, the cooks provided chicken, along with boiled corn and tomatoes. Irish stew and potatoes was another favorite. Black wheat bread and a little pat of butter always accompanied the meal. Sometimes fruit, such as cantaloupe, peaches, pears, or grapes appeared. This bill of fare, though not too terrible, never varied, and I was often hungry. Supper at eight o'clock consisted of weak coffee, a bowl of something slimy and sweet, and half a cup of milk. The dishes, cups, and utensils were routinely unclean—I suppose there was no one to wash them.

My roommate stirred and spoke to me in a raspy voice, evidence of her illness. For a week, she has had trouble forcing even a bit of gruel down her throat.

"Antonia, maybe today will be our liberation day."

"It is my fervent wish that both of us might receive a pardon today. I have a friend who is working on our release as we speak. For your sake, you need to try to eat more and take as many fluids as you can, as I see you are getting weaker day by day."

"I fear," she continued, "that I will not leave this place alive. Last night I dreamed that my mother and father were calling to me from somewhere far off."

This sent a shiver through me, as I too, feared that she did not have long to live. I believe that she had typhoid fever, which doctors here commonly refer to as "prison fever."

I felt the compulsion to give her hope, however. "Your husband and child await you at home. They miss and love you very much."

"Oh, if only I could see my loved ones again," she said. "The authorities last allowed them to visit me two weeks ago, and I miss them sorely. My youngest, Betsy, is probably toddling around the house now. I could have brought her with me, but didn't want to expose her to the poor conditions here."

"Why would anyone bring a child here?"

"If the husband is away at war, or the woman is a widow, she has no choice. There indeed have been a few children housed here recently."

At that moment, a footstep outside the cell door alerted us that someone was nearby our first floor cell. We were aware throughout our ordeal that certain guards enjoyed a perverse pleasure in spying upon us. When we washed or changed clothes, we closed our door, which seemed to be a cue for the guards to peep at us. I was tempted to jab the end of my ink pen through the peephole in the door, but fear of terrible reprisals prevented me from doing so. Often our door is wide open, as only punished prisoners remain locked inside their cells. A tin basin in one corner of the room serves as our privy at night, when peering eyes from the outside cannot see us. During the day, we have free access to the privy outside.

"Is someone there?" I shouted. I received no answer, but a sound of receding footsteps verified that our peeping Tom had moved on to more interesting subjects. More footsteps approached, the door opened, and a pair of hands placed two bowls of gruel and some stale crusts of bread on the floor inside our cell.

"Eat heartily, ladies," muttered the female servant.

"May we have some clean water?" I asked.

"I'll see what I can do," she replied.

Authorities permit inmates to keep small cakes and other non-perishable items in their cells as supplements. Abigail still had some left from her husband's last visit, and willingly shared them with me.

Many hours passed before the servant finally returned with a bucket of water. She left it inside our door and I cautiously looked within. Floating on top of the brownish-colored water were the ever-present dead maggots. I placed a piece of cloth, which I saved for this purpose, over the top of another bucket and strained the water as best I could. When it was as clean as I could get it, we drank.

I asked Abigail, "Do you feel like exercising for a few minutes in the yard outside?"

She wearily replied, "Whether I do or not, let us go out to receive some fresh air."

Besides exercise, I had a second motive for going outside. I always eagerly looked for my father and other villagers whom I know, especially

Preston Grigsby and Thomas Love. We were all prisoners. Union officers arrested us shortly after the March 8, 1863, raid on Fairfax Courthouse, when Confederate Captain Mosby and his men captured Union General Stoughton. My accusers claimed I "gave information" leading to the raid, but I received no trial to prove my innocence or guilt.

Soon, a guard indicated that we could leave our room to exercise. After walking around the courtyard for ten minutes, I felt disappointed to find that my father and friends were nowhere in sight. We then returned to our cell, where I took up ink pen and paper to write to my mother. I next met with a visitor who provoked a migraine headache forcing me to lie down. When I awoke, I then returned to the table to nibble on some bread. I had just begun when the door suddenly crashed open. Hands raised me from my chair, as Abigail watched with a look of horror on her face.

"Unhand me, sir," I demanded.

As the guard hustled me out without a word, I trembled to think what would happen next.

Chapter One

Coombe Cottage, May 1854

I just finished my art lesson and my busy school day finally ended. My other courses consisted of history, geography, science, grammar, mathematics, music, writing, and, of course, the Bible. Mrs. Baker, my English teacher and the school administrator, was bedridden with an illness, so another instructor orally tested me today in English, my best subject, and I knew that I had received high marks. I spent seven hours receiving instruction at the school each day, with one-half hour for lunch and recess. I enjoyed school—learning new things excited me and opened up worlds beyond what I could even imagine. This was my last month of the two-year school, and I would miss some of the girls who lived far away.

The private finishing school that I attended, Coombe Cottage, was the first of its type in Fairfax County. I felt privileged not only to be obtaining such a fine education, but also thankful that my father could afford the one hundred dollars per year that paid for tuition, room, and board. Rose Love and I, both sixteen, boarded at the school although we lived only a short walk away in our village of Fairfax Courthouse, Virginia.

We were going for a weekend visit to our respective families. It had rained today, keeping us indoors, and I was thankful to be outside breathing the fresh, spring air. I called good day to Frances Carper and other fellow students and departed with my best friend, leisurely walking on muddy Fairfax Street toward Zion Episcopal Church and the Gunnell's home. Although my family was Presbyterian, we often attended the Zion Church, as it was the only church in the village. I enjoyed the singing, and occasionally felt intellectually stimulated by Reverend Brown's message, but I could not say that I believed everything he said. Rose's family also attended there.

"Isn't Frances Carper a lovely person," I gushed to Rose. "When I first met her, even before talking to her, I immediately knew that she would be amiable. Often, I take an instant dislike to other girls before even getting to know them. I wonder why that is?"

"I think it is their eyes," said Rose.

"Whatever do you mean?" I asked.

"I can see kindness and sincerity in peoples' eyes. I believe that if we look beyond superficial beauty and stare straight into eyes, we can discern a person's true character."

"I'll remember to always look at eyes," I said thoughtfully.

"I wonder if Charles is helping your father in his shop after school today," Rose pondered.

Fourteen-year-old Charlie, my closest brother, had been part of our childhood band of friends. I suspected that Rose liked him more than she cared to admit. My father, E.R., was a well-known and affluent merchant in Fairfax Courthouse, population 250. There were about fifty wood-frame houses in our small, but growing town. Father's one-room mercantile store, one of three in the village, along with four taverns, a public grammar school, and Coombe Cottage made up the non-residential buildings. His store, located on Fairfax Street, contained such merchandise as clothing, farming implements, household goods, fabrics, and all sorts of miscellaneous items.

We were fortunate to have such easy access to the finer things in life. E.R., an indulgent husband and father, provided a comfortable, happy home. In addition to being a good businessman, he was also the handsomest man in town, tall and slender, with dark hair and brown eyes. When he smiled, the room lit up along with him—he exuded such good cheer and warmth to those around him. Father was a true Southern gentleman.

"It is a good guess that Charlie is working in the store," I answered. "He has been spending more and more time there since he has outgrown his boyish pursuits. I will miss his shenanigans, like scaring us with frogs, and jumping down from trees in front of us as we walk below. I suppose that now he will have to surprise us with the new parasol, called an umbrella. Father has just received some for the store."

"They are able to repel the rain," Rose commented.

We walked further on, turned the corner, and leisurely strolled past the courthouse. I had just transitioned from a back-to-front fastening bodice with a corset underneath and thought myself quite the grown-up young woman. It could not hurt to practice my womanly walk and coquettish mannerisms—just in case a handsome young man should cross my path. I prided myself on my golden brown hair. Prone to be a bit vain, I consoled myself with the knowledge that the Bible did state that a woman's long hair "is a glory to her." Why then must I wear it tied back or pinned up?

"Tell me, Rose," I asked, "do I look like a proper mademoiselle?"

"Oh yes, Antonia. If only I could have your elegant, refined features, large brown eyes, and beautiful figure and posture!"

I knew what she would say, for others had told me repeatedly throughout my life that I was an attractive and cultivated girl. I still needed to hear it—call it vanity, or pride.

Rose was rather plain-faced and timid with too-close brown eyes and mousy hair. Her legs were spindly and she had crooked teeth. Her personality and kind-heartedness more than made up for her faults, and I hoped that I could be so pious someday. Although I believed in God, I did not have the faith in Jesus that Rose and my mother had. I almost envied the simple beliefs and faithfulness that I saw in other people. Provable facts were important to me. How mind relieving and soothing to my soul it would be to just flow with the crowd and adopt the most popular beliefs of the day! My father always told me that my freethinking and spontaneity would get me in trouble some day. I hoped that he was wrong.

As we approached the corner and turned left onto Payne Street, where I lived, I saw my six-year-old sister, Pattie. She was playing graces with Mary, the six-year-old daughter of one of our slaves. The hoop got loose and headed toward us. Our beloved golden retriever, Star, barked excitedly as she chased after the hoop. I hugged her as she came up to me.

Rose laughed as she rolled the hoop back to Mary, who was wildly waving her stick. "Don't worry; you'll get better at the game as you get older," she called.

They ran away screaming, and I bid my friend goodbye and lifted my cotton skirt and petticoats to ascend the brick steps leading to the front door. Our house had a steep, hipped roof with a widow's walk. The front porch extended all the way across the front of the house. Two Windsor settees made out of bamboo adorned the porch.

It was a pleasant day, and the door remained open to let a breeze flow through the house. Mary's two sisters, aged nine and three, ran out the door as I entered and I immediately saw Mother in the parlor to the left, sitting in her favorite chair by the window, working on her quilt. Although not classically beautiful, she was nevertheless attractive—tall and stately, with light brown hair and refined features. Her fair, smooth complexion and sparkling hazel eyes attracted attention. A fine quilter, Mother sewed six even stitches to the inch, as a rule. The Ohio Star patterned quilt she was working on was all linsey-woolsey and cotton patches made from deep yellow greens, Prussian blues, Turkey reds, brown, and ombre. Although she took some of the patches from worn out clothes, many of our fabrics were store-bought. She preferred to make the entire quilt by hand, even though we had a Singer sewing machine. She said that it had a calming effect on her. Mother could also spin her own wool and flax, and knew all of the needle arts.

"How was school today, Antonia? May I help you with any of your schoolwork? Did you do well on your English exam?"

Although I attended school starting from age six, Mother tutored all of us whenever we needed help.

"You know I did well, Mother. English is the one subject that sings to my soul. May I piece together part of your quilt?"

"Yes, here is a needle, thread and two blocks. Pray sit down. Thank you, Daughter, for working willingly with your hands, as the Bible instructs us," she said to me in her melodious voice.

Picking up a pin from the floor, I chanted, "Find a pin and pick it up, all that day you'll have good luck."

I sat next to her in the other chair and began to sew. I thought my mother to be ideal because she enjoyed her role as wife and mother, and performed her tasks with ease. An economical house manager, she was quite devoted to me and my brothers and sister. She wore an indigo blue, floral cotton day dress that I particularly liked. The sleeves were close fitting and the dress had a pleated front. Mother's crinoline hoop skirt made her dress protrude in front of her.

"Mother, I made a small mistake in my stitch length. Should I pick it out?"

"No, the quilt should never be perfect, because only God can make things that are perfect."

After an hour, I set aside my quilting, and picked up the *Young Lady's Counselor*. The book, a guide to "true happiness," was a recent gift from my father. I was lost in the advice it put forth when Mother spoke.

"I saw a notice in *The Alexandria Gazette* today advertising the next term at the Buckingham Female Collegiate Institute. The term of five months starts next January. Father and I would like you to attend. Your cousin, Virginia Sangster, attended there seven years ago."

"Oh yes, Mother! Thank you."

I could barely contain my excitement. I had heard of the college for women in Gravel Hill, Virginia, but had not discussed it more than in passing with my parents. Perhaps in three months, I would make the arduous 127-mile trip by rail and coach to the backwards town of Gravel Hill. I would live away from home for the first time, and be on my own to make my own decisions.

"Too bad only girls attend there," I murmured softly to myself, wondering whether I thought too much about men and intimacy. I knew in my heart that it was not a proper way to think, although it was socially proper to portray the Southern belle to society. Virtue and modesty should be my guiding principles in everyday actions. It was important to learn deportment, and my mother was a patient teacher in that and all the other social graces I needed to know. I shifted my attention to my brothers, Charles, and nine-year-old Clarenville, and got up to greet them as they noisily entered the house. We called Clarenville "Clanie."

I paused by the hallway mirror and gazed at the reflection of a contented sixteen-year-old girl with brown sparkling eyes, surrounded by long, heavy lashes. My nose was not perfect, but I had no complaint. My full, pouty lips naturally curved up at the corners, giving me a happy countenance. I parted my golden hair down the middle and gathered it in a loose knot near the nape of my neck, as was the style. Overall, I could not complain about my lot in life.

Chapter Two

Horseback Riding, June 1854

Being mid-June, school was over, and I had the summer off before attending college in January. One of our slaves, Mathilde, quite talented as a dressmaker, sewed some new fashions for me. I thought to myself that I would be the best-dressed girl in school.

I decided to take advantage of the lovely day outside by enjoying a buggy ride. Rose joined me, and we made our way to the nearby barn where the buggy awaited us. We passed the summer kitchen and privy behind the house. Our livery boy, and all-around errand boy, James Norton, had everything prepared. James readied Molly, our sturdy horse, and Rose and I climbed into the open buggy with as much decorum as our long skirts allowed. With the reins firmly in my hands, I steered us down the lane. As we rounded the corner, I stopped the buggy, handed the reins over to Rose, and jumped down to the ground. Gathering my skirts up above my knees, I helped myself up onto Molly by bracing my leg against the buggy and swinging gracefully astride the gentle mare.

"Antonia Jane," Rose admonished, "no genteel lady would be seen riding astride a horse. What are you thinking?"

"That's what you say every time, dear friend. I can assure you that no wanton thoughts have ever popped into my head as a result of this activity."

She continued, "Wanton thoughts are not the worst of it. I suspect you have them, regardless. My mother always warned me of irreparable harm to our womanly areas."

"Ha!" I exclaimed. "You are such a prude. It will take more than a horse's back to de-flower me. Riding sidesaddle is not only uncomfortable and unnatural; it is quite unsafe, especially with no saddle on the horse. If society meant for all people to ride sidesaddle, men would be doing it too."

"But of course you realize that riding astride is more natural for men, as they don't have long skirts to maneuver," Rose commented.

"Alas, yes, you're right about that. I would like to own a pair of the waist overalls that Mr. Levi Strauss in San Francisco has designed," I replied. "How it would simplify my life."

"Again, you shock me with your wild and unconventional ideas."

"You should try it, Rose. It's freeing." I steered my gentle mare off the main road and across a field, heading for a narrow road that winded through the forest. We traveled about a mile. I felt open to share my inner thoughts to Rose—she and I being that close. Society frowned on speaking frankly about sexual and personal matters, but I figured close female friends had done so anyway since time began—how else would one learn?

"I love our village in the springtime!" I exclaimed to Rose. "The dogwoods and wild geraniums are my favorites. Such a fresh smell assails me and awakens all my senses."

"You are so poetic. Perhaps writing should be your hobby."

"Perhaps," I said. "I imagine I could earn some money by writing one day."

"I don't intend on ever having to earn money," Rose responded emphatically. "I hope that my husband will provide for me."

"Speaking of men, have you seen Reverend Boyton since he shaved his whiskers?" I asked.

"Yes, I attended a recent religious revival that he conducted. He is so masterful, but too old for me, I'm afraid. He won't be a bachelor long, I suspect."

"I have enticed Frances Carper to visit me with the promise that she would be able to see the new Reverend Boyton."

We meandered contentedly along the lane in silence, happy to be alive.

I twirled a buttercup under my chin and asked Rose, "Do you see yellow reflected on my face?"

"Yes, I do. It means you like butter, you superstitious old thing, you."

"Superstitions are fun, as long as they are not evil. The tea leaves left in my teacup this morning were in a straight line, meaning that I would go on a journey soon. Of course, that must mean my college trip. I sure wish you were going with me, Rose," I said. "Charlie teases me and says that the only education I need is for the bedroom and parlor, and to be an educated mother to my children."

"It's true that many men are ruined as boys by having an ignorant mother who diseases their minds," she replied hesitantly. "I'm quite sure that our children will have ideal models in us. What I like about you, Antonia, is that you have a definite moral sense of what is right and what is wrong. You are not at all equivocal about decisions or preferences, seeing everything as either black or white. I, on the other hand, see everything as gray and have a terrible time making any kind of decision."

We heard voices approaching us on the lane.

"Look who is coming!" Rose exclaimed, and our thought-provoking conversation ended.

Walking toward us were her brother, Robert Love, thirteen, and his friend, Lewis Helm, eighteen. Lewis was staying with the Love family for a few days, as his family lived in Loudoun County and he was here on business for his father, Joseph. The Helms were a congenial family, and along with Rose's family, the Loves, were close friends to my family. Most of the neighboring men farmed, and Lewis was learning the business to take over the family farm someday.

"Good afternoon, ladies," greeted Lewis. "It's a fine spring day for planting, bareback riding, or any other outdoor activity. Seeing the two of you in front of me, like visions from heaven, makes this pleasant day even more charming."

Lewis, six feet tall, dark haired, blue eyed, and very handsome, attracted notice wherever he went. My heart started to pound despite seeing him in his dirty, everyday work clothes, and needing a haircut and shave.

Robert only glanced between Lewis and us with a wide grin on his face. The subtleties of flirting were only beginning to dawn on him. Although he had an elder brother, James, to "show him the way," he remained naïve in many ways. I wondered if Lewis had confided in him about any romantic interests in passing.

"How are you?" I answered Lewis. Normally, a socially correct woman would not speak to a passerby on the street, especially if she was not the one to initiate the conversation. I, however, followed my own path, and reasoned that in the backwoods of Virginia, greeting neighbors with whom I had played all my life, did not count. Lewis held out his hand to Rose, who climbed down from the cart.

Reaching down to pick some sassafras in the woods, Robert suddenly exclaimed, "I just stepped on a snake hiding amidst the sassafras!"

Before I could admonish him to get away, the pit viper struck and bit Robert on his ankle. He shrieked from the painful bite and fell to the ground, groaning and grasping his ankle. The look on his face would have been amusing, if I had not seen the twenty-six inch snake slithering away. It was a Copperhead, also known as Highland Moccasin, unmistakable with its broad, triangular, copper-colored head, vertically elliptical pupils, and grayish brown with reddish-brown cross bands. Copperheads were endemic to our rocky and forested "neck of the woods," and were poisonous, but rarely caused fatalities, due to their small size. What worried me, however, was the place where the snake had bitten Robert. It was into his ankle— possibly the vein. This meant that the venom could be traveling toward his heart. There was not a moment to lose. I jumped down off my horse and ran to him.

"Robert," I said urgently, "can you hear me?"

Robert was lying on the ground, showing lassitude and shortness of breath.

"I'm fine," he said weakly. "Just get me home, please." By this time, the tissue near the wound site had turned a dark-purplish color. I knew that the venom caused blood and tissue poisoning, and turned questionably toward Lewis.

Lewis took charge. "Antonia," he urgently commanded, "hand me something clean I can use to constrict the blood flow above the bite."

Eschewing modesty, I shoved my dress thigh-high, exposing my bare leg, and yanked at one of my petticoats as hard as I could, ripping up the side of it and across and down the other side. I handed it to Lewis who applied it tightly above the ankle, but not as tightly as he would a tourniquet.

Using his knife, he made cross incisions one-quarter inch deep over the fang marks.

Lewis explained, "The venom must be sucked out."

"I will do it," I said, leaning toward the wound.

"Never," he said. "That is far too unladylike for you."

He sucked out the venom, consisting of mixed blood and lymph tissue, and spat the evacuated material into the bushes. As the swelling grew and spread ever higher, he continued to make similar cross incisions over the swollen area and repeated the onerous process. After ten such incisions, I said, "We need to get Robert to the doctor immediately." I got into the cart and then Lewis hoisted Robert into the cart with his head on my lap. Logic told me to keep the affected limb lower than his heart and I applied a little pressure to the wound. I coerced Rose to climb onto Molly's back, and Lewis and I, with Robert between us, rapidly returned to the village to the home of our doctor, William Gunnell.

Dr. Gunnell's office was located in his house. An outside door provided privacy for his family from the villagers seeking aid. One of the family's slaves, Winny, was hanging out laundry when she saw our situation and dropped everything to alert the doctor that we were coming.

Lewis and I supported Robert as we brought him inside and we quickly told Dr. Gunnell what had happened and what we had done to help Robert.

"Your quick action probably saved his life," Dr. Gunnell said. "I have seen copperhead bites before, but the particular location of this bite makes it deadly."

The doctor applied medicines, wrapped the wound, and gave instructions for Robert's care at home. The danger being over, we prepared to go home, our happy outing ruined. As I stepped through the door, I stumbled slightly over the raised threshold. Lewis reached out and steadied me by grabbing my shoulders. He held onto me a second longer than necessary. I thought to myself, "Maybe, just maybe, he will be a future suitor. He is indeed a kind person." I had a premonition that future events would intertwine us.

Chapter Three

Train Traveling to Buckingham, 1855

The day finally arrived. It was Monday, January 1, 1855, and I had packed my luggage with a new wardrobe suitable for a girl attending college. I slept fitfully last night, worrying about the dangers of traveling and unexpected delays. I had never been away from home for an extended period and feared being homesick.

Father pre-paid my bill for the next five months—$260 covered my tuition, room, and board, including fuel, oil lamps, candles, servant's ministrations, and washing and ironing of clothes. I had been up since six o'clock, as we had to be at Fairfax Station at seven-thirty for the train ride to Gordonsville, Virginia. The Orange and Alexandria Railroad just completed that route one year ago. Even so, the journey would take all day to get to the remote area of Gravel Hill, Virginia, where the Buckingham Female Collegiate Institute was located. It was 127 miles from Fairfax Courthouse, on the Richmond-Lynchburg stagecoach route. We would travel the last forty-six miles by stagecoach.

Porters would serve breakfast to us on the train, but Mother packed us a snack to take along for the coach part of the journey. Charlie loaded up the buggy to take us to Fairfax Station, where Father and I would board the train. Charlie closely resembled Father—tall and slim with dark hair and eyes. His thin face was clean-shaven except for a mustache.

He said to me, "I hope you have as good an experience at college as our cousin, Virginia Sangster. She has remarked on more than one occasion about the quality of the instructors, as they are often University of Virginia graduates."

Father replied, "I'm sure the quality has only improved in the seven years since she attended."

"Imagine, it took two and one-half days for her to get there, and it will take me only four hours by train and another thirteen hours by coach," I said.

We arrived at Fairfax Station in plenty of time for the seven-thirty departure. We found a few houses scattered around, but no real train depot—only a covered area with a bench to sit on. The train, which had left Alexandria at seven o'clock, was due any moment. Soon we heard the great shriek of the locomotive and a clanging bell that shattered the silence. Commonly known as a "4-4-0," the massive train came into view. These numbers described the wheel arrangement according to a system of steam locomotive classification. The first number indicated the number of wheels on the leading truck; the second listed the driving wheels; the last number the wheels on a railing axle.

We poked our heads into the gentlemen's car, where everyone smoked, and disgusting overflowing cuspidors were present. A rough-looking man spit a thin brown stream into one as I watched, repulsed. A porter directed us to the more genteel ladies' car, where both women and non-smoking men could sit. Father lifted my bags to the porter who stored them for us. Fifty people could fit in a car, and the well-upholstered seats were crosswise, each holding two persons. A narrow passage bisected the car, and a door stood at either end. Located in the center of the coach, a stove burned furiously, while greasy kerosene lanterns hung above the aisles. We sat in the middle of the car, and I slid into the window seat.

The courteous and hospitable conductor poked his head into our compartment to collect our fares of three dollars and fifty cents each, and remarked, "Welcome and enjoy your journey. William Mason designed this locomotive. Notice the highly varnished mahogany wood on the walls. We can reach speeds of sixty miles per hour, but our average is about twenty-five in good weather."

Father replied, "Thank you. We do have good fortune to opportune ourselves to the superior speed, safety, and comfort of this magnificent conveyance." He turned to me and inquired, "Did you know that the United States leads the world in railroad accidents?"

I nodded affirmatively, then laughed to myself. Father could be all-knowing at times. After all, this, his first train journey, certainly made him no expert on trains. I looked around the coach, then put my head on his shoulder and whispered into his ear, "There are some unattended ladies on this train."

Father murmured back, "Yes, it is happening more and more frequently, but I doubt any of them are as young as you."

Actually, at seventeen, I was relieved to have my escort with me, and prepared myself for the start of my journey. With a great lurch, the train started moving on a single track of rails, gathering speed rapidly. Looking around, I noticed that this car was about one-half full, with well-dressed people, for the most part. I supposed the fare kept the "riff-raff" away. A great many people were reading their newspapers, as was Father. The young porter started to distribute breakfast to the passengers. The meal consisted of hot tea, bread, cheese, cured ham, and fruit.

"Good morning, miss," he said to me with a charming smile. "Would you care for a breakfast?"

"Good morning, sir," I replied. "Yes, please." I contentedly started to eat, while gazing at the passing scenery. Mile after mile we traveled on through woods, hills, and farmland observing scenery much the same as the previous mile, but I enjoyed it nonetheless. We passed Sangster's Station, which consisted of a sign, water tank, and large piles of wood. We crossed the rickety bridge over Bull Run at Union Mills.

Soon we arrived at Manassas Junction. The depot was a one-story log building, about seventy-five feet long. Besides the depot, a new-looking hostelry and a few cottages marked the fledgling town. Several people boarded the train and we resumed our journey. We passed turnpike roads that for the most part had no gates or signals. The railroad-crossing gate, a relatively new invention, had not been implemented at every crossroad yet. I read the sign at one of these crossroads, "When the bell rings, look out for the locomotive." We passed a wooden bridge, serenely shading a rippling brook. Two young boys fished from the bridge, holding their wooden sticks with serious dedication to their task.

Faster than I could believe possible, we arrived at the train station in Warrenton. Some passengers discharged, and others joined us. After a ten-minute wait, we traveled onward to stops at Culpeper and Orange. The station at Orange, constructed of brick and iron, stood as a security against fire. We got out to stretch at Orange, and to use the outhouses near the station house. I had learned that car designers were just beginning to consider the "bodily needs" of passengers for long train journeys. One of the cars in our train had a lavatory, but for the most part, it was only in first-class coaches on trains that traveled much further distances than the one on which we traveled. Some companies went to extraordinary lengths to disguise the presence of such essential conveniences. Polite society was aghast, of course, that the topic of bodily needs was even raised. Naturally, lavatories took up space on the train, and were not revenue earners. I, personally, thought it was a sensible idea.

I enjoyed the time to myself, contemplating life. At home, I kept busy watching and playing with my siblings, or going to school, so free time seemed a luxury to me. I had a calm personality, good sense of humor, and loved games and pranks. I had never gotten into trouble with my parents, and didn't sneak or lie—it was against my nature. I had an intellectual curiosity about the world, more than any woman should have, which worried my mother, in particular. I called her old-fashioned, and she said I didn't "know my place." I believed myself to be forward-thinking and considered greater equality between the sexes desirable. For example, I maintained that the *Married Woman's Property Act*, as amended in 1849 in New York, benefited women in a positive way by allowing them more rights. Mother insisted, however, that the rights were burdens, better handled by men. I kept my views to myself when around Mother, but Father was more open to these discussions.

We had traveled for almost four hours and were approaching Gordonsville, the end of the line. The train slowed, and people were putting away their newspapers and gathering their belongings. Suddenly, the door at the forward part of the car burst open and an unruly character stumbled on-board towards us. Dressed in raggedy clothing, with stubble of beard, he appeared to be in his twenties. Father and I had previously exchanged places, and I sat on the aisle seat now. He glanced hastily around, spied my handbag, and reached down low for it. Without thinking, I jammed the point of my elbow upward as hard as I could, ramming his nose, and causing him to yowl and back away as blood trickled down his face. I cowered as Father stood up to protect me, but it proved unnecessary. Seeing a man's portfolio within hand's grasp, the thief grabbed it and exited the train by jumping far and rolling as he landed. He quickly regained his feet and ran into the woods, as swiftly as a deer. We could observe all this from our window. A few women were screaming by this time, and the victim blustered to the porter about the outrage of having his portfolio taken by the thief. The porter, clearly upset, stated, "This has never happened on this line before. We will notify the authorities once we stop."

It all happened so quickly, that Father and I just looked at each other in amazement. We had not reached the station yet, but the thief was long gone. I felt shaken, and grateful more than ever that Father was with me.

Chapter Four

Stagecoach Traveling to Buckingham, 1855

A s we approached the Gordonsville station and stopped, the scent of fried chicken in the air meant that the chicken vendors awaited us. Negro women with balanced platters of fried chicken on their heads served hungry passengers, like us, through open windows.

"Get your fried chicken here," shouted a vendor.

Father reached through, gave her some money, and our food was then passed back to us. We hurriedly closed the windows, as frigid air was blowing inside.

After we exited the train, we waited in the station for the stagecoach, along with two others. Father piled up my bags neatly, nearby.

Thirty-minutes later, a coach with six horses approached in a cloud of dust. We expected a thirteen-hour journey, as the stagecoach traveled only three and one-half miles per hour in the summer—even less now that it was winter. As the coach pulled up, we saw that there were already six passengers inside—three men and three women, and two men on the seat with the driver.

The driver's seat was the most desirable location, to reduce the bumps and jars over rough roads, but women were relegated to the inside seats. To reduce jolting, two leather straps known as the "thorough braces," which caused the coach to rock, rather than spring, braced the body of the coach. The coach accommodated fourteen passengers, besides luggage, post and the driver. Looking inside, I could see that each of the four fifteen-inch seats had room for three passengers.

The fare was five cents per mile, which made the cost of our journey two dollars and thirty-cents each for the forty-six miles we had to travel. My luggage exceeded the twenty-five pound limit, so Father had to pay an extra charge. Leather shades were available on the windows to block the sun and road dust. The driver scheduled a stop midway in the town of Rockaway, after traveling six and one-half hours.

The rotund driver, red-faced and whiskered, appeared slightly drunk to me, as he stood unsteadily on his seat and gave us new passengers a tirade of instructions:

> If a team runs away, sit still and take your chances. If you jump, nine times out of ten you will be hurt. Be sure to get out and stretch at Rockaway, and get some food if you wish.
>
> Don't keep the stage waiting.
>
> Don't smoke a strong pipe until after noon, and spit on the leeward side of the coach. If you have anything to take in a bottle, be sure to

pass it around, especially to me.

Don't swear, nor lop over on your neighbor when sleeping.

Don't ask how far it is to the next station until you get there.

Never attempt to fire a gun or pistol while on the road, it may frighten the team; and the careless handling and cocking of the weapon makes nervous people nervous.

Don't discuss politics or religion, nor point out places on the road where horrible murders have been committed.

Don't linger too long at the pewter wash basin at the station. Tie a silk handkerchief around your neck to keep out dust and prevent sunburns. A little glycerin is good in case of chapped hands.

Don't imagine for a moment you are going on a picnic; expect annoyance, discomfort, and some hardships. If you are disappointed, thank heaven.

Father had previously traveled by stagecoach, and had warned me that this would be an arduous journey, so I prepared for the worst. We ate our chicken meals at Rockaway, used the facilities, and then continued. Another father and daughter pair was now on the coach; they were going to Lynchburg.

The day wore on interminably, and I actually started feeling nauseous with all the jostling, as we hit rut after rut. The roads on the way to the school were soft, red clay, and very uneven and unpredictable. Deep gouges and mud potholes threatened the coach wheels at every bump. The scenery became more wild and beautiful the closer we came to our destination, with awesome mountains off in the distance. As we passed the town of Palmyra, we came to a scenic river called the Rivanna River. We crossed over the wobbly bridge and a stunning view revealed itself in every direction. It brightened my day considerably, and inspired me to draw it.

As nightfall approached, the roads did indeed get worse, and sometimes I felt that a particularly large rut would throw me right out of the carriage. My derrière ached, and the jostling of the coach pained my neck.

"Father, tell the driver to pull over! I'm going to be sick."

"Driver," he yelled, "stop the coach. My daughter is going to retch."

"Can't she stick her head out of the window?" the driver crossly responded.

"Don't be crass, man," replied Father angrily.

The driver grudgingly stopped, and after a brief rest, we continued.

"Hold on tight, Antonia," Father said. "With the darkening sky, it is more difficult to avoid the large potholes."

The past three miles had been particularly rough since we had left the main traveling road. We went around a curve through a wooded glen, and came upon a tavern and store on the right, lit by an oil lamp hanging outside. On the left, a stone wall enclosed what had to be the school, as I clearly saw the words "Buckingham Female Collegiate Academy" on a plaque. The oil lamp, still burning brightly, seemed rather unusual to me, as it was now midnight.

"Father, the school is obviously expecting late travelers."

"Let us out at the school," Father told the coachman.

The coachman complied by jumping down and opening the gate, so the coach could pass through. He then deposited us in front of the main building and removed our bags. He bid us farewell and left after assuring Father that he would stop again to take him back to Gordonsville the next day.

Father and I walked up the steps to the front door of the building and knocked on the door. A house slave, who curtsied as she opened the door, let us in.

"Welcome. My name is Sadie," she informed us.

We stood in the walnut paneled principal hall ornamented by carved cornices of great majesty. Along the sidewalls were ionic pilasters of pine, painted white, and the doorway had an ionic treatment. We gazed up at the ceiling of the hall to see a fanciful creation of modeled plaster. The staircases rising to the right and left were especially stately, shaped like hourglasses. Lit candles, in handsome brass candlesticks, hung throughout the hall, burning brightly. A large oil painting caught my eye by its tranquility. On closer inspection, the plaque indicated that it represented the settlement of Buckingham. The other wall displayed two steel engravings: one of the death of John Wesley and the other of the landing of the Pilgrims.

"In this hall," Sadie said, "the girls assemble for morning prayers."

I groaned inwardly, hoping that a nun-like life was not to be my future.

On either side of the hall, two library rooms displayed shelves, which must have held at least three thousand books in gleaming walnut cases.

"Most of these books were donated by Buckingham donors," Sadie told us.

She told us to wait there while she went to get "old Marster," Dr. Blackwell.

A tall, distinguished, dark-haired man, about forty-five years of age and formally dressed, walked towards us. His mustache and sideburns were neat and trimmed meticulously.

"I am the Reverend Doctor John Blackwell, the president of this collegiate institute. Good evening and welcome!"

Father shook Dr. Blackwell's hand and said, "I am very pleased to meet you. I am E.R. Ford, and this is my daughter, Miss Antonia Ford."

Dr. Blackwell bowed.

I said, "It is a pleasure to be here, sir, after traveling all day. We have been admiring the beautiful architecture, both inside and out."

"Yes, I have to admit that it is indeed a sight to behold. The building, built in 1837 on 120 acres, was the first chartered women's college in Virginia. It is 180 feet in length by thirty-six feet in width. It contains fifty-two rooms; some of them large lecture rooms. Enough about the place right now—you must both be very tired after your journey today. Miss Ford, I will have one of the servants show you to your dormitory, and have her help you with your bags. Mr. Ford, will you be staying the night at Mr. West's tavern?"

"Yes. I am pleased that it is just across the road. I also have to set up credit for Antonia at Mr. West's Buckingham Institute Store before I leave. The coachman will return for me tomorrow morning."

"Most of the girls have already arrived, and their escorts have left for home. A few girls will arrive tomorrow morning. You will find that Mr. West always busily runs his store and tavern because of this Richmond-Lynchburg stage route. Mr. Ford, won't you come back tomorrow morning to see more of the school and the grounds in the daylight?"

"Yes, I will be back."

I went to Father and kissed him. "See you tomorrow morning."

Dr. Blackwell asked Sadie, "Will you show Miss Ford to her room?"

"Yes, sir," she replied promptly.

Sadie led the way up the right hand flight of stairs, carrying one of my bags. We then turned right and walked a short way down a corridor to one of the dormitories.

She told me, "Mrs. Goff and old Marster's wife, Ol' Miss, are in charge of boarders. Mrs. Goff will give you the house rules tomorrow."

We entered the second door on the left. Sadie handed me my bag, and used safety matches to light the room's oil lamp. I observed four walnut bedsteads in this particular room with stenciled chairs, Boston rockers, and a walnut washstand. French prints graced the wall, between which hung brass candlesticks. Of course, a fireplace held a predominant place, embers glowing steadily. A frigid trickle of air flowed in through the cracked window. It appeared that the other women had already taken three of the four beds, so the remaining one near the window was mine. I placed my luggage there and bade Sadie goodnight. I unpacked my nightgown, changed, extinguished the oil lamp, and went immediately to bed, prayerfully thanking God for safe passage.

Chapter Five

Buckingham Female Collegiate Institute, 1855

The next morning I awoke early, peered out the window, and immediately felt depressed to see barren trees and red clay, the grass ugly and yellowed. Despite my initial reaction, I quickly dressed and put on my warm cloak, and without waking the three other women, ran down the hall and stairs. I fumbled with the doorknob of the front door in my excitement to see the grounds. Immediately before me, rows of holly trees surrounded a slate terrace. Farther on, a lane bisected what would be a meticulously manicured lawn in the spring. A long, tunnel-shaped rose arbor enclosed the lane for a few yards. I ran towards the tunnel, and turned back to gaze at the building. Behind the terrace, the main brick building seemed massive to my eyes. It stood three stories high, with wings of two stories. I walked back and saw a quaint little cottage located adjacent to the right wing with a sign, "President's Cottage." Some small boxwood edged a curvaceous brick walk, which led to a cozy white summerhouse. Many strategically placed small benches stood arranged around the brick walk for the students' leisure.

I walked to the back of the main building and saw the brick kitchen, the barn that housed a large herd of cows and flocks of chickens, the pigsty and yard, and a stable with accommodations for twelve horses.

"Hello," I cried as I stopped in front of the stable.

A Negro groom greeted me politely and waited expectantly. I spied a small wooden cottage and inquired of him its purpose.

"It be used to house and set apart sick students," he said.

Little did I realize the heartache I would later experience within that charming cottage. The boy sauntered back inside the stable. I returned to the front of the house and entered the front door. Father awaited me in the entrance hall.

"I am so happy to be here, Father," I said as I hugged him. "The grounds are lovely."

Father smiled indulgently and put his arm through mine. "I set up your account at the school store. Get anything you need, child."

We entered the dining room for breakfast, along with other young ladies and their escorts. Our student guide, Annie, informed us that the dining room had an eclectic assortment of furniture, obtained from the overflow of surrounding farmhouses. Situated against a wall I saw a fine walnut chest with two drawers, and an oil painting above.

We joined a group for breakfast at the long tables arranged up and down the length of the room. I spied my friend, Mary Helm, and her father, at another table and waved to them. After making some introductions, and partaking in small talk with our group, we ate a hearty meal before we left for the completion of our tour, as Father had to leave soon. Annie showed us one of the spacious lecture rooms, paneled in pine. We saw another pine lecture room, and some other rooms with plastered walls. All of them had interesting cornices and finely framed windows. We passed several study rooms, furnished with large desks and chairs.

Off the main hall, on the left next to one of the libraries, was located the music room, which contained a stage upon which there were four rosewood pianofortes. Several painted panels, set between the windows, represented the Greek muses. A prominent Buckingham politician had paid for the commission of these panels, Annie informed us.

Father asked, "Annie, are there strict guidelines for religious study?"

She replied, "Although the Methodist Episcopal Church of Virginia patronizes the school, the trustees also practice other religious affiliations. My fellow students and staff are Episcopalian, Presbyterian, Baptist, and of course, Methodist."

Religion, one of the courses of study, was fine by Father. I walked with him to the front door and promised to write as frequently as I could.

"Listen more to the Presbyterian teachings than the others," Father advised me.

"It's the same God, but I will use discernment in my studies. Have a safe trip, Father, and don't worry about me. I'll be just fine. Write me, and I'll do the same."

"You are indeed a loving and dutiful daughter. I will give Mother your love. I have no doubt that your strength of character and poise will sustain you in your new environment," he replied. We kissed each other goodbye, and then he walked away down the narrow lane to await the stagecoach.

I decided to return to my room and unpack a few items. My roommates introduced themselves as Mollie Jarratt, Maggie Branch, and Hortense Williams. Mollie was about my age, and after studying her eyes, I took an immediate liking to her.

"Mollie, what town do you hail from?" I asked her.

"I am from Jarratt's Depot, in Sussex County," she replied. "I am starting my second and last year here."

"Well, I guess you don't need to hear the house rules. I'm from Fairfax Courthouse, in Fairfax County."

We learned a little about each other until it was time for me to go hear Mrs. Goff's instructions.

"I'll see you at dinner today," I said.

I quickly descended the stairs to the principal hall and listened while Mrs. Goff gave the group the house rules.

"Ladies, I warmly welcome you to this fine institution. My husband and I are in charge of the boarders, and have a few house rules that we insist you abide by. First, besides Mrs. Blackwell and myself, there are two women faculty members, Mrs. Preot, the drawing, painting, and needlework instructor, and Mrs. Janey, our voice instructor. If you ever have any need of a sympathetic ear to talk to, please do not hesitate to contact one of us. We realize that homesickness is sometimes an issue, as well as other matters that would best be advised by other women.

"The Institute is responsible for the deportment of the young ladies that it boards. We cannot be responsible, however, for the behavior of the day students. Any discipline administered for breaches in proper deportment will be strict and impartial, but at the same time, kind and appropriate. All of you are debarred from interaction with the opposite sex, unless it is supervised by relatives or in the presence of the faculty. The strictest rules of propriety must justify this discourse.

"Church services will be held in the Institute chapel and young men from the Physick Springs Academy attend. A fleeting glimpse of them, and socially obligatory greetings, should be your only contact with the young men."

A chorus of sighs and groans reverberated throughout the hall at this announcement.

"Our first and foremost object is that you obtain a thorough intellectual education, attended by suitable moral restraints. I will consider anything else to be of secondary importance. You may think our rules strict, but sad to say, one of our former students found herself 'with child,' and ran away with her young fellow, to her ruin."

A few girls gasped in shock. Although her disclosure was disturbing to hear, things like this happened occasionally, even in Fairfax Courthouse.

"Your daily routine should consist of early morning private devotions followed by six hours of class work. A two-hour study time will be in your room, with lights out at ten o'clock. There will be room checks. If there are no questions, classes will begin in one-half hour."

"Ma'am," I interjected. "Do we have any social time?" I heard some girls tittering at my question.

She replied, "On occasion, musical soirées or public recitations may occur on Friday evenings. In nice weather, walking together outside can be calmly satisfying."

A bustle of conversation ensued at the unearthing of our meager entertainment.

My extensive courses of studies consisted of: Classical Literature, Intellectual Arithmetic, Science, Latin and French, Pianoforte, Drawing, Painting, Needlework, Penmanship, Modern Geography, and Modern History. Dr. Blackwell would give Bible lessons on Sunday. Mr. Arnaud

Preot, who taught the pianoforte, quickly became a favorite of mine. Natural Science and Ethics was with Mr. Potts. The teachers were all obliging. Class work, music, and drawing took up most of my day.

On Sunday, we convened in the Institute chapel. I felt curious to see the arrival of the Physick Springs Academy boys.

"They dress up in their best clothes," Mollie told me, "and walk the several miles from their school wearing their old shoes. When they are close to the church, they hide their old shoes in the bushes and exchange them for their freshly polished boots, which they had been carrying in a handkerchief under their arms."

I laughed at that tale—to think that the boys wanted to make such a good impression!

"Don't laugh. I, too, go to some trouble to look especially nice on Sunday. I put on my best white muslin gown, and wear my hair up, with a pretty comb to hold it in place."

"I have serviceable clothes, but nothing special," I said.

"Antonia," she rejoined, "you look especially nice without having to do anything extraordinary. You are one of the few natural beauties I have ever encountered. Think yourself lucky!"

As we sat in the pews, many glances were exchanged between the young men's and woman's sections. When we girls sang the school song, the boys looked at each other in wonderment, as if we were angels in disguise. I noticed one fellow in the adjoining aisle who had gone to sleep during the sermon. I nudged Mollie, and she too observed him.

"His name is Thomas Miller. He is also from my hometown. Isn't he just the handsomest boy in here?"

He startled awake and looked our way. His clear, green eyes sparkled in a face framed by golden, curly hair. The more I stared, the more his hair resembled a lion's mane. He raised and lowered his eyebrows quizzically a few times, and then a slow smile spread from ear to ear. I saw Mollie blushing. She fanned herself a few times, and then coquettishly returned Thomas' gaze. I imagined a budding romance beginning.

"Who is the handsome young man sitting next to him?" I asked.

"That is William Clapham. Do you fancy him?" replied Mollie.

I just smiled. His striking looks, dark hair, blue eyes, and angular face with a strong jaw intrigued me. Bella Redford, another classmate who sat next to me, overheard the whispered exchange. As soon as the service was over, and our teachers herded us out of church, she demanded to be included in shared confidences.

"Have you ever kissed a boy?" she asked me excitedly.

"Good gracious, no!" I exclaimed. Secretly, I have wanted to, but acted shocked, nonetheless.

Bella was no belle. She was heavy, big-boned, and rather clumsy and unattractive. Known as one of those people who talks too much, she had little to say for all the jabbering. I felt sorry for her, however, and tried to be kind to her. For some reason, she latched onto me as though I was her only friend. Perhaps that was true, but her eagerness to commune with me was one-sided. She followed me around like a big puppy and I had to learn avoidance tactics just to get some relief from her non-stop mouth. She was kind to me, however, so I endured her pestering.

Later, in the spring, I helped her with her classical studies, as I proved to be the better student, and she needed some study skills. Our current textbook, used by students of every age and either sex, was *Tooke's Pantheon of the Heathen Gods and Illustrious Heroes*. She must have felt quite grateful to me for my help, because after a particularly trying session, she took the book from my hands and wrote inside the cover, *Antonia is the dearest girl in school, the most amiable, at least I think so. Your devoted friend, Bella Redford.*

When Maggie Branch and I discussed the "Bella situation," we both agreed that the inscription was quite sickening!

Another time, upon opening my Philosophy textbook, I noticed a note that had not appeared on the first page the last time I looked: *Antonia is certainly very much in love with William Clapham. I think it will be a match.* The handwriting looked suspiciously similar to Bella's.

The months at school flew by. One June day, shortly before the term ended, I walked amongst the gardens to the gazebo while daydreaming of my beloved home in Fairfax Courthouse. Immediately to the left of the main building was a garden composed of flowering plants. The stocks and pinks, in particular, caught my eye. I rejoiced to see them and drew closer to smell their scents. I noticed a vegetable garden, not particularly bountiful, and I could spy an apple orchard in the distance, as well as hay and cornfields. My friend, Mary Helm, ran up to me shouting, "There you are. I've been looking for you. I just received a letter from Kate Carper and wanted to share the gossip with you."

Mary, a tall and thin brunette with high cheekbones, had arched eyebrows and a pug nose. After catching up on news, I unburdened myself to her. "I am so disappointed in Southern girls, Mary. I imagined them very warm-hearted, but they are the reverse, as chilling as icebergs, nothing like the Northern girls I am accustomed to at old Coombe Cottage. I'm so homesick sometimes, I cry myself to sleep."

She replied, "Southern hospitality and graciousness must be a myth."

"They are sissies also. In my typical fashion, I played a joke on Nannie McAgyle and Bella by putting a live spider in a little box on top of their shared desk. They screamed so loud upon seeing it, that a teacher intervened and scolded me firmly for the sin of a practical joke!"

"Do you plan on returning after the break?"

"I'm not entirely happy here. I do not know."

I found through experience, that not all people were as playful as I was. Learning to accept disappointment would help me get though life more serenely, I thought.

During the brief summer break, I stayed home nearly all the time. There was a great deal of sickness and one death in my family. Our cook died—the one who had been with Mother ever since her marriage. I never realized the pain of death before and slept in Mother's room for comfort. Mr. Whitehead, the preacher, seemed tall as a pine, reaching near to the ceiling, and was spare as well. He gave a good homily to all the mourners at her funeral.

Mother was pregnant, and I told her before I left, "I wish I could be here to help when the baby arrives." I shuddered when I said that, as it was commonplace for expectant mothers to make arrangements for their own funerals prior to delivery; so hazardous was childbirth and its after-effects. Mother was my rock and so dearly beloved to me that I could not imagine life without her.

I returned for a new term at my dear school, among my darling schoolmates. My homesickness resolved itself, and now I was happy again. I attended a great religious revival at the school, and watched my friends profess their commitment to Jesus. I, however, did not feel compelled to join them in their fervor.

I received post regularly from my family and the letter I had in hand, dated November 10, 1855, proved to be particularly "newsy." Mother had safely given birth to her fourth baby— a boy named James Keith. He had light hair, hazel eyes, and was a joy to the family. Father started a Yellow Fever Relief Fund in the village in September. He collected funds for people afflicted with the fever in Norfolk and Portsmouth, as they were having a difficult time with it, and needed more support than we could give.

Mother wrote that Frances Littlefair, aged ten, who was the youngest daughter of Horatio Littlefair, died of pneumonia on October 29. Frances was a playmate of Clanie's, and Clanie took it hard. The Littlefair family lived in Coombe Cottage, my beloved first finishing school.

I read with interest that my family's friend, Mr. Helm, had invested a good deal of money in this school. I suspected that he wanted to find favor with the directors seeing that Mary was a student!

I spent an uneventful Christmas at home, helping to care for my new brother with the awful yells, and returned to the school for the winter term. I asked Mrs. Blackwell if I could be a French teacher when I graduated, but she was noncommittal. The months rolled by, and on a dark, rainy June day, I traveled to Nannie McAgyle's home for part of our summer vacation. I felt less inclined to leave the school, as it became dearer and dearer to me.

In July and August, I was back in Fairfax Courthouse, and happily, Hortense Williams stayed with us for a week starting August 15. She was so lively and amusing, and we roamed the village together hoping to spy the very attractive and eligible Reverend Boyton, who was here every week. My friends and I spent carefree days during weekends that summer. Maggie and Gammia Edwards, and Anne Lerth, and I often lazed under the trees in my backyard, daydreaming and writing in our journals. One August evening, Maggie challenged me to write something witty inside my *Elementary Geology* book. Not one to decline a challenge, I wrote, "Sitting under the oak tree in the backyard with Gammia Edwards and a great big 'horse fly' took us for horses and bit us most melifferously."

Kate Carper stayed with us in September, and we canvassed the countryside in our buggy. When it was time to go back to school, we went together, escorted by my father.

Chapter Six

Life Lessons, 1856-57

Our journey back to school was uneventful, and I had a joyful reunion with my school chums. The instructors taught the same courses, but more advanced in nature. I had adapted very well last year to my surroundings and felt quite comfortable this year. My best friend, Mollie, had graduated on July 9.

Maggie Branch and Hortense Williams were still my roommates. Mrs. Goff told me that there would be some new arrivals during the January term. I felt very happy with the type of girls who attended this school, and relished the thought of making new friends.

Maggie had become a dear friend. We autographed each other's books and wrote poems to each other. We giggled and gossiped about fellow students, and agreed that we did not like Nannie McAgyle, as she was a teacher's pet. Maggie inscribed an original poem in the back of my book *Elements of Logick*:

Dearest Antonia,

If I thy face no more behold,
Thy name I cannot blot,
For memory will not be controlled,
Those n'er can'st be forgot.

Your Friend, Maggie.

My family wrote frequent letters to me. Sadly, my beloved infant brother James had contracted pneumonia and passed away. The onset, sudden and severe, caused death quickly. Mother and Father were devastated, of course. I hardly knew him, but cried anyway, feeling helpless so far from home. Infant mortality was so common that everyone breathed a sigh of relief if the baby survived his first few years.

Charlie attended Virginia's first high school, Episcopal, in Alexandria, known throughout the South as "The High School."

The year 1857 came upon us with a frigidly cold snowstorm that lasted all day. I expected Mollie's younger sister, Sarah Jefferson Jarratt, to arrive and take the fourth bed in our room. Surely, the snowstorm would delay her a few days. My predictions proved correct, and it was not until three days later that Sarah arrived, much the worse for wear, with a mud-splattered and torn dress, and a pale countenance. The rough roads apparently caused her to be severely motion sick on the journey. What a miserable start to her new life here! I fetched her some tea and crackers and tried to make her comfortable in bed.

"Sarah," I said, "tell me news of Mollie."

"Thomas Miller is courting her. He graduated the same time Mollie did. They were made for each other and will probably marry soon."

It was no surprise, remembering the looks they had given each other in church.

The next day, I met another new girl, Harriett Batte, from Sussex County. Tall, slim, and gorgeous, her long dark hair was styled in a French twist. Her midnight blue eyes contrasted with her dark hair. Harriet and I became fast friends, even though she proved to be somewhat shy. Her room, next door to mine, provided easy access for visiting each other after hours to giggle and talk about the teachers and other students. There really wasn't much else to talk about, as we were rather isolated from local and world news. The teachers tried to keep us informed about important news events that they conveyed to us from reading the daily newspapers. Only the censored news reached us, however, as we led a sheltered life.

My roommate, Sarah, prone to be precocious and headstrong, was not acclimating very well to life at school. She had trouble conforming to school rules and in completing assignments in subjects that she disliked. One evening, in March, Sarah and I were strolling leisurely in the garden, when we heard her name urgently called out from over the stone wall. Sarah immediately went over to the wall and started talking to a boy.

"Sarah, you know this is against the rules. Tell him so, and come back here," I enjoined her.

"I know him from church last week," she replied.

I couldn't help but think that this rendezvous had been premeditated. I left her there, and went on with my walk. When I passed by that way again, I heard noises on the other side of the wall. I peeked over and saw Sarah naked from the waist up lying on the ground with the boy's head buried in her breasts. I backed away, avoiding their notice and went back to the school. She received her first warning later that week when a teacher found her talking to the same boy off school grounds. A second warning meant that the Reverend would write a letter to her parents, and expulsion would occur.

A few days later, I returned to my room after dinner to find my dear friend Harriet, lying on her bed, sweating, with a delirious look in her eyes.

"Harriet, what is wrong?"

"I'm hot and feel queasy. I have stomach pains, diarrhea, and a headache," she replied.

"I'll go get Mrs. Goff." I calmly left the room, but once I was in the hallway, I ran.

A few minutes later, Mrs. Goff and I returned. She laid her hand on Harriet's forehead, looked her over, and said, "Harriet, we are going to move you to the infirmary."

Two male servants brought a stretcher, and they carried Harriet to the small wooden cottage that I had so admired my first day here. A doctor from town examined Harriet and after noticing the rash of flat, rose-colored spots on her abdomen, declared that she had typhoid fever. Luckily, there were no other affected students. The doctors segregated Harriet in the small house since the disease was highly contagious with a mortality rate of twenty percent. We had to wear scarves over our mouths and noses, and stay near the door when visiting. During the second week of isolation, Harriet fell unconscious on and off, while delirious. By then her parents had arrived. One of them sat beside her around the clock. The town doctor tried every remedy he knew, but nothing helped. Towards the end of the third week of her illness, Harriet asked for me in one of her coherent moments.

"True friend," she stated weakly, "promise me that you will do something great with your life. I know that my life is almost over. You, my first friend here, have remained steadfast and loyal to me always. You helped me get over some shy moments. I am forever grateful for your friendship."

"And I yours," I said. "Don't talk so, Harriet. Why, you look better today than when I last saw you," I lied. "I promise to lead my life as best I can, to help society." With that, I broke into tears and ran out the door.

The next morning, Reverend announced that she had died peacefully during the night. Her parents arranged to take her body back to Sussex County.

My sorrows were not to be over, however. Sarah had sneaked off the school grounds the previous Sunday to meet her beau. That day, Mrs. Blackwell needed to talk to her about her grades. She searched the school for her, but unsuccessfully. Staking herself at a good vantage point, she awaited Sarah's return and caught her in the act of kissing her beau goodbye while outside the school gates. To avoid embarrassment to both the school and the family, Reverend Blackwell allowed Mr. Jarratt to "withdraw" his daughter from the school. When students asked why she had left, the official statement from the school was, "she did not like it here!"

Attending to my studies with diligence, I passed all my final exams with high marks. Finally, it was my turn to graduate. I had a new light blue silk dress to wear that Mother made for me. My degree, issued on July 1, 1857, awarded me "Mistress of English Literature." All graduates were required to write an essay. Society considered it to be quite out of place, forward, and brazen for a girl to read her own essay. I was obligated to request a suitable person, such as a minister, or other prominent man to perform this service for me. Mr. Preot read my essay, ". . . we are the future of our great country, and our voices need to be heard. Our intelligence and resourcefulness will prove that the education of women and subsequent employment in a meaningful job is good for the economy and nation at large. Equality between the sexes, and, dare I say, between all people, is a high ideal in which to strive, and is possible in our lifetime."

The audience showed appreciation with enthusiastic applause. I purposely kept it short and sweet, unlike some of the girls who rambled on and on about nothing.

My father and eldest brother attended. They would escort me home. I admired my engraved diploma which read, "Antonia Ford—a young lady of unblamable morals and proficient in the elements of a liberal education."

"Well done, Antonia!" Charlie joyfully exclaimed when the ceremony was over.

"Now the only question is: What are you going to do next?" asked Father.

I could not very well tell them that I wished myself to be the next woman literary prodigy. I admired the writings of Jane Austen, George Eliot, and Charlotte, Anne, and Emily Bronte in particular. I wanted to keep my promise to Harriet to do something significant with my life, but was not sure which direction to take. I felt patriotic towards my country and zealous about living my life as a good person, in God's eyes.

"I feel that I have great opportunities," I responded. "I could be a school teacher or tutor. In fact, there may be an opening for a French teacher here at the school."

"That is a bit subservient, isn't it, for the daughter of one of the town's wealthiest families?" Charlie commented. "Perhaps marriage would be a finer calling for you."

Charlie did not say it with sarcasm or belittlement. Society considered marriage and motherhood to be great and wonderful callings for any female.

"I am in search of my purpose in life," I said. "It coincides with my faith journey, and the purpose that God has set forth for me."

"I'm still seeking," said Father.

Charlie pondered our statements, and then declared, "I feel closest to God when I am among others who feel the same way as I do. I only hope that I can fulfill God's purpose for me, before I go to His heavenly kingdom."

I ended the solemn conversation by saying, "I must bid my friends farewell. I will be back in a moment."

I hugged and kissed my classmates goodbye, not knowing when, if ever, I would see them again. Maggie Branch and I promised to write each other faithfully.

On the way home, Father mentioned that Mother was due to have another baby in November.

"How wonderful!" I exclaimed. "I'll have a new sibling to cuddle. By the way, how is everyone handling their grief over James' death?"

Father reflected inwardly for a moment then replied, "Your mother is kept busy with Clanie and Pattie. She is thrilled to be with child again. I believe it takes her mind off her sorrows. As for Charlie and me, we grieve inside ourselves, don't we, Son?"

Charlie nodded, and then asked, "Do you believe that James is in heaven, Father?"

"All people who never have the opportunity or are too young to receive Christ into their lives sit with God in heaven."

I have to admit, that statement gave me great comfort.

Chapter Seven

Party at Helmswood, August 12, 1860

We were on our way to a summer party at the Helm's plantation, Helmswood, located in Hamilton in Loudoun County. I particularly liked to visit there as Sophie and Mary were close to my own age and socializing with them was so much fun. The two sisters and I could talk frankly about anything on our minds, the same way that Rose Love and I could. The Grigsbys, Loves, Gunnells, and many other neighbors also would be attending. Dick Grigsby had been courting me for a year, and I especially looked forward to seeing him. As my family traveled in our carriage, Father and Clanie discussed the law passed by Georgia that forbade owners from manumitting slaves in their wills.

"It is only right and just, Father, that after a lifetime of servitude, the slave should be free."

Clanie thought himself the source of knowledge since he was attending "The High School" that our brother, Charlie had attended. His summer break allowed him some much needed rest and relaxation.

"Some Northerners think that that is not enough, Son. I even know some slave owners who have already given their slaves their papers and hired them as servants."

"What are you going to do, Father?"

"I think, eventually, I will give our slaves their freedom, with potential employment by me. They are almost a part of our family."

My sister, Pattie, gave a strangled cry and tears started rolling down her face.

"I don't want Mathilde to go away," she sobbed. "I love her."

Mother comforted Pattie and told her, "Let's not worry about that right now."

Charlie lived at Virginia Military Institute, starting his second year, along with his friend James Monroe Love. He emulated many alumni of that institute, including one of our village men, George Chichester, from the class of 1854.

The new baby, Frank, three years old, was the apple of my parents' eyes. He had curly, sandy brown hair, brown eyes, and long eyelashes. I truly loved the chunky, healthy, roly-poly little boy.

We arrived at our destination, and I hugged and kissed little Frank before running off to be with my friends. I ran inside the house and up the stairs to my friends' room, knocked on the door, and entered, party dress in hand. Although we had written letters, I had only rarely seen Mary since I graduated, and was anxious to catch up with her.

Sophie and Mary Helm shared a bedroom and excitedly gave me hugs of greeting. Sophie, blond and blue-eyed, loved to have the latest fashions, and showed her talent by being quite handy with a sewing machine. Unfortunately, although she needed spectacles for distance, she vainly refused to wear them, so we had to tell her who was approaching in social gatherings.

"Sophie," I laughed, "just how pink do you want your cheeks to be?" She was pinching her cheeks, while grimacing, to add a natural glow to her skin.

"The pinker the better." She observed me wriggling my nose. "Is something wrong with your nose?" she asked me.

"I hesitate to scratch it, because if I do, it means an old bachelor is going to kiss me!" I replied.

"Antonia, I see that you are still superstitious," said Sophie, reprovingly.

"More than I should be," I admitted.

After catching up on news and current beaus, we earnestly started getting ready for the party. Soon, dressed in our chemises, we arranged each other's hair and put finishing touches on our makeup. We splashed clove-scented water on our necks. Mary retrieved her little pots of scarlet and white powder and we mixed them to produce a pink rouge that we dabbed on our cheeks. My eyeliner was kohl, made from powdered charcoal. I produced a small pot of butter, beeswax and raisin-stained lip-gloss, which I applied artistically.

Mary, recently engaged to be married, was eager to converse with her beau, waiting outside. "I can't wait to be married!" she exclaimed.

"Well, you know, losing your virginity is one of life's mysteries that will soon be revealed to you," I said seriously.

"I've never thought of it that way," Mary replied.

Sophie asked, "What other mysteries of life do you expect, Antonia?"

"I have this philosophy of life that there are so few surprises in life that we have to savor each one that comes our way. The world holds limited experiences that are sacred, so it should be memorable when one of them happens to you. For example, our first great mystery revealed to us occurred at our own birth."

Sophie and Mary uttered exclamations of surprise.

"Second," I continued, "puberty is definitely a mystery that both boys and girls experience." I looked at my friends to see if they caught my drift, and they nodded knowingly.

"Marriage and our first experience of sexual intercourse is a big mystery we all hope to experience. I presume that we are all virgins and will remain chaste until our wedding night. Don't you wonder, imagine, and dream what that night will be like? I can't wait to find out what it feels like for two to become one and the expression of deep love that will come to me."

"I desire to get married," Sophie whispered. "Am I supposed to look forward to my wedding night? I've heard it can be painful."

"Nevertheless," I continued, not really knowing how to answer, "it is a mystery. Don't die wondering. When that act is accomplished, pregnancy is the next item on the list that is a true miracle. Who can know what it feels like to carry a child unless they go through it? We are all Madonnas. Childbirth, as dangerous and painful as it is, will be the next huge revelation. What could be more of a surprise than the gender of your baby?"

"What is left?" asked a worried Mary.

"Change of life is a mystery that is left, and, of course, soon afterwards, our own death is the last great unknown. Where will we go from this earth? What will our final reward be?"

"That is no mystery to me!" exclaimed Sophie. "All believers of Christ will be rewarded with a heavenly kingdom better than anything we could ever expect on earth."

"Ah yes," I murmured softly to myself. "The joy of being a Christian… Why does this state of being elude me?" Continuing our interesting conversation, I said, "Let's record our ambitions for the future. I'll act as scribe."

The three of us lounged in our undergarments on the bed while I recorded for all posterity, our ambitions:

> *Antonia Ford's idea of happiness—a big home in a city, with every luxury, wealth, and position that can be supplied. Oh, that I may attain it!*
>
> *This day at Helmswood, Sophie Helm's idea of happiness—to float on the topmost wave of fashion with ambition as her guiding star.*
>
> *Mary Helm's idea of happiness—a home, no matter how humble, lighted by Love's smile.*
>
> *We three will, if living, compare notes this day three years hence, to see how nearly we realize our girlish dreams.*

"Ladies, I will be the keeper of our wishes," I said. "We must be sure to experience our wildest hopes and desires."

"I happen to know that Dick Grigsby is waiting outside to talk to you, Antonia," said Sophie.

"He told me he would be here, and asked ahead of time to take a walk with me. He is eager, isn't he?"

Mary asked, "Do you love him, Antonia?"

I had to hesitate before answering. "I'm not sure I know yet what love is. I admire him, and like him better than anyone else I know. Is that love? Perhaps. Would I want to spend the rest of my life with him? Time will tell, I suppose. I still cannot give him too much hope for a commitment, if you know what I mean. Let's get our crinolines and dresses on and join the party."

Hoopskirts, or crinolines, were the rage, and we were all old enough to wear dresses that enhanced our figures. Sophie's originally designed pale, mint green dress, was Egyptian cotton with satin bows and lace inserts. She looked stunning. Mary's dress, also made by Sophie, was lavender dupioni silk, with three-quarter length sleeves and a plunging neckline. Although simple, it improved a figure that needed it. Mother made my ivory cotton dress decorated with pink ribbons, bows, and lace embellishments. By the time the three of us had our hoops on, there was barely room for us to walk. We left the room, descended the stairway in regal fashion, hoping that our admirers would be waiting earnestly. What a disappointment to find that they were nowhere to be seen.

Once outside, several young men immediately headed toward us to do the honor of fetching a beverage for us. Lewis Helm, aged twenty-four, and Dick Grigsby, aged twenty, rushed up to me and bowed in greeting. Dick, easily the handsomest man at the party, was six feet three inches tall with a muscular build. His light brown hair curled a bit, and he had large brown eyes with amazingly long lashes for a man. It gave him an interesting, exotic appearance. He smiled at me, and opened his mouth to speak, but Lewis beat him to it.

"Miss Ford, would you like lemonade, or iced tea?" asked Lewis. As heir to this fine plantation, he took the role of host. He was dapper in a different way than Dick, with dark hair and tanned skin, tall, and well-proportioned. Suitable in age and social status to me, both our parents encouraged our friendship.

"Why thank you, Lewis. A glass of iced tea would be refreshing." As Lewis walked off, Dick possessively took hold of my hand.

"Remember you promised to take a stroll with me. It looks like I have competition for your affections," Dick said.

I smiled at Dick. Besides being gallant and debonair, I liked the fact that he was mannerly and well-educated.

"Don't worry about that, Dick. You're first in my heart, presently."

He raised his eyebrows, and said in a hopeful tone of voice, "Does that mean we have an understanding, dearest?"

I laughed and shrugged my shoulders, as I stood up, releasing his hand. "I'm not ready for an engagement, if that's what you mean. Here comes Lewis with my iced tea."

Mary and her beau also joined us, and soon, a group of young people surrounded us, conversing, laughing, and enjoying the honeysuckle-scented summer day. I spied my friend, Rose Love, and her brother, Robert, and went up to them. They had lost their eleven-year-old sister, Laura, only three months ago. She suffered through a two-day illness, and then died of an inflammation of the stomach. My heart went out to them. This was their first social outing since Laura's death, and I hesitated to say anything that might bring them to tears. It had been almost exactly six years since Robert's copperhead bite, and I felt a motherly concern for him, considering the role that Lewis and I had played in saving him from a venomous death. I gave Rose a hug of greeting and then spoke to Robert, aged nineteen.

"How is that leg of yours? What a memory I have of the summer of your bite."

"I only think about it when I see the scar," he said ruefully. "I'm much more careful now about weed walking," he laughed.

"I hope my Charlie, and James, your brother, are getting some relaxation time at VMI in between all the studying they must be doing," I said.

"I hear it's rigorous," he responded. He shyly gestured for me to partake of the food that he had in a cloth napkin. "Have some potato chips!"

I tentatively tasted one, and found out that this new culinary treat was delicious! Robert went to get a refill on potato chips while Rose and I caught up on neighborhood gossip. Dick soon rejoined me, and after a suitable time, he and I walked away, hand in hand to meander through the grounds.

"Do you think that Abraham Lincoln will be our sixteenth President?" I asked Dick.

"Yes, Honest Abe has endeared himself to the public. I'm surprised you keep up with politics!" he exclaimed.

"I read *The Alexandria Gazette* every day. Isn't it exciting that the Pony Express can send news from Missouri to California in only ten days?" I asked.

Dick only smiled at me, and declared, "I have a present for you when we go back."

"Let's go back now. The crowd will miss us, and I love receiving gifts. What could it be?"

Upon returning, Dick presented me with a rectangular object wrapped in paper. When I opened it, I found a beautifully bound copy of Walt Whitman's newly published book of poems, *Leaves of Grass*.

"Thank you, Dick. I will treasure this always." I leaned over and placed a light kiss upon his cheek.

Chapter Eight

All Saint's Day Celebration,
October 31, 1860

Mathilde, our servant, escorted me to a social evening with friends. Clanie, away at "The High School," was not available to go with me. I did have to wonder why Mother and Father considered it safe for Mathilde to return by herself to our house, but it would not have been safe for me. I saw inequality and injustice all around me and reflected on how Jesus would have treated others. I felt guilty because of our class differences and the opportunities available to me that Mathilde would not have.

Mother didn't agree with us going out on All Hollow's Eve, for fear that we might "consort with the devil" and promote witchcraft. I had no such thoughts in mind. I only wanted to have a fun evening at the Love's house, with maybe some divination games involved. It was not often that young men and women had an opportunity to socialize in the evening, and I looked forward to it. I much preferred small intimate gatherings like this one, with close friends, as opposed to grand balls.

I had received a small hollow pumpkin with the invitation inside. An unknown person left it at our front door, and it caused a sensation when we found it there one week ago. I wore my best dress; a lavender taffeta, with three-quarter length sleeves. Lace decorated the square neckline and it buttoned down the front. My crinolines added just the right touch of elegance and showed off my slim waist. I wore a wool shawl over my shoulders, as the night was cool.

"Look," Mathilde said, wistfully. "I can see the smoke from the bonfire from here. I sure wish I had a party to go to."

As we approached the Love's front porch, all was dark. A pumpkin with a carved face lit inside by a candle, welcomed us. We knocked on the door and Ellen, their slave, answered it. Mrs. Love trailed behind her.

"Everyone is presently gathered by the bonfire out back. Please join them there." Mathilde bid me good evening and left. I hurriedly went around the side of the house and to the back, and there I saw my peer group of neighbors and friends—the Loves, Rose and Robert; Dick Grigsby; the Helms, Sophie, Mary, and Lewis; Richard Farr; John Esten Cooke; George Chichester; Martha Cook; and Mary Barnes. James Monroe Love and my Charlie were still at VMI in Lexington, Virginia, and the Institute did not permit them to return home for the first two years, which accounted for their absence from the party. Founded in 1839, VMI was the nation's first state military college. Robert Love and Dick Grigsby attended University of Virginia, but were home for a short visit.

"Good evening to you," said Dick with a little bow, charming as always.

"How are you, Dick?" I asked. He and I were still courting, and I always felt happy to see him. I could feel the heat from the bonfire, and hoped that it cast a glow over my face, adding a flush, where there might not otherwise be one, on this crisp fall evening.

"Now that you are here, I'm more than fine! Let the games begin," he shouted to the crowd at large.

A half-barrel stood ready, with apples bobbing in the water. By the light of the bonfire, we took turns bobbing for apples. When it was my turn, I daintily clamped my teeth into an apple, so pleased with myself that I had avoided getting my entire face and hair wet, when suddenly, a hand from behind pushed my face all the way into the water! I came up sputtering, crying, "How dare you?" in as mean a voice as I could muster. I turned around, and there stood Lewis, grinning from ear to ear.

He removed a handkerchief from his pocket and tenderly wiped away the water, while whispering, "I love you, wet or dry, angry or happy."

I composed myself, smiled, and said to the crowd, "What's next?"

The men planned the next game. We ladies had to close our eyes for five minutes, while they took balls of yarn and left a trail of yarn to their hiding places. When we opened our eyes, each of us chose an end of a yarn ball and followed it to its destination. I noticed some trails led to the woods, another to the house cellar, but mine led to the barn. I followed the yarn, walking carefully as the footing was unstable in the darkness. I could see a dim glow from an oil lamp inside. I walked through the barn door, advanced three feet, around the corner of a hay bale, and into the arms of Dick. He gently hugged me and bent his head to kiss my lips softly. My first kiss on the lips! Our kiss led to an intimate embrace. This went on for several minutes. When his hands started wandering, I knew it was time to return to the party. It wasn't that I didn't like what Dick was doing to me, but my upbringing told me to resist my natural urges. After a strenuous contortion to extricate myself from my compromising position, I felt my dress gape open in the front. Two buttons had popped off exposing my corset and breasts. Dick could not help but notice. I hastily wrapped my shawl around myself and picked up the buttons from the floor.

"Dick, I hear everyone re-gathering. Let's go before we are missed."

"If we must," he said, eyes glowing. "This kiss will have to last me another semester while at school. I hope you think about me fondly. May I write?"

"Of course, let's write each other," I said hurriedly.

When we reconvened, we all went inside. I repaired my dress and then rejoined the group. We ate and drank refreshments while a fiddler set up an area for dancing in the entrance hallway. Rose and I, and some of the other ladies gathered and decided to foretell our future husbands by throwing an apple peel over our shoulders. I went first, and saw a "J" form from the peel where it landed on the floor. This was the first initial of my husband-to-be. Again, I threw a peel over my shoulder, and the letter "C" formed itself on the floor.

"John Cooke!" someone exclaimed. "Do you fancy him?"

"He and I have spent some time together," I admitted.

"Well then . . .," Rose said, and archly raised her eyebrows at me.

Everyone else took her turn, amid squealing and a great deal of fun. What the men thought we were doing—I'm not sure, but they were off in their own part of the house, drinking and jesting.

The fiddler started playing, and the Grand March began in the entrance hall. Dick and I paired up for that, and for the First Waltz. Later, John Esten Cooke and I danced the Virginia Reel. A Contra dance followed, with Lewis as my partner. As the night wore on, I danced with all the men, flirted outrageously, and generally enjoyed myself to exhaustion. A late night buffet followed the dancing, and the fête ended, with everyone agreeing it had been a spectacular evening.

Chapter Nine

A Love Letter, April-June 1861

For one year, I had been sewing my own dresses on the treadle sewing machine, using only Virginia homespun fabric. I belonged to a Homespun Club in our village. I vowed to help Virginia by keeping the pledge that our citizens resolved at a public meeting held in Alexandria sixteen months ago:

> *That, by way of giving a practical issue to this meeting, and as the first step towards the attainment of Southern commercial independence, the citizens of Alexandria here assembled pledge themselves to use and wear no article of apparel not manufactured in the State of Virginia; and to buy all our hats, caps, boots, shoes, and clothing at home and of home manufacture, and induce our wives and daughters to do the same; and that the directors of our several railroad companies be and are hereby respectfully requested to pursue the same policy with reference to all articles required by their respective roads.*

Charlie was still away at VMI, and "safely put" as Father said, for war had started. The attack on Fort Sumter had occurred two months previously. Three units of Confederate soldiers, including ninety men of the Warrenton Rifles, sixty men of the Prince William Cavalry, housed in Zion Church, and sixty men of the Rappahannock Cavalry who slept in the courthouse, occupied our town. Clanie's high school had closed in May, so he was at home with us. Robert S. Grande, eighteen, and John Witworth, nineteen, were still boarders in our home, but would be enlisting soon.

The Yankee Government asked my family to take the Oath of Allegiance, but we refused. Our location, in Fairfax Courthouse, put us in a perilous position, as we did not know who might be occupying our city from week to week. We read that Willard's hotel, nineteen miles away in Washington City, was the Capitol defenders headquarters. Maryland, even closer, became a split state in the war, with brother fighting against brother, in many cases.

Father emancipated our seven slaves, and offered to keep them on as paid servants, if they so wished. One of our slaves and her three children left our employment to join her husband in a shantytown in Alexandria. We wished them well. Octavia chose to remain, as did Mathilde. Mathilde, a few years younger than Mother, was like a member of our family.

"Why would I want to leave?" she asked. "I am employed by good people, have a warm bed, and enough food to keep my belly full."

We took her point well, as there was a struggle for fuel, clothing, and food.

Most leaders in Virginia hoped that Virginia would remain in the Union, but with some specific federal concessions to Southern demands. Even so, a little more than one week ago, the people voted upon the Virginia Secession Ordinance. Fairfax County voted for secession with 942 approving and 288 against. William Dulany, an acquaintance of Father's, originally voted "no," but changed his vote to "yes."

"I convinced Dulany that a unified Fairfax Courthouse vote would give our village a sense of fraternity," Father remarked.

Clanie asked, "What happened after all of the counties voted separately?"

Father said, "John Bell represented Virginia's electoral votes when the Virginia Assembly met. He voted to secede, as all of Virginia's counties added together indicated a six-fold preponderance to secede."

"How will secession affect us?" I asked. "Is it legal?"

"Thomas Love and other attorney friends of mine agree that it is legal," Father said. "In addition, South Carolina, Georgia, Florida, Alabama, Mississippi, Louisiana, and Texas passed secession ordinances and joined to form the Confederate States of America, of which we are now part. I fear that the effect is a war that will take away the best and bravest our country has to offer. I fear for every family's future loss, and every young man capable of going to war," he wearily replied.

Mother patted his shoulders and smiled tenderly at him after glancing at Clanie.

"Mother and Father," I said, "now that I have graduated from the Institute, I need to prove my usefulness to society. Surely there is something I can do for the war effort?"

Father looked at Mother, and then said, "All that is expected from you in your station of life is to marry well."

"What if I don't find the right person for years? I'll be twenty-three in July, and although I have suitors—none please me enough to marry. Surely I could find a position as a schoolteacher?"

"I appreciate your offer, Antonia," Mother said, "but many schools are closing during this War Between the States. Besides that, we are wealthy enough that you don't need to work."

"My feelings of patriotism are caged inside of me. Yes, I am a woman, and not as strong as men physically, but surely there is a role for me to perform to help in the war effort? Perhaps I could nurse the wounded, or carry messages between enemy lines."

"Spying is dangerous work, Antonia," Father said dismissively. "Stay safe and watch over your younger siblings."

As I peered out of the parlor window, I saw our neighbor, Dr. William Gunnell, come to our door. I opened it and greeted him, "Good afternoon,

Dr. Gunnell, please come in."

"Good afternoon Julia, E.R., and Antonia," he replied. "I have just returned from a short trip to Alexandria, and have taken the liberty of retrieving your post from the post office there."

We were still a rural village and did not have daily postal delivery yet. Only forty-nine of the biggest cities had that convenience. We could count on one or two postal deliveries a week. Mother took the post from Dr. Gunnell while the two men situated themselves for a long talk, catching up on the news.

Mother handed me a letter. The return address indicated it was from Lewis Helm. Ever since he had enlisted in the army, after Fort Sumter, I kept my promise to correspond with him. It was the least I could do, I thought. I read the letter silently:

April 21, 1861

I still claim you with all my heart; you are so dear to me, though circumstances now indicate that I am anything else than dear to you, judging from your answer to my last communications. You seemed to have disregarded the arguments that I endeavored to prove in my last letter, or you recklessly read it. My letter was the bearer of warm, devoted affection to you, though it was of a sad and gloomy character. And in return for that, you scold me, and tell me that I have used a word that is bad to apply to a lady. The meaning of the word shapely is perfectly understood and is what I think, with no bad reflection on you. The advise you gave me about it, I will take kindly. I must insist that you take the same advise to yourself. How could you say that there is no engagement between us—only an understanding? If we loved each other, after a while there might be something more. Now Antonia, will you permit me to apply your language, how hard this was for me to bear. I tell you seriously, it was almost unendurable.

Now please tell me what I am to do? You have avoided answering the questions in my last letter. After all the affection and love that I have lavished upon you, you plainly tell me that you had not forgotten Dick Grigsby. Candor requires me to say here that I must have been mistaken, I understood you to say frequently last summer that you had forgotten him. I think it was upon that issue that I made known to you the fact that I loved you. I am sure that I told you at the time that my heart was yours, and I would have courted you sooner had I not thought that an engagement existed between you and him. I would rather go to my grave sorrowful than interfere with his love in any way. It's not necessary for me to give a synopsis of the whole affair. I know that you understand it, and I have too much confidence in you to ever indulge in the idea that you think that I have acted dishonorably or made a request that was unreasonable or improper in any way. Antonia, you tantalize me by giving me the conversation that took place at the depot with him. I was not aware that you had any conversations; by all the honor that is within me, so you see that was not the preposition that my letter was based upon. It was this: your conversation with my sister last summer about the engagement, when she gave me her opinion that she thought you <u>loved</u> Grigsby still.

Now in conclusion, I hope <u>your kind heart </u>will allow me to say to you that your letter does not give me the information that I asked for. Let me make one request before I close; that is please read my last letter carefully, <u>and I know</u> that a whispering voice will reinterpret it from beginning to end, and I feel that you will admit that there is nothing in it that <u>is improper or unjust to you</u>. Antonia, I have exhausted everything within me. Is it unjust to you and improper for me when I acknowledge that <u>I love you</u>, to ask will you love me in return, or to ask will you marry me?

I appeal now to your conscience and in order to see whether this anguish is unjust or not please take retrospective news of the manner in which I courted you, your letters to me, and my letters to you.

Please write before our mails are cut off. If this reaches you, it will be almost more than I expect.

Did you hear Mr. Carter? I think he is one of the finest men in the world. Our neighborhood is in a great state of excitement on the burning of the arms at Harpers Ferry by the Lincoln government, and murder of innocent citizens of Baltimore by Massachusetts plug uglies[1] and wide awakes[2].

Everyone up here now are secessionists; the next news will be that old Abe has left Washington, scared. These old quakes are all scared, until they look like "dun over tailors."
Write soon if you can.

Yours as ever,
Lewis C. Helm
Remember me kindly to Mrs. Ford.

I slumped against the couch and let the letter fall to the floor. I had to put an end to Lewis's false hopes.

---

[1] A street gang active in several East Coast cities.

[2] Young Republicans.

"Antonia, what's wrong?" asked Mother as she came to the couch to sit beside me. "I see that this letter has caused you anguish."

"Mother, trust me when I say that I will do what is polite and ladylike in discouraging the attention of an unwanted suitor. Lewis Helm imagines himself in love with me, and hopes to obtain my hand, eventually. I must write and end this notion." I left the parlor and went to my room to write.

The rest of the day noticeable Southern troop movements went through our village of Fairfax Courthouse. The call of men, rolling wagons and neighs of horses surrounded us. Captain John Quincy Marr, with the Warrenton Rifles, was here in town recruiting our young men to join his group. Many of our boys, on April 25, had enlisted in the 17th Virginia Infantry, Company "D," "Fairfax Rifles," commanded by Captain William Dulany. I wondered where John Quincy Marr thought he was going to get more able bodies.

On a pleasant Saturday in June, I stepped onto our front porch wearing a gray homespun dress with a scoop neck and capped sleeves. Although an old dress, the villagers expected nothing fancier for me to wear with the soldiers kicking up the dust. We tried to be more thrifty than usual, as supplies, including fabric, were now harder to come by. How did I feel about a war coming to my sheltered village and comfortable home? I felt scared. I had three brothers, but only Charlie was old enough to fight. I knew the neighbor boys who had enlisted, and feared for them. Some of them thought the war was going to be a big party. I wanted to do my part for the South, and thought that perhaps I could serve as a nurse.

Mother sent me to the Gunnell's house to borrow a cup of sugar for her baking. Mrs. Gunnell answered the door and let me in.

"How are you, Antonia?" she said kindly. "How is your family?"

The Gunnells were close family friends, and everyone thought the world of Mrs. Gunnell, a most godly woman. Her family, along with most of the village churchgoers, attended Zion Church.

"We're doing well, thanks," I said. "Mother sent me over to borrow a cup of sugar."

"Surely," she responded. "Come with me."

As we entered the kitchen, I noticed a stranger sitting in her kitchen drinking a cup of coffee. He looked a bit wild and disheveled for my taste, but glanced at me with keen brown eyes.

Mrs. Gunnell said, "Captain Smith, this is our neighbor, Antonia Ford. Antonia, this is Captain Smith."

"Pleased to meet you," he said while rising and bowing. "The Gunnells are kind enough to house me and some other Southern officers as we conduct our business in this village. I am part of the Warrenton Rifles, ma'am," he said respectfully.

"I'll pray for safety and courage for you and your men," I said. I bid everyone good day and quickly made my way back home. Loitering was not an option with so many strange young men about.

That evening, I prayed to a God, who I wasn't even sure existed, to provide safety and wisdom for my friends and acquaintances in performing their onerous duty.

Chapter Ten

Fairfax Courthouse Skirmish, June 1, 1861

At ten o'clock that same day, I retired for the evening, only to startle awake hours later by a great ruckus outside. Very close outside . . .

"I hear gunfire and cannons," said Clanie, running from his bedroom.

My parents, Clanie, and I huddled together in the parlor, wondering what was happening at two in the morning. We heard men shouting, horse hooves racing through the streets, and the clash of steel on steel. I hugged Mother close to me, in fright. Father held his shotgun and looked through the front window at the action outside. A bullet hit the side of our house, which made Father think twice about going out.

"There is fighting coming from the direction of the courthouse," Father said.

"I want to go, Father," entreated Clanie.

"You're only sixteen," said Mother. "You wouldn't be allowed to fight."

A man had to be at least eighteen years old to join the military. Men eighteen to twenty years old needed parental permission while those over forty-five, like Father, were considered by the government too old to serve. It was only a matter of time before Charlie joined up. That is, unless the war ended before he left VMI. A knock at our door interrupted my musings. Father opened the door a crack, gun poised, and saw our young neighbor, James Monroe Love, standing there. He let him in quickly, then shut the door, and latched the Yale lock.

"What are you doing out there?" Father asked. "Are you trying to get killed?"

"I was caught unawares," he said, "and needed to gain access to a friendly house. As yours was closer than mine, I am here for awhile."

"Do you know what is going on?" I asked.

"Company 'B' of the Union 2nd Cavalry has attacked us from the Falls Church Road. They are fighting against the Warrenton Rifles. I'm not even sure this information is correct, as it was difficult to find a person who wasn't running one way or the other."

We listened to continued gunshots for another fifteen minutes, followed by silence. Mother made us all tea, as the thought of sleep was impossible. When we heard what sounded like a rapid retreat through the streets, Father ventured out, his rifle loaded and ready. Captain William Smith and other men from the Warrenton Rifles, including Henry Gunnell, were running or riding through our main street.

Father yelled, "Did you chase the Yankees off?"

"Yes," replied Captain Smith, "but we are missing our commander, John

Quincy Marr. I am acting in his stead at the moment."

"Any casualties?" asked Father.

"One wounded, but no dead, thank God," he replied.

Father called for James to come outside, and promptly escorted him home.

The next morning, we found out the entire saga in more detail. Most of the villagers gathered on the courthouse lawn and listened as Captain Smith gave an account of the skirmish:

> We were fenced in, both on the right and left, by high board fences, and being armed only with carbines, we could neither escape nor resist a dragoon charge, except with the contents of our guns. We shot at them with all the might and force that our carbines could give, which so staggered them that they came promptly to the 'about face,' and returned to the run to reform. Then Colonel Ewell said to me, 'Governor you seem to have a taste for such matters, take the men and move them forward, while I dispatch a courier to bring up some cavalry which is at Fairfax Station.' I moved the men promptly, and on reaching a wagoner's shop, halted them, seeing a strong post and rail fence on each side of the turnpike over which the enemy was expected to return. The enemy did not return. Unfortunately and sadly, John Quincy Marr's body was found just southwest of here, in a clover field. 'Uncle' Jack Rowe found him.

Father said, "History has been made here. John Quincy Marr has the sad distinction of being the first Confederate officer of the war to be killed."

Chapter Eleven

Vienna Railroad Battle, June 17, 1861

On June 9, civic minded New Yorkers formed the Sanitary Commission during a meeting. Its purpose: "On the field or in the hospitals, supplies were to be distributed impartially to any and all who needed them, without regard to state or color of uniform, be it Union soldier or Confederate prisoner." We gathered together from our own supplies excess sheets, pillowcases, comforters, blankets, shirts, underwear, socks, and even some old quilts. I gave them to a person collecting these items in our village for immediate use by our own troops. Mother, Pattie, and I also made bandages for the troops. We were doing so when Father entered the parlor and said, "I need to go to Abram Lydecker's store in Vienna to receive some merchandise that I ordered."

Situated across the street from the railroad depot, Lydecker's store was a convenient location to pick up the goods.

"I'll go with you, Father," I said. "Is it safe to travel?"

"Vienna is occupied by the Union army now, but we'll be in and out of Lydecker's store quickly, and will avoid the part of the house where the officers are stationed. How will they know who we are anyway," Father remarked wryly.

The five-and-one-half mile journey by buggy took less than one hour. We had just loaded the last sack of supplies into our buggy and said goodbye to Mr. Lydecker, when we heard a great commotion coming from the south. The railroad bell clanged, men shouted, and musket fire was evident. Union officers piled out of Mr. Lydecker's house, currently their headquarters in the village. They had their weapons drawn and were looking around wildly. A Union sergeant on his horse came towards us after another moment went by and shouted, "We've been ambushed by the Rebels!"

"Where?" one of the officers asked as he went towards the cellar to retrieve his horse.

"One half-mile south, on the train track," replied the young sergeant.

"How do you know this?" another officer asked, "and why aren't you back there fighting?"

"I witnessed the ambush as I was returning here from business in that part of town. What is important, sir, is that four companies of the 1st Ohio Regiment are on the train that got ambushed. The engineer sounded the train whistle as it approached Vienna. This alerted the Rebels that the train was coming. Shots rang out, and our men jumped off the train to get cover in the woods and fight back. The ambush damaged the engine, and the engineer panicked and uncoupled the engine and passenger car and backed away in a cowardly and hasty retreat to Alexandria. I left to warn the townspeople at that point."

Father and I, in the buggy, were steadily retreating back the way we had come after hearing all that had been said. As we got further away, Father whipped our horse until he was frothing at the mouth, and we made a rapid journey back home.

After we had settled down and told our family the news, Father took the supplies to his own mercantile establishment. He then proceeded to tell any friends, business acquaintances and neighbors what he had witnessed.

The next day, *The Local News*, our village newspaper, had a more complete account of the skirmish. The 1st Ohio Regiment, a Union force consisting of twenty-nine officers and 668 men, was under the command of Brigadier General Robert Schneck. Schneck assigned the regiment to a work train installing telegraph lines along the railroad right-of-way from Alexandria to Vienna. The train consisted of a steam engine pushing a passenger car, a baggage car, and four flatcars.

The 1st South Carolina Volunteers, a Confederate force of over six hundred men and two light cannons, led by Colonel Maxey Gregg, was assigned to destroy the railroad water tank in Vienna. In addition, they were to disrupt Union railroad activity. The skirmish then unfolded as we had heard the previous day from the sergeant. The Rebels forced the Union force to retreat on foot, carrying several wounded and leaving six dead.

"The Union troops did not fully realize that our Confederate troops are still very active in Northern Virginia," Father commented.

"Mother," I said, "this was the first railroad battle in history, and just consider—I was almost part of it!"

"It's nothing to be proud of," she said shortly and sourly. "War is a terrible thing. Just wait until you're a mother. If mothers were in charge of the country, there would be no wars."

Chapter Twelve

Encountering Yankee Troops, July 16, 1861

Now that war was upon us, Confederate soldiers occupied Fairfax Courthouse and used our home as headquarters, as it was one of the biggest in town. Some of our men in gray coats were paying customers. Not only was our home important for housing officers, it was also considered an oasis in the storm. My parents' hospitality and graciousness made spending entertaining evenings here a relief from the daily pressures of war and decision-making for some of the men. We did our best to provide lively conversation and sometimes, even music for our "guests." I sharpened my social and political skills in order to take part in the conversations. I had to formulate and believe in my own convictions concerning slavery and other issues of the day in order to carry on intelligently.

The munitions of war were being stored in the Zion Church, and it was rapidly becoming dilapidated. The Willcoxon Tavern, also our stagecoach stop, had turned into a hospital.

To my dismay and alarm, Charlie left VMI to become a soldier. VMI was one of the few institutions of higher learning that actually stayed open during the war, but dear patriotic Charlie felt that he had to do his part. He came home for a short visit, then left and fell in with Colonel Kershaw's 2nd South Carolina Infantry.

On June 19, two days after the Vienna railroad battle, my childhood friend, Robert Love, enlisted as a Private in Company "K" of the 17th Virginia Infantry. My cousins, James and Thomas Sangster were in Company "A" of that same infantry. I hated the thought of my relatives and friends being in harm's way!

Only a few days previously, Virginia Governor Letcher issued a proclamation demanding "compulsory service" for our young men aged eighteen to forty-five. Only ten percent of each county's white males would be required to enlist.

Father, Clanie, and I set out for Alexandria on July 16, 1861. Father and Clanie needed to pick up some shipments, and I accompanied them. I suspected the real purpose of the trip was that Father had some important war information to pass on to someone in Alexandria. I often saw him talking to other village leaders across the street at the courthouse, and knew he wanted to do his part to help the Southern Cause. We planned on dining and spending the night in Alexandria, returning the next day. We set out on Little River Turnpike and reached the outskirts of Annandale. A boy on horseback galloped towards us shouting, "The blue bellies are one mile ahead—you'd better turn back!"

"How many are up ahead?" asked Father.

"It's hard to tell, sir," he replied. "It is the advance troops of Brigadier-General Irvin McDowell's army." He rode on without giving us a second glance.

"Father, if we go one-quarter mile further, we will come to the home of a school acquaintance of mine. Let's stop there and rest, and let the soldiers pass by."

Clanie and Father agreed, and we continued on to the home of William Garges, where my friend Mary lived. Father actually knew William, an influential and prosperous businessman in Annandale, from business dealings. We tied our buggy in the back of the house, to attract less attention, and then knocked on the front door. Mary herself answered.

"Antonia, what a surprise," she said, upon seeing me on her doorstep.

"Mary Garges, this is my father, E.R. Ford, and my brother, Clanie."

Father said, "Very pleased to meet you, Miss Garges. I know your father. Is he here? We have had a report that a group of Yankees are imminent, and we wonder whether we could impose on you to let us rest inside until they pass through."

Mary, a nice-looking woman, with blonde hair curled in ringlets, sparkling blue eyes, and a curvaceous figure, had been a new student when I was ready to graduate, so I knew her, but not well. Mary let us in, and called for her father. A medium-tall man, with dark hair came towards us. The ever-popular mustache and mutton-chop sideburns decorated his face. He had a serious expression when he and Father shook hands and we quickly explained our predicament to him.

"It's best you stay put for a bit," he agreed. "My wife will serve you some tea."

We entertained war news back and forth for one-half hour, when we heard loud knocks on the door. Mr. Garges answered the door.

"I am Major Wadsworth, General Irvin McDowell's aide-de-camp. On behalf of the Union army, I commandeer this house for a temporary Union headquarters."

"I'm not happy about this," Mr. Garges said, "but seeing as there is nothing I can do about it, you may come in."

After a suitable rest time, Father and Clanie, who had stayed out of sight, decided that they needed to continue on, but felt that it would be too dangerous for me to accompany them.

"If the Gargeses don't mind, Antonia, I will impose on them to let you stay the night, and we'll pick you up on the way back, tomorrow," said Father. "I don't rightly know if it's more dangerous to take you with us, or leave you here."

Mrs. Garges, an older version of her daughter, replied in a worried voice, "It is you who might mind, Mr. Ford. Generally, the officers are polite and well-behaved, but they will have to be even more so with two lovely young ladies in attendance."

I looked at Father and said, "I feel comfortable here Father, and have quite gotten over my desire to accompany you to Alexandria. Please let me stay overnight?"

Father and Clanie looked at each other, nodded their heads at each other, and left.

Mr. and Mrs. Garges, who were staunchly pro-South, reluctantly took having the enemy in their house in stride. We made the best of it that evening. After dinner, we retired to the parlor to hear Mary play the piano. The gentlemen, including Major Wadsworth and a few other officers, drank whiskey. I flirted shockingly, trying to find out any information that would be helpful to my Southern soldier friends. General McDowell had already retired for the evening.

"How long do you plan on being in this area, Major?" I asked breathlessly, as I batted my eyelashes and gazed steadily into the major's dark eyes.

"Oh, just as long as it takes to get the job done, Miss Ford," he returned evasively.

"Are you actually in charge of any men yourself?" I asked.

"I am an aide-de-camp to General McDowell. My duties consist of assisting and attending to the general as needed as he interacts with the public at large. I receive and bear orders, and can act in his stead, if needed. I am his right-hand man. So, you see, it is the general who is in charge of six thousand men, not I, my dear."

I filed that information away for future use.

Midnight approached, and the men had been drinking steadily all evening. A rotund officer named Major Stone talked my ear off for the past hour and I almost nodded off when he said, "We will soon sweep the Confederates out of their holes with a flanking maneuver up the Warrenton Pike and across Bull Run above the Old Stone Bridge."

"Major," I said, "How can you be so free to speak of your army's plans in front of me?"

"My sweet," he replied, "I'm afraid that this plan is in action now. There is no savior who could keep the Rebels from being gamely routed by us. With Hunter's, Miles's, and Burnside's brigades nearby, we are ready for battle."

"Please excuse me, all," I said, "as I am weary from traveling today, and will say goodnight."

Mary and her Mother left with me and we retired for the evening. As we went upstairs, I discussed with Mrs. Garges what I felt I had to do the next morning.

"I cannot wait for Father to pick me up on his return journey," I said. "There is important information that I must relay to our troops. I beg the use of one of your horses to carry out my mission. I need to leave first thing in the morning."

"Mr. Garges should be the one to go," said Mrs. Garges.

"He would be killed for sure before getting to our lines. A woman would be less suspicious."

"I will discuss this with Mr. Garges when he retires. I'll let you know in the morning."

I shared a bed with Mary that night. I was restless, could not sleep, and felt an urgency to pass on the important information I had heard. Would morning never come?

Chapter Thirteen

Prelude to Battle, July 17, 1861

At five-thirty the next morning, July 17, Major Wadsworth was conspicuously missing from breakfast. He had left earlier, to join up with some of the troops heading towards Fairfax Courthouse. General McDowell, however, greeted me pleasantly.

"Good morning, Miss Ford. You are up early."

"Good morning, General. I wish to return to my home in Fairfax Courthouse, and request a pass for safe travel."

He thought me to be a Federalist at heart, so he issued me a pass for safe return, not knowing my true plans. The Garges had their swiftest horse saddled and waiting for me—a lively, sable-colored horse with a well-kept mane. Mrs. Garges supplied me with a canteen full of water, and some provisions wrapped in a cloth.

"Please tell Father and Clanie the situation," I said to Mr. and Mrs. Garges. "Help me in any way you are able in explaining my compulsion," I pleaded.

"Godspeed, Antonia," Mary whispered as I mounted the horse.

I left, feeling frightened and foolhardy, but worthy and justified in my actions. I rode for hours, pressing the horse as fast as I thought he could go without wearing him out completely. Back home, our recent houseguests, some high-ranking Confederate officers, had spoken rather freely about our troop locations, so I knew where to go. I knew I had to reach the Confederate lines and General Beauregard with my information. My brother's life and the lives of boys I grew up with depended on it. Of course, there were formations of Union troops everywhere, which made my journey more difficult. I had to stop when accosted and show my pass. I took alternate roads and short cuts that I knew about in order to avoid as many troops as possible.

Because 1861 was a wet year, the roads were rutted and muddy. I stopped to rest the horse periodically, and to let him drink from streams, but for the most part spent the entire day urging the beast onward. Although I had to travel only thirteen-and-one-half miles, with all the stops and detours, it took much longer than it should have.

At four o'clock, I arrived at Bull Run, beyond Centreville. I don't know what the men thought to see me, astride my horse, not riding sidesaddle, with a morning dress on, my hair wild and unencumbered, and with red and watery eyes.

"Can someone direct me to General Beauregard," I shouted with as much authority as I could muster. "I have important information about enemy troop movements to tell him." I must have seemed believable, because a soldier held my horse, while a sergeant lifted me off the horse and onto the ground.

"Come with me," the sergeant said.

I waited outside the general's tent for several minutes, as he was speaking to someone else. I overheard the statement, "Stuart's Black Horse cavalry are ready, sir." Indistinct murmurings of approval were the response. A captain then exited the tent and walked away. The sergeant accompanying me spoke to the guard outside General Beauregard's tent for a moment before opening the tent flap and ushering me inside.

"Who are you and why are you here?" gruffly asked the general.

"I am Antonia Ford of Fairfax Courthouse, and I have firsthand knowledge of battle plans being laid by the Yankees to trap you, sir."

"Please go on," he said.

I proceeded to tell all that I had heard the previous evening. After I finished, General Beauregard looked thoughtful, thanked me for the information, and the sergeant summarily ushered me out of the tent and walked away. Since there was no more business to keep me there, I started to mount my horse. At that moment, from behind me, a soldier grabbed my arm!

Chapter Fourteen

Battle of 1st Manassas, July 17, 1861

You, ma'am, are under arrest for suspicion of being a spy and giving us misleading information."

"I protest. I am a Southern lady, patriotic to the cause of the South. What evidence do you have against me?"

"In these days, suspicion is enough. You will have to come with me."

The soldier took me that evening to the village of Brentsville, south of Manassas. The courthouse, clerk's office, and jail were located on the main street. He led me to the jail where I had a cell to myself. I had food and water to drink, and had a chance to relieve myself in the privy. A guard lounged and gawked at me from outside the jail door.

"Please let me out," I begged to him. "I have a brother, Charlie, who is with Colonel Kershaw's Infantry. My father, E.R. Ford, is a respected businessman in Fairfax Courthouse, and a staunch supporter of the South. You can check these things out! Ask Jeb Stuart or John Mosby!"

"We are doing so, ma'am," the guard curtly said.

I made myself as comfortable as possible and tried to sleep. The bare dirt floor felt cruelly hard and I slept fitfully.

After soldiers from my own side incarcerated me for twenty-four hours, the same sergeant who had escorted me here came to release me.

"Our apologies, ma'am for this mistake. Your story checked out, and I will now take you back to Fairfax Courthouse."

"Thank God!" I exclaimed. "I hope you haven't done anything to my borrowed horse," I added sarcastically.

"Your horse is here, miss," he replied. "Let's get on our way."

We returned via a circuitous route in order to avoid being seen by the Yankees. It took far longer than it should have, but we finally backtracked our way to Fairfax Courthouse and to my home. It had never looked so good. The sergeant left me at my house. I opened the front door and Father and Mother ushered me quickly into the parlor.

"My God, Antonia!" exclaimed Mother. "What were you thinking to put yourself in such danger? Where have you been? We thought you were dead."

I knew I had seriously alarmed Mother for her to use the word "God" in her exclamation.

"Father, Mother," I cried, "You know by now, that the information I learned was important enough to spread to those in charge. I have saved people I love by the information I gave General Beauregard. Don't be too harsh." I then explained what had occurred.

Father only clutched me to him, weeping, as if I was lost and had been found again. "It is an outrage that our own army treated you so."

Mother told me what had happened here yesterday. "I awoke to hear the sounds of wagon wheels, horses' whinnies, and men shouting. I looked out my window and could see the Confederates taking down their camp, and Bonham's men moving out. To where, I did not know. As the day went on, the temperature rose to ninety-four degrees, and I pitied the retreating men in their hot uniforms, no doubt thirsty. It seemed that our troops had just cleared town, when, at eleven-thirty a.m., Yankees started pouring in. You can imagine, without your Father here, I was frightened. I saw some slaves out and about, and a few of our local elderly peering at the troops. I was brave enough to stand in my doorway and observe the procession. Our recently departed Southern troops had left their heavy belongings, such as knapsacks, behind on the streets."

Father stated, "Clanie and I were just making our way home, when we observed our Confederate flag being lowered from the courthouse flagpole, and a United States flag raised."

Mother continued, "I was quilting in the parlor, when I heard a commotion through the window. A local youngster ran by shouting, 'They're ransacking the printing office!'"

"Aren't you afraid our house will be looted?" I asked, panic-stricken.

Mother assured me that since Yankee officers were using our house now as headquarters, their men would dare not trespass.

"General McDowell was here in town, mid-afternoon yesterday in order to send a dispatch to Washington," Father said. "Last night, he spent the night in our home, and left early this morning, for Sangster's Station. He appeared to be feeling poorly, but as to the nature of his complaints, I had no idea."

Too tired to entertain further discussion, as it was late, we went to bed.

Not until three days later, did weary, wounded and bedraggled Union soldiers stagger in retreat through Fairfax Courthouse. Their officers still came and went through our front door, so I was not surprised to hear a knock upon the door. To my dismay, Major Wadsworth stood on the porch, along with Major Stone. I'm not sure who was more surprised—they or I.

"Majors Wadsworth and Stone," I stammered, "what an unexpected pleasure it is to see you again so soon." I hoped and prayed Major Stone did not remember what he had told me in his drunken state, while in Annandale.

"A pleasure indeed," Major Wadsworth replied. "I understand this house is our headquarters, and I need to attend to some business for a few hours. In addition, I need to see that stragglers and worn-out soldiers are not left behind during our retreat."

"Retreat? Does that mean the battle was a Confederate victory?"

"Our carefully planned surprise attack seemed to be not such a surprise," he said wearily. "The damn Rebels routed us, with an estimated three thousand casualties on our side versus 1,750 Rebel dead. We are falling back to Washington City, and will be gone by dusk."

I turned away to get Father, a smile upon my face, knowing that the first major land battle of the war had resulted in a Southern victory, perhaps due to my timely information.

Chapter Fifteen

John Mosby, August 26, 1861

One steamy evening, at ten o'clock, I heard a rapid knocking on our door. I opened it and saw through the dark, rainy gloom my friend, John Singleton Mosby, a private in the 1st Virginia Cavalry, supported by a fellow soldier and a Negro. The men had tied up their horses out front. John looked much shorter than his five feet ten inch height, as he leaned heavily on his men. There were two revolvers at his side. His normally intelligent, sparkling blue eyes appeared clouded with pain; his sandy hair mussed and his brown hat crookedly ajar. Being fair complexioned and beardless, John looked more youthful than his twenty-eight years. I usually received a nice smile from him, but at present, it was all he could do to greet me through his obvious agony. The two other men carried his thin and wiry body into the parlor where Mother and Father were reading and then the soldier left. The other man was Aaron, John's servant.

John explained, "I received a fall from my horse this evening, while on picket down at Falls Church, which came near to killing me."

Father took John's hat and his horrible looking, raggedy, dirty jacket, and Mother fetched some blankets to cover the sofa so that John could recline while continuing to tell us his tale.

"There were only three of us at our post; a large body of cavalry came dashing down towards us from the direction of the enemy. Our orders were to fire on all. I fired my gun, started back toward where our main body was, my horse slipped down, fell on me, and galloped off, leaving me in a senseless condition in the road. My comrades caught my horse and brought me here to your house, as we knew I could get good care here."

Right away, Mother chimed in, "Of course you and Aaron can stay here. We will nurse you back to health." Mother and Mathilde had cooked John many breakfasts in the past after he had stood picket the night before.

Mathilde brought some soap, water, and clean bandages. John hobbled into the kitchen and while he sat, we bandaged all his scrapes. His hawk-like nose bled profusely. Father went to get Dr. Gunnell.

"I do not believe that any bones are broken, but perhaps some bruised ribs," Dr. Gunnell said, after examining John. "Whoever applied these bandages did a good job. Stay off your feet for a few days, and I believe you will be back to health in about a week."

Afterwards, Father helped him upstairs, and made sure he reposed comfortably in Clanie's room.

The next day I had opportunity to find out more about John Mosby. Our friendship, purely platonic, would always remain so, although I found myself attracted to him. His devotion to his wife was touching.

"I have been married to my wife, Pauline Clarke, for about four years now. We have a daughter, May Virginia, and a son, Beverly. I miss Pauline and the children tremendously, as I so infrequently get to see them."

During the next week, while he stayed with us, I discovered what a true Southern gentleman he really was. Although reserved, I found him to be thoughtful, with a sharp mind and quite well read. His intelligence, boldness, resourcefulness, and scrupulous honesty were all good traits for the lawyer that he was. As he recuperated at our house, we had many opportunities to take very short walks to help exercise and limber his aching muscles, which his horse bruised terribly by falling on him.

Towards the end of the week, we decided a longer walk was in order. We turned right out of my house onto Payne Street, and then turned right again onto North Street.

He told me about his college days. "I went to the University of Virginia in 1849, but was expelled for shooting and wounding a fellow student in a quarrel when the student disparaged me. The court fined me one thousand dollars, and sentenced me to one year in jail for unlawful shooting; however, the Governor of Virginia released me after six months in jail. While I awaited my trial, I persuaded the prosecutor to lend me some law books, as I expressed interest in the law. Following my release, after my sentence was annulled, I was admitted to the bar and opened a law office in Bristol, Virginia."

"Have you had many important cases?" I asked.

"Not many. The practice of law is not only arguing in court. There are mundane items and lots of paperwork that take time. The war interrupted my practice."

We turned right onto Merchant Street, walked one block, and then turned right onto Fairfax Street.

"Tell me the history of this building," John asked me. He pointed to a brick, two-level home that had eight windows facing the street. A central chimney divided the roof of the long, narrow building. A wood fence enclosed the front yard.

"This is the oldest residence in town, built around 1805, on land once owned by Richard Ratcliffe. It has been used as a post station and stagecoach stop."

We walked on in companionable silence.

"John, which side do you think will win this war?"

"I've heard it said that this war should be over soon, but I have my doubts. I fear that the South is doomed, but I, for one, must defend the soil I love so much."

"On August 26, the Union forces were surprised and routed by our men at Kessler's Cross Roads in West Virginia," I stated.

"That is true," said John. "For every punch, the Federals give a counterpunch. On August 29, Union troops in North Carolina captured Forts Clark and Hatteras. The Federals then garrisoned the captured Confederate forts with only one man lost on their side. They strategically seized our coastal defenses to enforce the blockade."

"It is the lack of essential supplies that hurts the South more than anything else," I said.

We had circled the block and returned to my house on Payne Street.

"I think I will be leaving you tomorrow," said John. "I need to be where the action is."

"If your body is mended, then that is what you must do."

Chapter Sixteen

The Helpful and the Hopeful, September 1861

Now that war was full upon us, it would be unseemly to cavort around and pursue a good time, but life did go on. We knew that Charlie had survived the battle at Manassas. The gentleman who clerked for Father and boarded with us, John R. Gunnell, had just left this month to enlist. Although having the same last name, he was no relation to our neighbors, and I hoped that the 8th Virginia, in Pickett's Division, would keep him safe at Camp Johnson. I always felt that John's persona was an odd mixture of studious intellectual contrasted with brawny, rugged outdoorsman. He helped my family in any way he could, especially with the bookkeeping for Father's business. I sensed that he was attracted to me, but I thought him too old to be a proper suitor to me.

My family made the best of things, and luckily, for us, we had the means to keep ourselves well stocked with food, clothing, fuel, and other essentials. Many nights our entertainment consisted of our family playing cards together. On occasion, a group of young people would meet at one another's homes for games. A preponderance of young women congregated at these gatherings, as our village boys showed no shyness about enlisting. Often, the gathering was a quilting bee.

My current quilting project, a diamond pattern, consisted of tatters and scraps of cloth from old clothing. I made bandages out of anything that was big enough, so my diamonds were very tiny indeed. I was careful not to quilt on Sunday, as it was the Lord's Day. On Sundays, I attempted to comprehend what I read in the Bible, especially the teachings of Jesus, but my concentration was half-hearted.

Eager to help in some way, Mother and I went to Jerusalem Baptist Church, known as Payne's Church, in order to nurse the wounded. Located three miles away, we took our carriage, along with one of our former slaves, who drove us. We brought a basket of medical supplies, including bandages, and some very tattered and worn linens and blankets. We went through a dense forest on the main road leading from Fairfax Courthouse towards Fairfax Station, and then came upon the large, brick church, built during the Colonial times. A graveyard surrounded the church. Many of the gravestones were so old that I could barely read the names. The yard, however, was rapidly filling up with new burial places—those of our brave soldiers. Every week, there were more and more occupants of these barren, unadorned, headstone-less mounds. Only the heaps of dirt identified them as graves, marked with plain wooden crosses with carved names.

Mother and I entered the decayed, arched doorway, and stepped onto the paved floor. The raised pews had old-fashioned high backs. Medical personnel had pushed them into a formation that made nursing to the sick more convenient. Each pew became a bed, and contained one or two wounded soldiers, with the overflow on pallets on the floor.

The old pulpit, sounding board, and reading desk graced the front of the room. On one side of the room on the wall were the Ten Commandments, the Apostles' Creed, and the Lord's Prayer in large gilt letters. The decrepit stove provided heat in the winter. While we worked there, a small boy, about six years old, entered the hospital.

"Bread for the sick and hungry," he cried, while going from pew to pew, handing out slices.

"Where did you get the bread, young fellow?" I asked.

"Mama baked it," he replied. "We are not members here, but Mama says we have to help the sick soldiers as best we can."

"Your Mama is correct," I said. "You are a dear boy. I see your basket is empty. You run along now and tell your Mama we said thank you. A hospital is no place for a little fellow like you. Scat!"

Every week, Mother and I made the trek and did what we could for the Manassas wounded. When our village hospital, the old Willcoxon Tavern, had occupants, we worked there, too. Sometimes I hid myself and cried over the suffering I witnessed.

Our village was once again under Southern control. Generals Beauregard and Johnston moved their headquarters here on September 17. Jeb Stuart and his men, along with John Mosby, had been here since July 23. We could count on *The Local News* reporting a skirmish every two to three weeks. I knew John Mosby instigated the raids, as he came to our house often and told us his exploits.

One of my frequent suitors, John Esten Cooke, was due at my door shortly to give me some important news. At promptly eight o'clock, just as night fell, I heard his knock on the door.

"Good evening, John," I said as I opened the door, with a wide smile on my face. John amused me tremendously and had good stories to tell.

"You are a sight for sore eyes, my dear," he said to me, as he kissed my outstretched hand.

His small brown eyes gazed intensely into my eyes. Although thirty-one, he looked youthful with a thin, angular face, and luxuriant dark brown hair. His handlebar mustache and goatee gave him a debonair appearance.

"Come into the parlor. I have the teakettle on. Would you like some tea?"

"That would be splendid," he said, as he entered the parlor and removed his hat. "Mr. and Mrs. Ford, Pattie—good evening to all of you," he said with a courteous lowering of his head and a bow.

My family had met John many times over the years, and always felt that he would be a good match for me. Although I had warm and friendly feelings for him, I couldn't see myself as his wife, and had previously told my parents so. I entered the parlor with a tray containing our tea and set it on the table.

"I've come here to tell all of you that I will be serving as a sergeant in the Richmond Howitzers, 1st Company. I will be going to Leesburg in one week to join the group."

Pattie, ten years old, knew little of life and death, and clapped her hands excitedly.

"Go get those Billy Yanks!" she shouted gleefully.

"Pattie, it's time for bed, honey," Mother said wearily, as she escorted her out of the room.

"Why do you feel you must do this, John?" asked Father.

"I have to stand up to what I believe is tyranny," he responded. "My sense of duty, ethics, and morality compel me to fight against a government, which I feel is imposing too much of its will on the day-to-day actions of its people. I am not fighting for slavery, which I believe to be an evil institution."

"Well stated!" I chimed in. "I, too, believe that slavery is evil. What my heart cannot bear is the threat of losing people dear to me."

"Am I one of those people?" John asked ingenuously.

"You know you are!" I exclaimed.

"The entire Ford family is fond of you," Father said. "With that sentiment, I will tend to some bookkeeping. Good night to both of you."

"Good night, sir, and pray for me."

"I will indeed," Father said.

Now that we were alone, John moved from the armchair to the sofa where I was sitting. He smiled at me and took my hand in his.

"Will you truly miss me?" he asked tenderly.

"I will pray for your safe return," I said, speaking in a louder and stronger voice than I meant to.

"I didn't think that you prayed. You've never talked about religion much."

"I'm not sure that Jesus Christ died to save us all from sin, but I believe in God, and will pray for you every night. You could say that clouds of doubt cover my spiritual sky."

John put his arm around me and we sat companionably for an hour chatting about people we knew and especially news about friends and neighbors serving in the army.

"I must leave you now, my precious. I will write and hope that you write back."

"The post is erratic, but you can be sure I'll write cheerful letters to you."

At the parlor door, John brushed his lips lightly against mine, and left, looking back once, longingly. Mathilde closed the front door and I went up the stairs to my bedroom where my sister slept soundly.

Chapter Seventeen

Aide-de-Camp, October 7, 1861

After the Northern debacle at Manassas, General McClellan now commanded the Union troops. The Union army occupied a line from near Fairfax Courthouse almost to Leesburg, excluding our village. In contrast, the most advanced outpost of the Confederates was at Centreville.

On this dry autumn evening of the seventh day of October 1861, the foliage sparkled in all its glory. At eight o'clock, I heard the sounds of horses outside our fence followed by some sharp knocks. Father cautiously opened the door to find two of our soldiers, known to us all.

"Come in, gentlemen," said Father. The men came into the parlor where Mother, Clanie, and I casually sat. They removed their hats and held them by their sides. I could not help but notice the black, plumed hat that I had seen before, even before I noted the man himself. General James Stuart stood, smiling, accompanied by John Esten Cooke.

"Good evening, all," said John Esten Cooke.

I ran up to him and let him kiss my hand while saying, "What a pleasant surprise! I've enjoyed our correspondence, but a personal appearance is even better."

"I believe you all know my good friend, cousin, and compatriot, Brigadier General James Ewell Brown Stuart, otherwise known as Jeb."

"John and my dear wife, Flora Cooke, are cousins," clarified Jeb Stuart.

Jeb, a handsome, strong looking man with blue eyes and auburn hair, had an erect, soldierly bearing that, along with his full beard and handlebar mustache, gave him a refined look. He approached me and kissed my hand, as well as that of my mother's.

"What gives us the honor and pleasure of your company tonight?" asked Father.

"Why, the honor is ours, and we hope to be able to relax and socialize with these beautiful women, young Clanie, and you, sir, while having pleasant conversation and dare I request—music?" replied Jeb.

"Even better," Mother quickly replied, "you must spend the night. I'll have Octavia prepare a sleeping place for you."

"I can't turn down such a generous offer, ma'am. My men are camped nearby. Did you know that John has just become an ordinance officer in my cavalry?" asked Jeb.

"And you," Father pointed out, "have recently been promoted from Colonel to Brigadier General."

"Very observant," Jeb replied. "The promotion came through on September 24, following our great success at Manassas."

"You are too modest, Jeb," said John. "What he did not tell you is that he screened Johnston's movement to Manassas, and, in the fighting of July 21, made an effective charge. Colonel Early said that Stuart did as much toward saving the battle as any subordinate who participated in it."

"Bravo, sir!" I exclaimed.

Mother instructed Mathilde, "Prepare a tray of blackberry cordial and shortbread, please. This is a cause for celebration."

Father asked, "Would either of you gentlemen care for some bourbon?" Receiving affirmative answers, he prepared drinks for our guests.

"Have you seen your little daughter and son recently, General?" Mother asked.

"My sweetheart, little Flora, 'La Petite', is the light of my life. She just turned four—I look at her, and I see my wife in her face. James Jr. is one year old. I rarely get to see them, and I miss them, as they are in Lynchburg, Virginia."

"I'll play some pieces on the piano," I said. I knew that the general was not a card playing man, so that form of entertainment was out of the question. Being a devout Christian, he did not swear, as did so many of the military men; nor was he prone to any vice that I knew of. He did not drink a drop of alcohol. He was a family man who loved his wife and adored his children.

I started out playing "Glory! Glory! Hallelujah!" Jeb had a clear, ringing voice, quite in tune. Obviously, the men needed this respite from their troubles.

"How about 'Dixie?'" queried Jeb.

We all sang along to that rousing and inspirational marching song. My favorite was "The Bonnie Blue Flag."

"And 'Here's to Brave Virginia! The Old Dominion State,'" I sang.

As the night went on, the effect of the consumption of bourbon and blackberry cordial became apparent to all. I had not seen Mother so happy since before Charlie went to war. The men's demeanor became boisterous and loud, the women giddy. Non-alcohol imbibing Jeb, the personification of wild courage, superb manhood, and indomitable gayety, always had a laugh at his lips and a song behind it. Several hours went by as the men smoked and drank. They held lively discussions concerning everything from supplies to slavery.

"Thank you for your letters, dear Antonia," said John Esten Cooke. "Your recent visit to Leesburg was especially welcome. It afforded me the opportunity to visit you while you stayed with Miss Hattie Fadely. I especially enjoyed hearing the details you gave me concerning your part in warning General Beauregard about the advancing Northern troops at Manassas."

"General Ewell came to see me personally, to thank me."

John responded, "I don't wonder at General Ewell's coming to see you.

You deserve that compliment, at the very least, leaving out of view the fact that I reckon the old fellow—pardon my disrespect—knew where a sweet face and musical voice were to be found."

"Hear! Hear! To a brave and courageous young lady. I was particularly angry to hear how you were treated when you brought the message to Beauregard," said Jeb.

Clanie laughingly suggested, "Antonia should be part of your staff."

"Mrs. Ford, may I impose upon you for a piece of paper and a pen?" said Jeb mysteriously.

Mother fetched the items and we waited patiently to see what mischief Jeb was conjuring. After several minutes, he put the pen down and took out his sealing wax and using his signet ring applied an impression on the paper. He stood up, and with a flourish and a bow, presented me with the document, signed by him. I read it to the group:

TO ALL WHOM IT MAY CONCERN:

Know ye, that reposing special confidence in the patriotism, fidelity and ability of Miss Antonia Ford, I, James E. B. Stuart, by virtue of the power invested in me, as Brigadier General in the Provisional Army of the Confederate States of America, do hereby appoint and commission her my Honorary Aide-de-Camp, to rank as such from this date.

She will be obeyed, respected, and admired by all the lovers of a noble nature.

Given under my hand and seal at the Headquarters Cavalry Brigade, at Camp Beverly, the seventh day of October, A.D., 1861, and the first year of our Independence.

J. E. B. Stuart
Brigadier General, CSA

Everyone in the room started clapping and cheering at the conclusion. I laughed so hard I could barely speak. I could feel my cheeks redden with delight at the impish prank.

"Thank you, General!" I gushed. "I will consider this one of my most cherished possessions. Never doubt the loyalty of my family, and our continued assistance to you and your men, however you might need us." I proudly gazed at it again.

"Mr. Ford, I must formally thank you and your family for the information thus gained throughout this first year. Anything further concerning Yankee troop movements or plans that you can convey to me will be vastly appreciated," Stuart said. "The high command in Richmond also sends its thanks for your secret dispatches."

Chapter Eighteen

Our Home is Searched, Winter 1861

General Stuart now had his headquarters in my village, while John Mosby continued to attack picket posts in the nearby places still under Union control. Our soldiers busily constructed small semi-subterranean huts out of logs chinked with mud. They buried the sides of the huts underground to make them warmer and use less wood. Of course, despite these conservation techniques, the construction further depleted our nearby sources of firewood. As each hut hastily was finished, six to eight men would occupy it, savoring the warmth it provided. Winter approached, and the troops of both armies were short on supplies. On November 23, 1861, a Union foraging raid in an area close by known as Flint Hill made it unsafe to be on the roads. Even our own troops posed a danger to us, because they viewed every traveler with suspicion. Father obtained a letter of safe passage from L. Herman Brien, Assistant Adjutant General. We hoped that this would prevent our own troops from shooting us, assuming that they would stop to read first.

Headquarters Advanced Forces   November 25, 1861

*   The Bearer, Mr. E. R. Ford, has permission and is authorized by General Johnston to procure supplies for the family at Fairfax Courthouse, and will therefore be allowed to go from the C.V. on the Little River Turnpike as far as W. Sampson Beach, about two miles and return, as often as he may desire.*

By Command of General Stuart
L. Herman Brien
A. A. Gen

A skirmish occurred on November 28 in Vienna, Virginia, also quite close to Fairfax Courthouse.

Another month went by. We had a subdued Christmas, as we had not heard from Charlie in a while. On December 29, we finally received a letter from him. He wrote: *I think that I have committed myself as regards the artillery and I am not sorry for it—because it is my inclination to go through the war.*

On December 31, John Esten Cooke sequestered himself in our house to help us say goodbye to the old year and welcome the new one. I told him during that visit that his friendship was dear to me, but I could no longer consider him a suitor.

"May I still visit you and write you, Antonia?" he implored.

"Please," I begged. "I would be upset if you did not."

We passed the evening casually playing parlor games with my entire family.

On January 8, 1862, I read in *The Local News* that another foraging raid by the Federals occurred in Flint Hill. So far, we had been lucky that our own supplies were untouched, perhaps due to protection by Lieutenant John Singleton Mosby.

We received another letter from Charles, stationed in Gainesville, Virginia, on March 5. The line he wrote, that was also my fervent prayer: *I will endeavor to do my duty to my country, and hope I will get safely through.*

Meanwhile, Confederate General Johnston had moved our troops further south for logistical and strategic reasons. Our village was now unprotected and I felt vulnerable. This uneasiness caused me to fret, bringing on one of my bothersome migraine headaches. My portent of doom came to fruition a few days later, in the early evening, when I witnessed a Lincoln cavalry skirmish. I heard a group of men outside, and opened the front door a crack to try to determine in the near darkness from which army they were. A Yankee and a Confederate soldier struggled on the road in front of me. The soldier dressed in gray thrust his short dagger into the chest of his opponent. A fountain of crimson sprayed into the air and the Union soldier fell, screaming in agony. He convulsed once or twice then all was quiet and still. The other soldier ran to rejoin his comrades. A Yankee officer located on the courthouse lawn ordered in a booming voice, "Perform a thorough search of all the houses, men."

I quickly shut and locked the door and told Mother and Father what I witnessed. Father swiftly gathered some papers from his desk in the parlor and hid them under a loose floorboard. I went to my room to fetch some incriminating letters, maps, and my aide-de-camp souvenir from under my mattress, as I didn't want them to fall into the wrong hands. Although too late to hide them better, as I heard fists battering on our front door, I hid the papers in my crinoline hoopskirt and quickly ran down the stairs and into the parlor. I calmly took up my embroidery while Father opened the front door. I spread my skirts in a wide circle around the chair, touching the floor. Mother worked on her quilt. Two Union soldiers entered our home. I could see from my chair that the taller soldier appeared rough and burly, with dark hair and beard, and cruel eyes. He outranked the shorter soldier who seemed more genteel and had a cautious air about him. They started searching the upstairs. Pattie clung to me, crying, while Frank sat at Mother's feet. Clanie scowled and tried to look ferocious and brave, while standing near the fireplace. Father escorted them from room to room and presumably picked up the items that the soldiers threw to the floor. Finally, the only room left was the parlor.

"I wish to search this room, ma'am," said the shorter soldier to my mother.

Mother nodded her head, while continuing to sew.

"Search all you wish," I said calmly, not lifting my eyes from my sewing.

At the end of the search, with nothing in their hands, the taller officer in charge said to me in a rude voice, "Stand up."

I looked up, more furious than ever in my life, and said, "I thought not even a Yankee would expect a Southern woman to rise for him!"

Almost losing control, his face, red with anger, he bowed stiffly, and with the abashed junior officer remaining behind, left our home without a backwards glance, slamming the door in response.

The junior officer said, "You are indeed a woman to be reckoned with."

At this point, I slumped wearily against the edge of the chair, trying to console Pattie. Mother rocked Frank, and Father poured a shot of bourbon.

The officer turned to leave. I stood up to help straighten things, when one of the hidden papers fell from my hoopskirt onto the floor. Hearing the noise, the Yankee came to me, picked it up, and handed it back to me politely without looking at it. I recovered quickly by saying, "My embroidery design is useless without the color chart. Thank you kindly, sir."

He then left, shutting the door behind him.

Father came to me, wide-eyed, and asked, "What have you there, Antonia?"

I replied, "It is a map of shortcuts that I drew for Mosby."

"I see, Daughter. Do you realize the peril that you just caused yourself?"

I did not answer.

"You need to keep anything that might be incriminating carefully hidden. Do you have somewhere safe in your room to hide your documents?"

"Yes. I'll see to it right away." Before I could go upstairs, I heard some shots ringing out, and knew that the two sides had converged again, somewhere in our small village.

Many instances during these uncertain times, I wondered when the right man would come along for me to marry. I decided to pray to God for his safety, knowing that he must certainly be alive, even if I did not yet know his name.

Chapter Nineteen

Joseph C. Willard, April 9, 1862

The Army of the Potomac occupied our quiet village again as a military outpost. They had been here since early March. Yesterday, I watched squadrons of cavalry swarming over our hills on their horses with their sabers drawn. They looked like little boys playing cowboys and Indians. Some of them, sadly, were young boys.

I carefully walked around our village, in the lightest of rain, enjoying spring's beauties, but avoiding war's eyesores. I saw from a distance the white camp tents of the Union army. I passed by the ruined structure which was formerly my Uncle Brower's newspaper office—destroyed by the advancing Federal troops.

As I walked by the old Zion church site, I shuddered to see what the Union soldiers had done, out of necessity, to keep warm. The church was an empty shell, stripped of its very soul to supply firewood for the troops. The remnants of our town's place of worship stood starkly against the clean, blue sky.

Robins sang and crocuses bloomed, but I felt heartsick with worry for my friends and relatives fighting this God-awful war. As I returned home, my musings continued, even as I climbed our front steps. I turned around to see that the light misting had stopped, and the sun was trying to break through, when two men rode up on horseback; one a Union officer, the other apparently his servant.

"Is this the Ford residence?" the officer asked me politely, in a baritone voice.

A handsome man, mature, dressed in the blue uniform of a Yankee captain, faced me. His light brown, curly, side-parted hair framed his face, and the ever-popular mutton-chop sideburns adorned his cheeks. Large, brown, soulful eyes on a kind and gentle face caused his ordinary features to become extraordinary.

"Why, yes," I replied in honeyed tones. "You are at the correct residence. What is the nature of your business, sir?"

"I am Captain Willard, a staff officer of General McDowell's, and request that this house be used as his headquarters." He bowed his head, almost shamefully.

"Our home has been a popular choice, sir. Let me find my mother. I am Miss Antonia Ford. Please come in," I said as I opened the door wide.

I noticed several neighbors openly staring and listening to the interchange. They had seen both Southern and Northern soldiers headquartered at our home, and knew our staunch "secesh" viewpoints. Still they stared and whispered behind our backs.

Captain Willard gave the reins of his horse to his servant, Jim, and followed me inside, removing his hat as he entered our home. He left his leather haversack by the door. I showed Captain Willard into the parlor, and then quickly walked into the kitchen to bring Mother to the captain.

"Good afternoon, madam," he said, rising to his feet when we entered the room. "I am Captain Joseph Willard. General McDowell has requested your hospitality, yet again, and the loan of your house for his headquarters for the next few weeks. The general, Colonel Schriner, and a few of his staff would like to stay here, if we may," he said politely, yet firmly. Although he spoke to Mother, his eyes flitted occasionally to me.

"Yes, you may stay here," Mother said. "I have a son fighting for the South, however, so you'll understand if I am not whole-heartedly as amiable as usual. My husband is away on business."

Mother didn't mention that his business had to do with the Confederacy.

"Understood perfectly, madam. I would feel the same way in reverse circumstances."

"Excuse me now, Captain, but I have to get back to my cooking. Antonia?" she asked questionably.

"I'll show him out, Mother, when we finish our arrangements." I had been through this scenario before, with both Union and Confederate staff officers, and so felt competent to handle matters. Mother left the room.

The officers would use one of our upstairs bedrooms. We were a family of seven—nine counting our servants, Mathilde and Octavia, so the army could not very well commandeer all our bedrooms. Not if they wanted Mother's hearty breakfasts served. We had long ago rolled up and stored our fine Wilton carpeting from the parlor and dining room floors. The mud on the men's boots would have ruined the carpets in no time. We were lucky that no bummers, that is, foraging or marauding soldiers, trespassed in our home, or stole all our stores of food. The government's military rules did not allow foraging, but it still occurred. I told the captain what the sleeping arrangements would be and at what time Mathilde would serve breakfast.

I couldn't help but notice how soft-spoken and genteel this captain was. I looked him squarely in the eyes, smiled, batted my eyelashes, and said, "How long have you been away from your family, Captain?"

"I have two brothers, Henry and Caleb, whom I see frequently. We are all in the hotel business. Henry and I run Willard's hotel on Fourteenth Street in Washington City. Since the government commissioned me in 1862, Henry has handled many of the day-to-day tasks. Unfortunately, he and his wife recently decided to move back to Hudson, New York, to escape the wartime danger. I suspect they will return after the war. We have a good person overseeing the hotel."

I knew that Willard's, the finest hotel in the city, served now as Union headquarters. It was "the place to see and be seen" in polite society, and the brothers were known for their wit and charm. Their restaurant offered fine dining. My family more often frequented Brown's Hotel, where the atmosphere was as distinctly Southern in character as it was Northern at Willard's, the rival house. What a pleasant surprise to find this successful businessman in my home!

"I have dined there before. How is business, by the way?"

"Booming, miss! We sometimes have one thousand guests at a time, with three or four to a bed. We manage to maintain high standards, nonetheless."

"Are you able to see your brother and other family members often?" I asked, unashamedly fishing for further information.

"I used to meet with Henry and his wife, Sarah, fairly often, as my unit is stationed in Washington. I also own a home, one block north of the hotel at 613 Fourteenth Street, near G Street. Edwin, my eldest brother, is a soldier. Back home, in Westminster, Vermont, my youngest brother, Cyprian, is a farmer. I have two married sisters, Mary and Susan," he said quickly and dismissively.

I did not see a wedding ring on his finger, but as he seemed reluctant to talk further about his family, I thought it best to end that topic of conversation.

"Are you stationed with General McDowell in Arlington?"

"At times, yes, but I am able to spend a good many nights in my own home."

"I'm curious—how do you travel here from Fourteenth Street, sir?"

"I travel across the Long Bridge. It is a wooden, mile-long toll bridge across the Potomac River. By, the way, your town's plank roads are dreadful. The warping and rotting of the wooden planks could easily maim a good horse."

"I have been across both the Long and Chain Bridges. My mother and I used to shop in Washington City before the war. I remember when the Chain Bridge was rebuilt after the first one was swept away by a flood. I also know that the Aqueduct Bridge is being used to transport your troops and supplies from Georgetown to Alexandria."

"Perhaps, miss, you know too much! I am not at liberty to comment on your last statement."

"My goodness!" I laughed. "I am an educated woman and I do read the newspapers. I ask for nothing that is not already common knowledge! Tell me, what does one do with one's horse in the city? Do you rent a stable stall?"

"That is a good question. I'm fortunate that the hotel has its own stable behind the hotel, so I am able to quarter my horse there."

"Is it true what I've heard about the dereliction that the city has become?" I asked.

"You would be well advised to avoid the south side of Pennsylvania Avenue, an area where pickpockets, prostitutes, and con men abound."

I thought, how refreshingly outspoken and honest this man was. Perhaps I should have been embarrassed to hear him use the word prostitute instead of Cyprian, fallen woman, or camp follower, but I was not. No credit to me, I thought wryly.

"I have completely forgotten my manners, Captain. May I serve you some tea?"

"That would be kind, miss. My superiors will be arriving this evening, but I have no urgent business to attend to just now other than the urgency of keeping you company."

"Oh, you say so!" I said in a spirited manner. "Flattery will get you nowhere! So, your comrades would be arriving no matter what our answer was to your request for housing?"

"This is war," he said abruptly.

I went into the kitchen to set up the tea tray.

"Antonia!" exclaimed Mathilde, "why are you talking so long to that man? You don't have to serve tea to the enemy!"

Mother added, "We go beyond our limits by allowing the men to relax in our parlor and drink our whiskey in the evening. I serve them breakfast in the morning. How the neighbors must be talking about the sociable Fords!"

"You are so right, Mother. I must say, though, that this captain strikes me as a man any woman would want to know, enemy or not."

I returned to the parlor and found the captain looking at some tin plate daguerreotypes of family members, with Charlie's picture in his hand.

"This must be your brother, who is serving for the South."

"Yes, this is Charlie. Of all my siblings, he is my favorite."

"Your family is firmly for the South, then, I imagine?"

"'Oh yes, I am a Southern girl, and glory in the name…'"

Captain Willard finished, "'And boast it with far greater pride, than glittering wealth and fame.'"

I just looked at him. The silence lasted a few seconds before I stammered, "So you are a man of poetry also?"

"Like you, I read the newspaper every day, and happened to see that poem published. It has become popular."

We drank our tea in companionable silence. Our clock chimed four o'clock. I broke the silence by blundering forthrightly into war talk again.

"Skirmishes in Flint Hill and Vienna have been occurring fearfully close to home. Tell me, is the Star Fort in Vienna being occupied by North or South?"

A fleeting smile crossed Captain Willard's face, and then he said with a straight face, "My dear, if I told you that, I would have to kill you."

I burst out laughing. I could see that I had met my match in Captain Willard. No slips of the tongue would be emerging from his mouth. I played a patriotic tune on the piano for my companion, and then he left, after cordially bidding me good evening.

That night, in bed next to Pattie, I could hear through the bedroom window the usual commotion from the camps. I quietly left the bed to peer out and could see twinkling lights from the campfires. Band music played and soldiers sang energetically. I climbed back into bed, the music lulling me to sleep, along with dreams of the interesting man I had met today.

Chapter Twenty

Battle of 2nd Manassas,
August 1862

Clanie and I, in Father's store, were listening to the men talk about war news. Although it was not fitting in a time of war to worry about my appearance, I did start to feel a bit shabby and deprived as far as clothing went. Even my merchant father had to search high and low for bales of cotton that workers could convert into yarn. Pattie, Mother, and I resourcefully learned to use a spinning wheel far more skillfully than we really desired. I read an editorial in the newspaper:

> *There is a great deal of wool in the country, and a large crop of flax will, no doubt, be grown in many parts of Virginia, North Carolina, and Tennessee; but cotton warp constitutes the basis of all our textile fabrics. How can the people obtain this indispensable article? The coarse yarn spun by machinery is scarce and very costly; and though we see the cotton burned in the face of the invader, raw cotton cannot be obtained in many portions of the interior at any price.*

I could attest to this fact. I had four un-tattered day-dresses left. One was a plain blue linsey-woolsey; another a tan checked homespun; and the other two dresses were from before the war.

I noticed a thin, older man, who looked like a peddler. He was probably a sutler—one who followed the armies to sell food and supplies to the soldiers. He described to the other customers a charge of the Black Horse Cavalry at Cub Run during the first Manassas battle:

> The Fauquier cavalry advanced in a wedge form, then opened, disclosing a battery, which fired upon the regiment, and then the cavalry, charged upon the opposing regiment, hemming it in on all sides; and, cutting right and left with tremendous blows, each blow powerful enough to take off a man's head. I never wish to see such a charge again.

Charlie's friend, James Monroe Love, now in the Black Horse 4th Virginia Cavalry, had left VMI to enlist in the Terrible Black Horse when it first organized, and became "conspicuous in the Troop for gallant conduct."

We received a letter from our former bookkeeper, John Gunnell. He wrote, *I have been wounded during the Battle of Williamsburg on May 5.*

My wounds are not life-threatening, however. Pray for me.

Our last letter from Charlie had been at the end of May, and we did not know where he was presently, as his location was secret.

Rose Love and her mother, Sallie, entered the store. Their gaunt faces appeared ravaged with grief. On May 31, Robert T. Love died from the wounds that he received in the Battle at Seven Pines located south of the Chickahominy River in Henrico County, Virginia. Both sides claimed victory in the two-day battle. I went up to Rose and hugged her, which caused a bout of crying that I tried to soothe by murmurings of sympathy and compassion.

"I know, Rose. It is so hard. But, every day that passes should get a little easier."

I could not help myself. Now I was crying with her, while remembering the day a copperhead had bitten Robert. How young and innocent we all were that day.

"I loved him so much, Antonia. He was the sibling closest to me in age. I do not know how I can go on. I could not bear it if this evil war takes James from us too. He was cited for gallantry by General Jeb Stuart, you know."

"Yes, I did hear that, from the general himself," I replied softly.

Rose and her mother purchased what they needed and left the store. As they departed, Mrs. Gunnell entered with a wild look on her face.

"They've taken our cousin, Joshua, to Old Capitol Prison!"

Old Capitol Prison was located in Washington. The Yankees often locked up Southern sympathizers on suspicion of "assisting the enemy" or being on the roads without a pass.

Father added, "How are Eliza and the children taking it?"

"As well as can be expected," Mrs. Gunnell replied.

Clanie paced animatedly behind the counter of the store, a scowl on his face. "I want this war to end soon. Maybe if I joined up, I could help achieve that goal…"

"Don't you dare, Clanie!" I interrupted. "I worry about Charlie every day. Besides, we need you to help run the store."

Father agreed, saying, "What little is left to run. Look at the bare shelves. Where am I going to get new supplies with the Northern blockades active? Since the Union army has interrupted the railroad service, it is almost impossible to obtain the basic necessities for the store. I have to go into Alexandria and rely on friends who sympathize with the South, but pretend to be Northerners to obtain some of my supplies. Other times, I am able to get things from the privateers who attack Northern vessels on the high seas."

Clanie teased me by saying, "Antonia, John Esten Cooke manages to send little trinkets to you by various means. Maybe you should find out where he gets them!"

It remained true that John was still courting me, despite my talk with him last year. He was promoted to captain in July, and I admired him for many reasons, but I did not believe I should continue to accept his gifts to me. Too dangerous for him to be in the village with the Union army here, a civilian messenger delivered his letters and parcels to me.

Surprisingly, Major Willard, recently promoted, stopped by to visit me occasionally. When I was not at home, he left his card. He often brought with him some hard-to-obtain food items or other small luxury gifts for the family. It seemed to me that he could have spent his time better with military activities, but I was flattered nonetheless by his attention, enemy attention though it was.

On August 25, my aunt, Augusta Brower, came to stay with us for a few days. It had been raining for several days and the roads were muddy. She arrived with her traveling dress covered with spattered mud.

"I think my dress is ruined," she bemoaned as she entered the front door.

Mother said, "I'll get Mathilde to clean it. She works wonders."

Augusta came up to me and gave me a warm hug.

"How are you Antonia?" she asked me.

"Worried. But then, everyone is worried, aren't they? Federal officers occupy our house some nights, but on other nights, we are alone. Father and Clanie are away in Richmond at the moment."

At five o'clock one evening, my aunt and I were talking in my room when we heard men's voices coming from the back of the house, and I moved closer to the window in order to hear them better.

A young Union officer exited the privy. He spoke to another officer waiting to use it. "Pope needs reinforcements at his right flank near Thoroughfare Gap, west of Gainesville and Manassas. That's where we are headed."

I looked at my aunt, and she had such a serious look on her face that I exclaimed, "We need to do something!"

She nodded and we put some plans into action. She and I were of a like mind when it came to patriotism. We listened to war talk, and gathered information from visitors in town concerning troop movements of both sides. There was no one to carry the message to General Stuart, so my aunt and I went to the stable and hitched a team of horses to our carriage and started on the twenty-mile trek to his camp in Gainesville. It rained steadily as we sloshed along.

"Dear Lord, Antonia, slow down. We will lose a wheel in these ruts. It is beginning to get dark, and we'll not be able to see them."

"I feel that haste is our mission to get this critical message to my friend. Besides, God will protect us."

As we rode along, we had to avoid prowling Union troops. Occasionally, scouts blocked our way, stopping our horse and carriage, but they allowed us to go through the roadblock when they saw that we were only two women alone in the carriage.

Finally, we reached Stuart's camp in Gainesville, and soldiers directed us to his tent.

The sentry announced, "Major-General Stuart, there are two ladies here to see you."

The general came out of the tent and gazed at us with an angry look. "Are you trying to get yourself killed?" he asked.

"We heard some Union officers talking. Pope needs reinforcements at his right flank near Thoroughfare Gap. We thought this information was important enough to convey to you."

"My God, you're right," he said thoughtfully. "Thank you very much, ladies. You need to leave now. It is not safe to be in the camp with us. I will have one of my men escort your carriage back home."

"No, don't do that," Augusta said. "There are too many Union sentries to encounter, and a man in uniform would draw fire upon us for sure. We put our safety in God's hands tonight and trust that He will get us home safely."

"Amen to that," said Jeb.

We did make it home safely. On Wednesday, August 27, all the Union sympathizers in my village left, as the Confederates had possession again. I read an account of the events of August 26-28 in *The Local News*:

> *On the evening of August 26, after passing around Pope's right flank via Thoroughfare Gap, Jackson's wing of the army, along with Stuart's cavalry on the extreme right, struck the Orange & Alexandria Railroad at Bristoe Station and before daybreak August 27 marched to capture and destroy the massive Union supply depot at Manassas Junction. This surprise movement forced Pope into an abrupt retreat from his defensive line along the Rappahannock River. This seemingly inconsequential action virtually ensured Pope's defeat during the battles of August 29-30 at Manassas because it allowed the two wings of Lee's army to unite on the Manassas battlefield.*

General Pope's army had sixteen thousand casualties, with 8,500 wounded—the Union's bloodiest loss so far.

On the morning of August 31, Southern troops rapidly marched through our village in pursuit of the retreating Northern army. Union forces occupying Virginia retracted back into Maryland across the Potomac. Our village was firmly under Southern control again.

General Stuart visited us at our home to thank us for all we had done.

"Our mutual friend, John Mosby, also provided service that proved to be a shining record of daring and usefulness."

"Thank God he is safe," I said.

"I lost my plumed hat and cloak to pursuing Federals at Manassas, though," he added ruefully.

"But you didn't lose your life," I pointed out.

"Thanks to you and your aunt, many Southerners during that campaign owe their lives to you."

Chapter Twenty-one

Battle of Chantilly, September 1, 1862

Mother and I had recently made a trip into Washington City to see some friends and do a little shopping. I wore one of my new purchases—a floral print silk dress with three tiers of flounces. With its long sleeves and rich hunter green color, it seemed very appropriate for autumn, I thought.

On a rainy, September 1 evening, feeling bored and restless from sheltering myself indoors all day, I heard a knock upon our door. Mathilde showed Major Willard into the parlor.

"Good evening Mrs. Ford and Miss Ford. General Ricketts and his staff are outside and request the use of your house. We have just fought a vicious battle at Chantilly."

Thunder rumbled in the sky and a big boom cracked, making me jump.

Father, at that moment, entered the parlor, "Good evening, Major Willard."

"I just explained to your wife and daughter that we need your house as headquarters again."

"Very well," he replied. "It is risky for you, however. There are many of our men passing through."

"Mathilde, go to the summer kitchen and prepare some food for these men," Mother ordered.

Many of the staff went to the stable to sleep after eating. General Ricketts and Major Willard decided to spend the night inside the house on the floor. At around midnight, the sound of additional horses alerted us, and Major General Pope arrived. Again, Mother and Mathilde prepared a very nice supper for General Pope, even at that late hour. I overheard General Pope speaking to General Ricketts,

"Generals Stevens and Kearny were both killed today. I ordered my army to make a retreat, and realizing that we were still in danger in this village, ordered a retreat all the way to Washington. I estimate that we lost thirteen hundred men today—more than the Confederates did. Some of the wounded are being brought to the old hotel in this village."

"My God!" General Ricketts exclaimed. "Who would have thought that the Rebels could out-maneuver us again?"

Major Willard, who had remained silent up to this point, opined, "It sickened me to see innocent lives of our young men wasted. They cried out to their mothers in their last breaths. I have no stomach for battle and pray that the end will come soon."

I drew Major Willard aside with a "come hither" look and comforted him as best I could, as he was obviously agitated and upset.

"I sympathize with both sides of the war," I said. "I have many loved ones and friends fighting and I pray for their safe return. My mother and I do what we can for the sick and wounded whom we encounter."

"When I fought at the Battle of Cedar Run one month ago," said Major Willard, "the house of Mr. Shoermax was a hospital. There were beautiful Southern women like you ministering to the sick and wounded. I thank God for people like you."

"Do you thank God for me?" I could not refrain from fishing for a compliment.

"You are an angel in disguise," he said reverently.

The next morning, General Pope wrote a letter of protection for my family's home before departing. It would prevent ravaging of our stores, and would allow us to move about the surrounding area without harm. Major Willard handed it to Father.

"Thank you for providing this letter," said Father.

"It was the least I could do for you after your kindness to me and my fellow officers."

Mother said, "If you ever have the opportunity to go to Missouri, where my people are from, you must visit my family there. They will receive you warmly."

I could not cease staring at Major Willard. There was something intangible about the man that attracted me more than any other man.

"I pray that you will be safe, Major Willard," I said.

He rode off with the general and his men, waving goodbye.

That night, our troops entered the town, chasing the last stragglers of the Union army. Surprisingly, I heard a familiar voice in the house—Charlie's! He and his friend, Sergeant George W. Shreve, came to stay the night, along with some Confederate officers. His happy homecoming had to remain short, however. I was so preoccupied with serving and entertaining the officers that I barely was able to speak to Charlie. I overheard George Shreve say, "Charlie and me eat together, and even share a blanket sometimes. We have been together in all the local battles. He is like a brother to me."

It warmed my heart to know that his friend, George, watched out for him. The next morning, everyone left, and the house seemed as quiet as a tomb.

Chapter Twenty-two

Nursing the Wounded,
August-December 1862

Now that two battles had occurred, one at Manassas and the other at Chantilly, the wounded men in town needed to be nursed back to health. Most of our men were taken to Richmond hospitals, but for various reasons, some came here.

Mother, Pattie, and I donned our oldest clothing, and, with aprons tied securely around our waists, pockets bulging with essentials, we walked across our street and along Fairfax Street. We each carried baskets with clean strips of cloth to use as bandages. These cloths, too tattered to use in quilts, had been our slave's plain muslin garments. Each of us also had a supply of writing paper and a pencil.

We entered the front door of the old Willcoxon Tavern and the predominant smell that assailed us was the stench of unclean bodies and festering wounds. The next thing we noticed was the cacophony of moans, screams, and "dead silence."

"Mother, I cannot do this," Pattie complained piteously.

"You can and you will," replied Mother sternly. "Imagine if our Charlie lay wounded somewhere and the relief that someone like you could bring him."

I gazed at the main room, where red-eyed men were lying on straw pallets on the floor with bloodstains and other body fluids everywhere. As I walked towards a back room, the screams coming from that direction became louder. The bare-armed army surgeon, working on a soldier, wore a bloody apron that was a horror to behold. Two able-bodied men held the injured man down while the surgeon amputated a leg below the knee. A wooden knife handle, in the victim's mouth for him to bite down on, stifled his cries. The surgeon poured a half-filled bottle of whiskey over the wound and I surmised that some had also gone down the poor soul's throat prior to the amputation. My mouth felt sour and dry, and I trembled, my fear was so great.

"Are you a nurse?" asked the doctor. "I need you. Now."

"No," I stammered.

"It doesn't matter what you are. Get over here," he ordered gruffly.

Morphine and other painkillers were in short supply, but I noticed a collection of jars and decanters labeled "opium pills, laudanum, and chloroform" on the table near the doctor.

"Press on the wound with this," he said, handing me a bloody rag, retrieved from a basin that looked none too clean. He continued his grating with the murderous saw as he spoke to me. By this time, I gratefully noticed that the wounded soldier had lost consciousness. I did as the doctor asked, averting my eyes from the horror before me. From start to finish, the operation had taken only five minutes, but it seemed far longer than that to me. Doctor tossed the leg below the operating table where I was horrified to see a heap of other limbs splayed this way and that. He cauterized the wound using the end of an iron implement heated glowing red in the fire, wrapped the stump with bandages, and motioned for the two men to carry the still comatose man away.

"You did a fine job, miss. What is your name?"

"Antonia Ford."

"This army needs more heroic, sensible women like you to nurse the wounded. There are far too many lily-livered Southern belles who faint dead away at the sight of an injured man."

I thought his description of many of my genteel counterparts a bit harsh, but said nothing.

I went back to the main room to find my mother and sister tending to the wounded, many of them half-naked. Mother was writing a letter home for a soldier who looked like he would not survive the night. He had a discolored, unnaturally swollen abdominal wound. A minié ball had punctured the wall of his abdomen, exposing his intestines, with the inevitable result of peritonitis and death. Pattie lifted a cup of water to the lips of a young patient who could not have been much older than thirteen years. Perhaps a drummer boy, I thought.

I surveyed the scene, the unimaginable agony, and a tear rolled down my cheek. I brusquely wiped it away and sought my best use.

"Nurse, nurse," I heard behind me. I looked to see a disheveled young man weakly raising his head. I walked over to him, stepping over bodies.

"Yes, soldier. How can I help you?"

"Will you give me some water? I cannot use my arms or legs."

I went to the water jug and removed the tin cup from my apron pocket. The water did not look too clean, but we were in desperate straits.

"Here you are," I said gently. "What is your name?"

"I am Johnny Jackson, from Centreville. Will you write a letter for me?"

I took out my paper and pencil and he dictated a short note:

Dear Mother,

I am in good hands. Do not worry about me. I will see you soon, or meet you at the pearly gates, God willing. You have always been a good mother. I love you.

Your son, Johnny.

"I will take personal responsibility to make sure your mother gets this," I said tenderly.

I stepped outside for a moment to breathe some fresh air. A stately middle-aged man in a white shirt with turned back cuffs, tanned brim hat, and dark beard and mustache came towards me. A tiny notebook peeked out of his shirt pocket. I felt apprehensive, not knowing his intentions.

"Good morning, miss," he said politely.

"Good morning, sir. May I help you?"

"'I am weary. I have just witnessed battle. Lo! the war resumes . . .'"

"'Again to my sense your shapes . . .,'" I continued. "You enjoy Walt Whitman's poems too, I see."

"I am Walt Whitman," he replied with a chuckle.

My mouth opened in astonishment to think that my favorite poet stood before me, talking to me.

"Why were you at battle, sir?" I asked timidly.

"I arrived at Manassas on the 29th. I remained on the outskirts, observing the battle from a distance. The troops behaved with great coolness, courage and in perfect order."

"I have a brother, Charlie, fighting for the Confederate states," I said.

"My brother fights for the Union, and as for me—I am an observer."

"How did you make your way here?"

"I left Manassas battlefield at eleven o'clock on the 31st and bivouacked that night at Centreville. I left the latter place September 1 at five o'clock a.m., arriving at Chantilly at dusk. A sharp engagement raged there in the woods, through furious rains, lasting until ten o'clock at night. I left there at three o'clock a.m. and arrived here soon after sunrise. I will leave for Alexandria and Washington this afternoon."

"You must be exhausted!" I exclaimed.

"I am. What is this place?" he asked, pointing to the Willcoxon Tavern.

"It is now a hospital," I replied. "My mother, sister, and I are working here as nurses."

"I met a brave woman while at Fairfax Station. Her name is Clara Barton. She and four other women brought supplies there from Washington. Under the supervision of Dr. James Dunn, she and her assistants cared for three thousand wounded soldiers."

"How dangerous that must have been for her," I murmured. "How did she tend to soldiers with no hospital?"

"She laid straw on the ground and treated the wounded in open fields. Using candlelight, she worked all night to care for injured and dying soldiers."

"What a risk for fire, with all that straw nearby!" I said.

"She is very brave and would not leave. She is probably still there working without sleep."

"Sir, we have no inn in town presently. Pray come with me and rest at my house for a few hours. It is only across the street. My father is home and will see to your comfort."

"That is kind of you, Miss Ford. I will take you up on your offer."

I walked with him back to my house, introduced him to Father, and then went back to the hospital to continue working. When I returned home at the end of the day, he had left hours before.

During the next few days, reports came in about the battles and heroics. The South claimed a victory for both battles. Clara Barton remained until orderlies evacuated all the wounded by rail on September 2, taking the last train out of Fairfax Station. As she rode away, our troops burned the station that had served as her headquarters.

Three days later, I read an article in *The Alexandria Gazette* entitled "Willard's Hotel Crowded with Officers." I wondered where Major Willard was right now. Mingling with the officers? In his home? On a battlefield somewhere?

As our wounded men's conditions stabilized, doctors transported them to Richmond, sent them home, or sent them back to the battlefield. The men in town had constant burying tasks, travel being too difficult for the families of the dead to claim the remains of their loved ones.

We obtained a copy of the September 10 *Alexandria Gazette* and read:

> *Medical Inspector Coolidge remained behind after General Pope's retreat to care for the wounded. He reported to the Surgeon General, "The removal of our wounded from the battle-field was completed Tuesday afternoon, the 9th instant, and the last trains of ambulances arrived at Fairfax Seminary Hospital, Alexandria, early Wednesday morning.*

During this month, Abraham Lincoln was drafting the Emancipation Proclamation. The proclamation declared, "That all persons held as slaves" within the rebellious states "are, and henceforward shall be free." My spirits soared when I read this liberating statement in *The Alexandria Gazette*. The piteous institution of slavery was repugnant to me now, even though my parents were former slave owners. Unfortunately, the proclamation would not take effect until the next year.

On September 17, the Battle of Antietam, in Maryland, occurred, and our ex-clerk, Corporal John Gunnell, wrote, *I have been wounded again. Provide fervent prayers, as I think my luck cannot hold out further. This horrible battle was worse than your most gruesome nightmare.*

We received a letter from Charlie on September 22, 1862. Now in Company 2nd of Stuart's Light Horse Artillery, he wrote, *The army has promoted me to Lieutenant 2nd class, and although I am healthy, many of the men around me are dying from various diseases or infected wounds.*

The autumn and early winter brought some dismaying events to our lives and our loved ones. On October 2, Preston Grigsby, the eighteen-year-old brother of Dick, rode past the village lines without a pass. A Yankee soldier stopped him on Little River Turnpike, and asked him to take the Oath of Allegiance. He refused, provoking his arrest, and was sent to Old Capitol Prison in Washington. Dick wrote me letters urging my family to take the oath, simply to protect ourselves from the Federals.

On November 3, in Lynchburg, Jeb Stuart's beloved daughter Flora died. While camped near the Rappahannock River, an officer telegraphed him that his child was dying. He replied, "I shall have to leave my child in the hands of God; my duty to my country requires me here."

Edward G. Ford, a cousin, purchased supplies from my father's store on November 18, and was journeying on his way back to the farm when the Federals stopped and arrested him. They eventually had to release him from jail, when they could not obtain any evidence of his wrongdoing. The officials subjected most of the arrested men who refused to take the oath to a similar inconvenience.

The evening of December 28, around nine o'clock, I heard guns firing from the picket posts outside our village, on the Alexandria pike. I heard couriers galloping on the road outside our house yelling, "Stuart's cavalry is surrounding the town!" Other couriers had different reports, resulting in a madhouse of confusion. Wagon wheels rolled and creaked, and horses neighed. I jumped every time I heard a gun go off. My stomach hurt, and I paced the room nervously.

Father said, "Perhaps there will be a skirmish at daylight. We need to stay inside and keep our weapons close." His loaded revolver lay on the table beside him.

Mother said a prayer aloud for God's protection, and she and Father retired for the evening.

Feeling impervious to danger, I disobeyed Father and went out the back door to use the privy. The privy door creaked open as I stood in front of it and a dirty, bedraggled Confederate soldier carrying a lantern came out, his private parts exposed. He leered at me and lunged forward to grab me. I turned and ran to the back door, slamming it shut, and locking it behind me. When I looked back, he was laughing and had not even bothered to chase me. I kept that indiscretion to myself, and went to bed, thoroughly frightened, unable to sleep for several hours.

The next day dawned with no battle at hand. Stuart's cavalry had circled the town and moved north to Vienna.

The 11th Army Corps was encamped here in Fairfax Courthouse, and typhoid fever made its rampant path through the population. We barely went out of the house for fear of contracting something from the air around us. In January, a measles outbreak struck our village. When the Corps moved south, compatriots left behind many soldiers, sick, once more in Willcoxon's tavern.

Chapter Twenty-three

Annie Jones, March 1863

I had spent all day in the old Willcoxon tavern-turned-hospital nursing the wounded. Many of those I cared for had measles, and doctors quarantined them in our village. I must have contracted measles and survived it as a child, as I seemed immune to this contagious disease. As I walked home on Fairfax Street, an attractive woman I had never seen before came up to me.

"Excuse me, miss," she said. "I am looking for the headquarters of General Stoughton."

"You are close," I replied. "He and his men have commandeered Dr. Gunnell's home. Let me show you the way."

We headed west on Fairfax Street, and passed the courthouse. This nicely dressed woman appeared to be just a few years younger than I was. It would be a pleasant distraction to have someone with whom to talk, as there were not many women my age around.

"I am Antonia Ford," I told her.

"My name is Anna Elinor Jones. I am originally from Cambridge, Massachusetts. You may call me Annie."

"You are a long way from home Annie. What brings you to Fairfax Courthouse?"

She shyly said, "I always wanted to be a nurse, but when orphaned, I had to support myself. The war caused me to be nearly destitute, and to keep from starving to death I had to search for work. In Washington City, no one would hire me, even to nurse to soldiers, because they said I was too young. I became what is known as a vivandière."

I dredged up my language skills and realized that the term "vivandière," from a mixture of French and Latin, meant "hospitality giver."

Although somewhat taken aback, as I had never conversed with a "fallen woman," I wracked my brain trying to think of something to reply.

"Are you paid by the Northern military officers?" I finally asked.

"Oh, are you asking me if I am a Cyprian?"

I was embarrassed, but replied simply, "Yes."

"I prefer to think of myself as a guest of certain officers, providing them with creature comforts and conversation. In return, they provide me with things I need: a place to live, transportation, food, and sometimes money. Some vivandières travel with soldiers for little or no pay as sutlers, mascots, or nurses, while others fight alongside their male counterparts."

By this time, we had reached the front of the Gunnell residence, but our conversation was so interesting, I continued, "Surely women don't fight alongside men in the battles?"

"It is uncommon, and the women are usually sent home once they are found out. You must realize that vivandières are often the only females seen by men for weeks on end."

We stopped under the shade of an oak tree to continue our conversation.

I boldly went on, "Aren't you afraid of contracting a social disease? I have read that this problem is rampant among the men." I had never discussed anything like this with another person—not even Mother. Such conversations were usually taboo in today's society, but my curiosity prevailed.

"Yes. That is a concern of mine, which is why I only consort with high-ranking officers. Some Cyprians provide 'horizontal refreshment' for five dollars to anyone who can pay the price, but you see, I am more selective. General Custer is one of my prior companions," she said proudly.

I shuddered and looked around to see if any neighbors observed us conversing. I reasoned that since she looked so respectable, no one would think ill of me for talking to another woman. I felt determined to befriend this wayward person and to show her an alternative way to live her life.

"My family has started to take in travelers as paying customers because our only tavern in town is now a hospital. Can I persuade you to stay with us instead of with General Stoughton?"

She looked at me with amazement. I supposed that she was not used to kindness from respectable people after they learned what she was.

"I will keep that in mind," she said slowly. "It is good to know that I have options."

I was reluctant to allow her to go just yet without providing her with some moral advice to contemplate. For heaven's sake, *The Young Lady's Counselor* had plenty of advice on preventing ruination! Searchingly, I asked Annie, "Do you have any religious beliefs?"

"I don't know much about the Bible, if that's what you mean," she responded.

"The Bible tells us that our bodies are the temple of the Holy Spirit, which is in us. Also, the worth of a virtuous woman is far above rubies."

Annie glanced down bashfully at her discreet décolletage. I followed her eyes, and added, "You know, my Mother always asked me, 'Are you dressing to be chased, or to be chaste?'"

Annie laughed at me. "Are you trying to save me?" she asked.

"I'm probably not saved myself," I replied. "I do know that the Bible says that every temptation we experience is common to man. God is faithful and will not allow us to be tempted more than what we are able to bear. He will provide a way to escape it."

"Do you believe that?" Annie asked. "What kind of temptations could a refined lady such as you ever have experienced?"

"Yes, I do believe it. I have prayed for deliverance from temptation on occasion. I have indecent thoughts in my head from time to time, especially after one of my suitors visits me. I have by nature, a passionate temperament, and have to curb my appetites to appear respectable to my friends, family, and society, and to myself. Believe me, I have prayed to God many times about this."

Annie became silent. I thought I should change the subject—perhaps I had gone too far.

"Perchance you can help nurse the men to health in the village homes and tavern that have been made into hospitals? I could show you what to do. After all, these men are Northerners, as you are."

"I would like that," she said. "In return, would you like to be invited to any parties that General Stoughton hosts? I'm sure I could get you an invitation . . ."

I interrupted, "No, I really can't do that. First, the soldiers are my enemies. I have a brother and many close friends who are in the Southern army. Second, it would not be proper for me to be around riotous drinking and ribald activities. But if you could tell me when and where the parties are occurring and who will be attending them, I would be eternally grateful to you."

She looked at me knowingly and intelligently. Annie had more to her make-up than her looks, I thought.

"Why sure, I could," she said. "Let's meet at the Willcoxon tomorrow, and I'll start my nursing apprenticeship."

I wished her good day, and made my way home, secure in the thought that I had done a service to someone in need.

Chapter Twenty-four

Stoughton's Capture, March 8, 1863

O n Tuesday, March 3, Captain Mosby had been a guest at our house for three days and nights, disguised in citizen's dress. We enjoyed many rides together through the countryside. He missed his wife, Pauline, and his two children, and wrote to them frequently. While we took our rides, I gave him all the information that I could recall concerning enemy movements. These included the number of forces in the neighborhood, the location of the camps, the places where officers' quarters were established, the precise points where the pickets hid, the strength of the outposts, and the names of officers in command. I told him the layout of Dr. Gunnell's house, as I had attended many parties there, both before and during the war.

"Brigadier General Stoughton is not shy about throwing parties in the good doctor's house," I said. "I have seen him about town, but have never been formally introduced to him. I have had occasion, however, to endure the ribald flirting by a British chap by the name of Colonel Sir Percy Wyndham. He offered his services to the Federal Government, and is in command of the Federal cavalry in the area."

I told him about my new confidant, Annie. "Annie and I worked side by side in the hospital giving comfort and aid to those who needed it. Sometimes we just wrote letters for the soldiers. She gave me some details about General Stoughton's drinking habits that I think you will want to know."

"Please, tell all," he eagerly requested.

"He drinks a lot, and cannot hold his liquor. Annie says that once he hits the bed, he is out for the night."

"Does Annie spend the entire night with him?"

"Sometimes yes, sometimes no. She has her own tent pitched in the yard behind the house."

"Tell me about the Yankee boarders staying at your house this week."

"General Stoughton's sister and three of his aides have been with us for about one week now. You must have seen them going in and out."

"Yes, I did notice. I cannot take the chance that one of them may recognize me, so I do not stop to chat with them. I will leave that to you. Do they all dine at Dr. Gunnell's house?"

"Yes, thankfully we don't have to feed them! General Stoughton invited my family to a big party at the Gunnells this Sunday. Everyone of substance in town was invited, but, of course, my family will not be attending. Annie will be there, however."

"I hope to gain some useful information for the Southern cause," John told me. "What seems to be innocuous information may prove to be vital.

Keep up the good work."

On Sunday, March 8, General Stoughton's mother arrived from Washington, and came to our house to spend the night. She planned to attend the party where her son and daughter would be.

"Can't I persuade you kind people to enjoy a night of merriment?" Mrs. Stoughton asked Mother and Father.

"You'll have to excuse our absence, ma'am," Father said politely.

That night, we retired as usual, around ten o'clock. We heard Mrs. Stoughton and Miss Stoughton, as well as the aides, enter the house at midnight, with the rumbling sound of thunder in the sky.

The next morning, early, I heard pebbles hitting my windowpane. I put on a cloak, and looked out to see who it was, and saw Annie. I ran downstairs and opened the front door.

"Come in," I said. "It's chilly out. What are you doing here so early?"

Annie whispered, "Dr. Gunnell's home was raided last night, ending with General Stoughton and his men captured. Sir Wyndham was fortunate to be socializing in Washington City, or he would have been caught too!"

By this time, Mother, Father, and Clanie came downstairs, curious. We went into the parlor and sat down, while our other guests slept off their imbibitions of the past night.

"Start at the beginning," I begged her.

"A splendid party was held, with all of Stoughton's officers present, and as many women of Fairfax who would come. Plenty of champagne flowed non-stop, and a regimental band provided dancing music. Everyone felt so gay and happy. The party broke up about midnight."

"That was when I heard General Stoughton's mother and sister come in," I commented.

"I was in the same room as General Stoughton, sleeping," Annie said. "I had not overindulged and I had my wits about me. Someone pounding on the front door awoke me, but the general still slept. I got out of bed, threw my clothes on, stepped carefully around the empty champagne bottles, and peeked out the window. The house clock chimed two o'clock. It was raining, with lightening and thunder. In the room next to mine, a staff person, named Lieutenant Prentiss, opened the window, and asked the reason for the intrusion. Someone outside announced that the 5th New York was carrying dispatches for the general. I heard Lieutenant Prentiss stomp down the stairs and open the door. I heard pounding footsteps coming up the stairs and to the right, where my room was. A man dressed in the uniform of a Confederate captain, whom I had seen before in the village, but whose name I did not know, pulled back the bedcovers, raised the general's nightshirt, and slapped his rear."

"It had to be John Mosby," I murmured. At this point, Father was having a tough time keeping a straight face.

"The conversation between the two men went something like this," continued Annie:

> "Get up, General, and come with me," the Confederate soldier demanded.
>
> General Stoughton replied in a groggy voice, "What is this? Do you know who I am sir?"
>
> "I reckon I do, General. Did you ever hear of Mosby?"
>
> "Yes, have you caught him?"
>
> "No, but he has caught you."
>
> "What's this all about?"
>
> "It means, General, that Stuart's cavalry has possession of the courthouse; be quick and dress."
>
> "Is Confederate cavalryman General Fitzhugh Lee with your Rebel group? If so, I insist you take me to him as we were classmates together at West Point."
>
> "Very well. Now dress—and be quick about it."

Annie continued her story, "I watched the general gaze at himself in a mirror as he slowly and fastidiously dressed for the journey. The Confederate soldier lost his patience and had two of his men assist the officer while the third guarded Lieutenant Prentiss. I slipped out of the room quietly, then down the stairway and across the hall to the parlor, where I continued to watch and listen. The parlor was in a state of disorder after the party the preceding night. There was trash littering the majestic large fireplace. Some of the mantle place objects were scattered, broken on the floor. Mud covered the carpets. I felt sorry for the Gunnell family. After another moment, the captors hurried the two Federals downstairs and out the front door. As they were leaving the house, one of the Rebels handed the general his watch, which he had overlooked as he dressed."

"How many Southern men were there altogether?" asked Father.

"I saw two men guarding the horses, and four others who actually went into the house. I heard General Stoughton complain that the Rebels were not giving them enough time to saddle the horses, so they were compelled to ride bareback to wherever they were going. I followed them on foot as far as the courthouse. It was nearly three-thirty a.m., and panic and confusion reigned, as scores of Yankees in the area around the courthouse looked for a place to hide."

"We slept through the whole thing," said Mother.

"I saw the column of horsemen leaving, and they had only gone a few hundred feet when a naked man leaned out and shouted at them from a second-story window of the house directly across North Street from your house."

"Joshua Gunnell's house!" Father exclaimed. "That is where Union Colonel Robert Johnstone and his wife are staying."

"Colonel Johnstone demanded that the horses be brought back. He ordered, as commanding officer of the 5th New York Cavalry, that the horses remain to get their rest. He did not realize that it was Rebels beneath his window! Two Confederates went through the front door to capture the officer. They encountered the officer's wife, who stalled the men. They came back empty-handed. The whole Confederate group with their prisoners and captured horses rode southward into the night."

"Do you know where Colonel Johnstone ended up?" I asked.

"I only found out this morning as I was coming over here. It seems that Colonel Johnstone had escaped through the back door and concealed himself beneath a privy in the yard."

We all could not help but laugh at the ridiculous picture that made—to imagine a naked man cowering underneath the privy for hours! We hoped that Colonel Johnstone would find his way to a bath before going near anyone.

Later that day, at Father's store, we learned that it was indeed Mosby and twenty-nine of his men who had carried off that raid. The raiders had captured a Union general, two captains, thirty enlisted men, an Austrian baron, and fifty-eight horses by riding into and out of a garrisoned village without firing a shot or losing a man.

Chapter Twenty-five

Frankie Abel, March 11, 1863

The backlash from the raid just would not end. All of the local newspapers as well as the *Washington Star* and *New York Times* had their own versions of Mosby's daring raid. The *Times* reported that the Rebels took every horse that could be found, public, and private, for a total of 110. Not entirely true—our horses remained. Mosby also took as prisoner the telegraph operator, who frequently wired dispatches for the Yankees. I said good riddance to him!

I sat on the Windsor settee on our front porch enjoying the afternoon, when a curiously dressed woman descended from her carriage in front of my house. Her dark complexioned face had plain, mannish features with her hair tightly pulled back from it. Dressed drably in calico, she carried a large traveling bag in her hand. She paid the driver, who left immediately. As she walked up to my door, she greeted me in an unusually low-pitched voice.

"Hello. Is this the Ford residence?"

"Yes, it is."

"A woman in Annandale told me that I could perhaps get temporary lodging in your home. I have money."

"I will have to ask Mother," I said. "Wait here." I brought Mother to the porch.

"It is dangerous for a woman such as you to be unattended and wandering around the Virginia countryside. What brings you here?" asked Mother.

"I am on my way to Culpeper to meet up with General Fitzhugh Lee. I have some dispatches for him. You see, my views are secesh, and the place where I lived in Baltimore, Maryland, is definitely pro-Union. It became very uncomfortable for me to be under the same roof with my Yankee cousins."

"How long do you plan on staying?" asked Mother with a gentler tone to her voice.

"Only two nights," she replied. "I have a particular time and place that I am to meet the general."

"Come in then. You can stay in the same room as Antonia and Pattie if it will be only a few days. What is your name?"

"My name is Frances Abel. You can call me Frankie."

"Come with me," I said. I showed her my room and introduced her to Pattie.

Pattie, who was a lovely, although sometimes impetuous, adolescent, offered to share her chest of drawers with Frankie.

"You surely do not want your clothes to get wrinkled do you?" she asked.

Frankie hesitated, and then replied, "Why of course, you're right." She started pulling things out of her bag.

She had a dress, some chemises, and some personal items. When she removed pants, coat and a vest, Pattie and I just gaped in amazement.

"Men's clothing!" exclaimed Pattie.

"I have come upon hard times, and had to make do with sturdy clothing that I can find to fit me," she explained.

We looked at her large-boned frame, then looked at each other and shrugged. Something did not quite check out with Frankie. She had money to pay us for lodging, had arrived by carriage, and yet had to resort to men's clothing? A few women in the army posed as men, but these women were not highly respected or admired, when found out. The army simply sent them home, in disgrace. A woman's place was not in battle—only as nurse or cook.

As the day and evening went on, Pattie, Frankie, and I became acquainted. We found Frankie to be quick-witted and amusing. Her stories of Baltimore and life up North interested us. She had dinner with us, and we took note of her good manners.

That night, with the candle flickering eerily, Frankie delighted us with the poem, "The Raven," written by Edgar Allen Poe.

"Did you know that early in 1830 Poe lived in my town—Baltimore? Sadly, after moving around, he ended up dead on a Baltimore street."

Frankie certainly endeared herself to us, and we apparently to her. She was all ears and clamored for more as we related wartime adventures that had occurred in and around Fairfax Courthouse.

The next day, feeling sorry for Frankie, I found a few accessories that I could spare from my meager store, and gave them to her. She seemed genuinely pleased to receive the gifts.

That night, before bedtime, almost in a party atmosphere, we exchanged confidences about all sorts of things. We talked about the men in our lives, ambitions, parties, and of course, the war. I reached under the mattress and pulled out a ribbon-bound pile of letters and keepsakes to show her. I proudly held out my souvenir commission from Jeb Stuart.

"Here is my prized possession," I said, while handing it to her with a flourish. She read the document, with amazement showing on her face.

"Tell me how you got this, Antonia," she said.

I relayed the evening back to her, trying to convey the prankish nature of the little compliment bestowed on me.

"What else do you have there?" she asked.

"Just the usual—love letters, correspondence between soldiers and myself, some little maps of local areas that I drew to amuse myself," I replied carefully.

We extinguished the lamp and went to bed.

The next morning, Frankie started packing her bag.

"You will need a carriage to get to Culpeper," I said. "I will have Father arrange to have one pick you up."

"That is kind of you," she responded. "I will never forget you, Antonia."

"Likewise," I said.

Frankie left at about noon, with hugs and kisses from all of us, as we had made her a part of our family, if only for a few days.

I spent the afternoon quilting, but felt restless for activity. I had always enjoyed horseback riding and decided that I needed some fresh air on this pleasant March evening. I went into the stable and asked the groom to prepare my favorite horse. From behind me, a voice said, "Good evening, miss."

I turned to see Major Willard!

"I had business in town, and wanted to talk with you again," he said simply.

"As you can see, I am ready for a ride. Would you care to join me?"

I led my horse to the street, where his waited patiently. We mounted our horses and cantered west through the countryside, enjoying the last rays of the sun peeking through the trees. We talked about the war, philosophies on life, and army living. We came upon a turn in the road to find a civilian on a fine thoroughbred horse. Captain Mosby faced us. I maintained my composure, as this civilian obviously intended on greeting me, because he slowed his horse and had a wide grin on his face.

"Good evening, Miss Ford," he said civilly.

Blurting out the first pseudonym that came to mind, I calmly replied, "Good evening, Mr. Ruse. This is Major Willard, of the Union army."

Major Willard said, "It is a fine evening for a ride, sir. What brings you out on such an evening? Are you not afraid of marauding soldiers, or Mosby's men, ready to attack you for your fine horse?"

"I am out for the same reason as you, sir: to enjoy the refreshing autumn evening. As you can see, I am well protected with my armaments. But you are more fortunate than I, to have such a lovely companion to ride with you."

"Indeed," he responded warmly.

We conversed for a few minutes, then bid our farewells to Mr. Ruse, and went our own way. After returning home, Major Willard said his goodbyes, and headed for Washington. I had a secure feeling inside as I watched him ride away. When I told my parents about the narrow escape with Mosby, we laughed, but somewhat nervously.

That day, we received another letter from Charlie saying that his promotion to Full Lieutenant 1st Class occurred on February 15, 1863.

Chapter Twenty-six

Arrested, March 13, 1863

On the snowy morning of March 13, I was bedridden with a severe migraine headache that caused me nausea and vomiting, and Mother was taking care of me as best she could. I must have eventually slept, for Mother gently awoke me.

"You must come downstairs. A man named Sergeant Odell has some questions for you."

As I entered the parlor, I heard Father ask, "What is the occasion of your visit?"

"I am Sergeant John Odell. I regret to say, sir, that my men and I are here to search your house."

"Who ordered this?" asked Father.

"Lafayette Baker, head of the Secret Service division," he replied. Sergeant Odell then addressed me, "Antonia Ford, will you take the Oath of Allegiance?"

"No," I said quietly and firmly.

He asked the same of Mother and Father. They also declined to take the oath.

"Then I am afraid I must search the premises," he concluded.

Two other men entered our home and started their search. Sergeant Odell headed directly upstairs and inquired of my mother to direct him to my room. Father and I followed them upstairs and observed Sergeant Odell going directly to my bed. He lifted the mattress and withdrew the bundle of letters that I kept there. It seemed almost as if he knew where to go. He slowly smiled as he glanced through the bundle. At last, he pulled out the document given to me by Jeb Stuart.

"This seems to be a military commission from General Stuart," he said jubilantly.

"It is a compliment from a personal acquaintance, nothing more," I stated emphatically.

"That remains to be seen," he said as he continued to rifle through my papers. "This one seems to indicate another raid for tomorrow night," he said, while reading a letter.

"I have letters from my brother and other soldiers that are precious to me. Nothing here would interest you. May I have them, please?"

"These will be used as evidence, miss," he said.

He pulled out eighty-seven dollars in Southern bank bills and Confederate notes.

"That money is mine," I stated.

"You will get a receipt," Sergeant Odell said.

He continued to search my room, messily going through my chest of drawers and looking for loose floorboards. When he finished his search, we rejoined the other two officers downstairs, who had searched the rest of the house.

"What did you find?" asked Sergeant Odell.

One of the other men replied, "I have a large quantity of Southern and Confederate money and evidences of debt amounting to the sum of $5,765."

Father objected. "You know the Confederate money is not worth anything. Why do you feel you must take it?"

"It is evidence that you are secessionists," replied Sergeant Odell. "If you were true to the Union, you would have United States notes."

"Mr. Ford, I have an arrest warrant for you and your daughter. I charge you both with giving information that led to the late Confederate raid on the courthouse and, being secessionists. I also charge Miss Ford with being a commissioned Southern officer. I will give you both a minute to pack small bags, and then you will have to come with me."

I cried out and ran to Mother, hugging her. Mother had tears streaming down her face. Father started shoving the men out of the house, but when they drew their pistols and aimed them at the lot of us, he backed down.

"This is an outrage," he shouted. "We have housed officers of your army here, and done whatever we could for the sick and wounded that have straggled through our village."

"But isn't it true, sir, that you have also housed Rebel officers here?"

No one answered.

"I will give you five minutes to get packed, and then we must go. Mr. Ford, you will go with the officers over there."

"Where are you taking my family?" Mother asked.

"Mr. Ford will be incarcerated in Old Capitol Prison in Washington. Your daughter will be in the women's wing, called Carroll."

Mother immediately demanded, "Take me in her place. She is innocent and would not be able to survive the incarceration with her poor health," she lied.

"Your turn may yet come, ma'am," Sergeant Odell said wryly.

I quickly went upstairs to my room and packed a traveling bag with some extra clothes, my Bible, stationary and ink pen, embroidery materials, Federal currency, and *Leaves of Grass*. Mother came with me.

She whispered, "I will get word to everyone—John Esten Cooke, General Stuart, and especially John Mosby. Surely they will vouch for your innocence."

"Be sure to get word to Major Willard, if you are able. He is the only one that can help me now. Be strong Mother. I'll write, and hopefully, Father and I will be released soon."

An ambulance transported Father, along with our neighbors: Joshua Gunnell; William Powell; our Sheriff, F. S. Murray; E. Ostrander; T. M.

Williams; and R. Newman.

The driver helped me into another ambulance. I imagined that these conveyances were more plentiful than coaches were. Another neighbor, a merchant, Mr. John Taylor, already occupied a seat in the disgusting, bloodstained ambulance.

Mother shouted at Sergeant Odell, "Can't you see how pale and sick she is? The jostling about in the ambulance will do her in! Have pity!"

Sergeant Odell only replied, "Good day, madam."

I got inside and started my journey to Old Capitol Prison. I asked the driver to stop twice, so that I could retch. I slumped against the seat, but the jostling only made my headache worse. Finally, we started up a steep hill. I could see the Capitol in the near distance. Amongst the trees, I saw some brick buildings. The bottom half of the building had been whitewashed. We had reached our destination.

Old Capitol and Carroll Prison, the women's wing, adjoined each other. Additional structures extended on each side of the buildings. The two-story edifice had windows with iron bars and no glass, similar to those found in a jail. I saw a three-story back addition obscured by the front building. Two armed guards paced the perimeter of the buildings. A ledge of stone supported an iron railing, which surrounded the grounds of the nearby capitol.

I exited the ambulance at one of the entrances to Carroll Prison. It pulled away to take Mr. Taylor to his building. Upon entering the front door, I entered a large hall with benches on both sides of the corridor. Sergeant Odell stopped before one of the open doors and indicated for me to go in. Beside the door, a placard read "William P. Wood." The large room contained only a desk and a few scattered chairs, with two men seated.

"Mr. Wood, I am delivering to you, another of Uncle Sam's boarders, a prisoner named Antonia Ford," Sergeant Odell announced. He then bowed and left.

Mr. Wood rose from his desk chair and came forward. He looked about forty, medium in height, well proportioned, with light brown hair and clean-shaven with a fair complexion. He appeared solid, as if he could hold his own in any brawl. His bright bluish-gray eyes looked me over curiously, then he indicated for me to sit down and he did the same.

"Miss Ford, I know your family, as we met last summer. Regretfully, I have to incarcerate you, but it may not be for long. Prisoner exchanges occur frequently here. We will do our utmost to see that your needs are met, but you will find that the Carroll most definitely is not as comfortable as home."

"Who is this seated man? Has he no manners for not rising when a lady enters a room?" I asked.

"I am Lafayette Baker, head of the Secret Service," Mr. Baker said, rising from his chair. Tall and thin with sandy, wavy side-parted hair, a dense red beard, mustache, and mutton chop sideburns, he somewhat resembled Abraham Lincoln.

"You recently had a woman visitor in your home named Frankie Abel. You showed her the document that General Stuart gave you and bragged that you were one of his commissioned officers," Mr. Baker said.

"That, that was just a joke," I stammered. I thought to myself that Frankie Abel sure had me fooled!

"You told Miss Abel about the times that Captain Mosby had visited you, stayed with you and rode with you," he continued.

"Yes, that is true," I said.

"Surely you passed to him important information," Lafayette Baker pressed.

"We talked about the weather and politics. Nothing more," I lied emphatically.

"Why have you, in the past, pretended to be a loyal Unionist?" he asked.

"My family had to get along and survive. The Union army commandeered our home many times, against our wishes. I have a brother fighting for the South. It is no secret. You would have cooperated in exactly the same way my family did were you in our predicament."

"Yessss…your family," he said slowly.

"Leave my family out of this affair. I alone am responsible for my sentiments and actions. As much as I would have liked to do the things you charge me of, I am physically unable to travel around as you think. I have done no spying for either side. The only assistance I have given either side is as a nurse."

"Miss Ford, I formally charge you with holding a commission as an officer of the Confederate army, and communicating information which resulted in the recent capture of General Stoughton."

"You don't have evidence!" I exclaimed. "I deserve a trial and a lawyer for legal advice."

"You just had your trial, Miss Ford," Lafayette Baker replied. "The preponderance of evidence does not necessitate anything further."

Mr. Wood chimed in, "It is highly irregular for anyone here to have access to a lawyer for legal advice. I must deny that request."

"May I see my father, who is also incarcerated here?" I asked Mr. Wood.

"Yes, that can be arranged. I will permit you to receive and write letters, although I will read them first. I will also allow you an occasional package from home that I will inspect, of course. A parlor is available where visitors may see you for fifteen minutes a day."

Mr. Wood said, "Take a seat please. I need to record your arrest." He produced a clean piece of paper and started asking me questions.

"Your name?"

"Antonia Jane Ford."

"Of what state are you a native?"

"Virginia."

"Your age?"

"Twenty-five years."

"Where are you from now?"

"Fairfax Courthouse, Virginia."

"What is your profession?"

"I have none."

"Where were you arrested?"

"In Fairfax Courthouse, Virginia."

"Have you taken the oath?"

"No."

"That will do, miss."

He recorded all my answers on the paper, along with a physical description of me, and then asked me to sign the paper to authenticate it. I requested to read my arrest sheet:

> *Antonia Ford is a native of Virginia—aged 25—resident of Fairfax C.H. Va. rather delicate in appearance—is a defiant Rebel pleads especially for her family, and says she alone is responsible for her sentiments and actions—has a Rebel Commission from the Rebel General Stuart, which she declares he gave her as a compliment and as a personal acquaintance. She acknowledges the will but asserts her <u>physical inability</u> to participate in any manner in this national strife, and positively denies having done a single act for or against either part, but claims having assisted the sick and wounded of both sides.*

Mr. Wood called to a guard who came into the room.

"Escort Miss Ford to her cell. She is to have the cell for distinguished guests."

"Very well," said the guard.

We walked through a dark passage and then outside into a large yard, through a door and into another passageway. We walked midway down the hallway and stopped before a closed door. A guard, lurking nearby, opened the door and said, "Walk in. This is your quarters."

He handed me the list of rules to read, then left, leaving the door open.

Spider webs adorned the corners and ceiling of the room. I set my bag down on the dirty floor, and went to the window and peered out. I could see coal or lumber, as far as my view extended. A building labeled "Sutler's Store," stood at the rear end of the courtyard, where the daily papers could be purchased for twenty-five cents. Although I currently had no cellmate, my guard told me to expect one soon.

I called to the guard, "I would like to purchase a newspaper."

He allowed me to go unescorted to the sutler's store. Inside, I found essentials such as toothbrushes, combs, soap, and various other toiletries. Whiskey and playing cards were for sale. I purchased a *Washington Star*, and used the outdoor privy on the way back to my cell. Once back inside, I sat down to read today's paper. I read a letter written by a soldier at Fairfax to a friend in Vermont:

There is a woman living in the town by the name of Ford, not married, who has been of great service to General Stuart in giving information, etc.—so much so that Stuart has conferred on her the rank of major in the Rebel army. She belongs to his staff. Why our people do not send her beyond the lines is another question. I understand that she and Stoughton are very intimate. If he gets picked up some night he may thank her for it. Her father lives here, and is known to harbor and give all the aid he can to the Rebs, and this in the little hole of Fairfax, under the nose of the provost-marshal, who is always full of bad whiskey.

As I read this, I thought this was indeed, very bad for my case.

Figure 1 - Antonia Ford
(Library of Congress, LOC,
c. 1860)

Figure 2 - Joseph C. Willard
(LOC, c. 1862)

Figure 3 - Jeb Stuart
(LOC, c.1861)

Figure 4 - James P. Love
(VMI Archives, c.1860)

Figure 5 - John Mosby
(LOC, c. 1861)

Figure 6 - Antonia Ford
(LOC, c. 1855-1860)

Figure 7 - General Stuart's New Aide
(Harper's Weekly, 4/4/63)

Figure 8- Charles Edward Ford
(VMI Archives, c.1860)

Figure 9 - Gunnell House
(City of Fairfax, c. 1861)

Figure 10 - Ford Residence
(City of Fairfax, c. 1950)

Figure 11 - Buckingham Female Collegiate Institute
(Wm. and Mary College Quarterly Historical Magazine, c.1845)

Figure 12 - Fairfax Courthouse
(Fairfax Public Library, c. 1904)

Figure 13 - Fairfax Courthouse
(National Archives, c. 1863)

Figure 14 - Old Capitol Prison
(National Archives, c. 1860)

Figure 15 - Fortress Monroe
(LOC, c. 1862)

Figure 16 – Willard's Hotel
(LOC, c. 1853)

Figure 17 - Willcoxon Tavern
(City of Fairfax, c. 1861)

Figure 18 - Vienna Railroad Station (U.S. Army
Military History, Carlisle Barracks, c. 1876)

Figure 19 - La Pierre House, Philadelphia
(Free Library of Philadelphia, c. 1876)

Chapter Twenty-seven

Prison Life, March-April 1863

The next day, the sun streaming in through the bare window awakened me. I had small bites on my body from the bedbugs and lice that inhabited the straw mattress. At nine o'clock, the guards checked each cell to make sure the prisoner was still there. After that, a servant brought me breakfast—leftovers of the previous night's dinner. I whiled away the day by reading and sleeping. A servant delivered to me a few belongings from home that had arrived in a thoroughly ransacked bag. I still awaited my trunk.

A servant bringing me dinner interrupted me at three o'clock.

"What is this?" I asked her.

"It is Irish stew," she replied, while closing the door after her.

Along with the Irish stew were bread, butter, an apple, and a jug of water. I ate sparingly, as I never had much of an appetite in the aftermath of a migraine headache.

After dinner, looking through the window, I saw that it was exercise time in the courtyard. Feeling that mingling with strangers would be unwise for me, I hesitated to go out, until I saw my father. I walked to him as rapidly as I could.

Although against the rules to converse with fellow prisoners, I threw myself in his arms, exclaiming, "Dear Father! How awful our lives have turned around for us to be in this place." I told him what had happened to me since we last saw each other.

"Antonia, don't fret. I believe we shall be set free soon. Are you being treated decently?"

"Yes, don't worry about that, Father. I have a cell to myself right now. It is dank and smelly, but I will carry on."

Father replied, "I am located in the central wing in a second-story room, called Number Sixteen, allotted to political prisoners. It has a huge cylinder stove, a triple tier of bunks, some benches and stools, and two pine tables. We are among one hundred prisoners, but the number will rise. Do you have Federal money to buy necessities?"

"Yes, Father," I said. I hugged him tightly to me, and then returned to my cell.

On Sunday mornings, Mr. Wood roamed through the building corridors shouting, "All you who want to hear the Word of God preached according to 'Jeff Davis' go down into the yard; and all you who want to hear it preached according to 'Abe Lincoln' go into Number Sixteen." I went faithfully to the

"Jeff Davis" version, praying fervently for my release.

The March 16 *Alexandria Gazette* referred to me as a "young lady, at or near Fairfax Courthouse who had been arrested." The *Washington Star,* not so kind, actually mentioned me by name. How cruel, I thought, to besmirch my name and reputation!

Three days later, after I had exercised outside, a guard awaited me back at my cell.

"You have a visitor," he said. "Come with me."

We went past the main front door to a tidy, small parlor. He told me to await my visitor.

The officer of the day instructed me. "You are to speak in a distinct volume so that I can overhear your conversation. Interviews are generally limited to fifteen minutes, but occasionally I will grant thirty."

My visitor entered the room. Major Willard came up to me, took my hand, and said passionately, "This is an outrage! You no more deserve to be here than I do! I have many friends in high places and will use my influence to get you released. I have asked to be reassigned from McDowell's staff to that of General Heintzelman, officer-in-charge of troops and prisoners in Washington."

"My mother acted quickly to get word to you about our capture," I said.

"While stationed at the front, I sent a messenger to your village to send a telegram to headquarters. Your mother went up to him and asked him if he knew me. When he responded affirmatively, she gave him the message."

By this time, I felt shaky and weak. I almost laughed with relief. "Will you work to get my father released, also?" I asked.

"Of course, I will," he said.

He gave me a parcel that the officer of the day had searched. It contained some small cakes, bread, cheese, and some fruit.

"I have also brought you today's *Alexandria Gazette*."

"I appreciate that. As you can imagine, there is not much to occupy my time here other than my needlework and reading."

"I will try to visit you every day, Antonia," he said.

The officer of the day broke in, "Passes to visit the Old Capitol are obtained here on Tuesdays and Fridays."

"We will see about that!" exclaimed Major Willard. "Stay out of my conversation with Miss Ford!"

"Major Willard, we have no understanding. We are supposedly enemies. Why are you doing this for me?"

"I am a person of small words. Do you believe in love at first sight?"

I could feel myself blush, and then said, "Perhaps. I thank you sincerely for your attentions. I believe in predestination; therefore, what will be, will be. Only time will tell."

After more small talk, Major Willard left me, and I went back to my cell. I sat still, staring off into space, thinking about my protector, Major Willard. I then opened the *Gazette* and read that another neighbor, Mr. Amos Fox, had been arrested.

Yesterday's *Washington Star* reported, "We believe it has been determined to remove from the immediate vicinity of the Federal lines, in Fairfax, all residents not known to be reliably loyal."

That explained a lot.

The article that intrigued me most in today's news concerned Frankie Abel. My arrest night also turned out to be hers, in Washington. She had not gone to Centreville at all. When arrested, she wore male attire and gave her name as Frank Tuttle. After being permitted to go back to her boarding house for the night, she had to report to the authorities the next morning. Accordingly, the next morning, she appeared dressed properly as a woman and gave her name as Francis Abel, of Baltimore. She said Colonel Fisher employed her as a detective, and that she frequently went about disguised as a man. Lafayette Baker required her presence as a witness against some people who were currently under arrest.

"A wolf in sheep's clothing," I thought. How she had fooled me!

I read on. There was a long editorial on the capture of General Stoughton written by his uncle, E.W. Stoughton of New York. I felt relieved to read:

> *Mr. Ford and his family were highly respected in the neighborhood, although it is probable that, like most of the residents there, they were unfriendly to the Union cause. I have information which leads me to believe that General Stoughton had no acquaintance whatever with either of the female members of Mr. Ford's family. He, of course, believed them respectable, or he would not have placed his mother and sister under their roof.*

I resolved to mention this to Major Willard the next time I saw him, to help my case.

It was common, Father told me, to receive notes from fellow prisoners through ingenious means. I found out exactly what that meant, as I heard a scraping noise coming from the wall. I observed a dull metal knife blade poking through my cell wall. Grabbing my own knife from my dinner tray, I inserted mine into the crack in the wall. Soon, a rolled up message arrived, between the two blades. Often, the news from other female prisoners was more amusing than important. We all delighted, though, in deceiving the guards, and breaking the "no communication" rule.

That same week, I had a visit from my friend, John Esten Cooke. He came disguised in civilian dress, in order to avoid arrest, and signed the visitor's log using an alias. We faced each other in the parlor.

"My dear Antonia, I am using every influence I have to get you out of prison. I have contacted General Jeb Stuart and enlisted his aid. He said he would write a letter to the newly promoted Major Mosby asking for whatever evidence he could furnish of your innocence as involving the exploits at Fairfax. He must have done so, because Adjutant General Ferguson wrote a letter to Major Mosby requesting that he send a statement to Fitzhugh Lee's headquarters stating that you had nothing to do with the capture of General Stoughton and men. We want to get you an unconditional release."

"Thank you. I worry for my father and the other arrested villagers. Will you put a word in for them too?"

"Certainly. Is there anything you need? I have brought you a packet of food."

"Mr. Wood is actually very kind, and allows me whatever I wish to have. He says that compared to some of the women prisoners, who have since left, I am a model prisoner in decorum and etiquette. Will you see my mother anytime soon?"

He whispered, "I dare not go into that village unless I, too, want to end up here."

"How did you get a visitor's pass to visit me?" I whispered.

He looked at me and rubbed his fingers together, indicating a bribe.

"What do you do here to occupy your time? You must be lonely."

"Actually, jail is a sociable place. The separation of prisoners is impossible. The men mainly play cards. Muggins—or Old Capitol, a domino game—is also popular among all of us. I am embroidering a lace cap and collar set which is so intricate that it steadies my nerves and makes the time pass by."

When our visiting time ended, he left, telling me to have faith and not to despair.

Every day seemed much the same as the one before. I now had a cellmate, named Abigail Williams, not a strong person, and I thought she would not fare well on the greasy beans, fat, and other meager rations and chilly conditions that were our lot.

I read from the March 28 *Alexandria Gazette:* "Army of the Potomac. A circular issued yesterday suggests that the presence of ladies in camp is no longer necessary or profitable, and an immediate hegira of crinoline will ensue."

I thought that it was about time someone uttered a statement like that.

On April 15, I received a letter from my Mother that she had written two days previously:

Fairfax April 13, 1863
My darling Child,

I have not received a single line from you since the sad morning of your departure from home, nor have I seen anyone who could tell me how you were or how you were looking. I have longed for one line saying you were well. I have seen several who could tell me how your Father was. Keep up your spirit—by so doing your health may be better preserved. You were so sick the morning you left I feared seriously you were not able to stand the trip but trust in God my dear child he is able to accomplish all things will not let us fall if we put our trust in him. He has said call upon me in the day of trouble I will deliver you.

We are all well. All your brothers, Pattie, and darkeys. Mary has been sick but is now well. She has been very anxious to go to see her mother but has not been able to get a pass. Since I hear your Father's favorite (of past summer) is the superintendent of the C. Prison, I am much better satisfied. If Mr. Wood will allow it, I will write you a note soon again. If only one line to let me know how you and your Father are, will be a good comfort to me. To your Father tell him not to feel uneasy about home—we are getting on very well.

Your devoted MaMa, Julia Ford.

Everybody that knows you sends love to you. Tell Father to try to keep up his spirits and not to trouble about Frank's eyes. Lizzie, Murrys, send much love. All the neighbors are well except Mrs. Gunnell.

I cried with relief to get that letter—it had been one month since my arrest. I had written Mother several letters, but apparently, she had not received any of them. I took out stationary and pen, and composed a reply to my mother:

My dear Mother,

Mr. Wood has given me permission to write for my trunk, of which I gladly avail myself—being as you may imagine in much need of clothes. I am very comfortably fixed and very well; so is Father. I see him occasionally. We don't want you to feel uneasy or distressed about us, we really are doing very well; and but for the separation would be satisfied. Please Mother make a clean sweep in gathering up my things, for (I don't want to distress you, but you must know it) I shall see Richmond long before Fairfax Courthouse. If it were possible for you to leave home how glad I should be to see you; but I suppose it can't be affected. Father says you had much better take the oath, if you can conscientiously.

All the gentlemen from Courthouse are well—tell Mrs. Powell, Benceley says his health hasn't been as good since Jan., as it is now. Tell Mary I leave you in her care. Tell Pattie not to cry her eyes out.

Tell Frank Father talks of him every time I see him. Tell Clanie to fill my place for you. If you can't come to see me, do pray write, in that case; put your letter in an unsealed envelope directed to me, and then in a sealed one to Wm P. Wood... Carroll Prison. Mother can't you come down once while I'm here? We don't know when we'll meet again, and I'm so anxious to see you. If you can possibly get off bring Frank. I'm at a great loss for work, please put some in my trunk.

Give my love to the family, Mary included, and all who inquire. Please send to me the following essentials: plumes; bows; china mug; tea; spool cotton #18, 24, 30, 36, 40, 70; Les Miserables; music of "Bonnie Blue Flag" and "Dixie"; buckskin gloves; stationery. Place them all in small bags then put neatly in larger ones, for gentlemen take a peep in.

Keep any of the articles I've written for, if you want them for your own use.

Most affectionately your child,
Antonia Ford

Chapter Twenty-eight

A Startling Revelation, May 1863

"C aptain Willard, are any efforts being made for my release?"

I was in the visiting parlor with Captain Willard on a pleasant May morning. His almost daily visits meant so much to me.

"Antonia, in March, General Stuart wrote a letter to Major Mosby. My sources tell me that he asked for whatever evidence Mosby was able to furnish of your innocence in the exploit at Fairfax—so that he could insist upon your unconditional release. We are still waiting for that letter."

I looked at him with despair.

"I know it's difficult for you. I'm personally working on obtaining your release. I think that perhaps a prisoner exchange is your best option. Be prepared, as you will probably be sent South, if this scenario plays out."

"Where south?" I asked.

"Prisoners are sent by train to Baltimore, then by ship to Fortress Monroe, Virginia. From there, you steam to City Point, Virginia. It is a small port town located at the confluence of the James and Appomattox Rivers. You are released there."

"Do you have any news from Fairfax Courthouse?" I asked.

"Yes, Dr. William Gunnell and his wife have moved away."

"I suppose they felt unsafe and annoyed at sharing their home with the Federals."

Major Willard looked at me, took a deep breath, and started speaking.

"Antonia, I've known you a little over one year. I've seen you almost daily during the last month. There is something that I need to tell you."

I looked at him warily, not knowing what to expect.

"I am married."

"Married!" I exclaimed. For a long moment, I was too stunned to react. Then I stood up from my chair and advanced toward him, hands on hips. "You, you, scoundrel! How could you lead me on and even declare your undying love towards me, with this disgraceful fact?" I felt angrier than I could ever remember, and I'm sure my voice echoed throughout the first floor of the prison.

"Before you judge me so harshly, I need to tell you my story. Then you can choose to forever banish me or not."

"Very well, Major Willard. Pray tell me," I said, more calmly than I felt as I reclaimed my seat.

"In 1844, as a twenty-four-year-old, I moved from my home in Westminster, Vermont, to Troy, New York. I worked briefly at the New York and Troy Steamboat Company. Seeking more genteel work, The Astoria House in New York City employed me in 1845. While I was there, I behaved as many young men do. I attended parties, gambled, and drank excessively. I capered with young women of the town, and was in no hurry for marriage, I can tell you that! I accepted an invitation to a party by an acquaintance from work, who introduced me to the daughter of the house— Caroline Moore. As the evening went on, we conversed, danced together, and had a pleasant time. Caroline, twenty-five, had no marriage prospects, even though from a financially desirable family. Only average in appearance, she seemed slow in some ways. For example, I asked her about current books, and she indicated that she did not enjoy reading. She had not furthered her education by going to a finishing school. I continued to see her, perhaps out of a feeling of pity towards her and an obligation towards the friend from work."

I interrupted his story. "This story does have a conclusion, I hope?"

"Yes. Please indulge me and listen on. When I visited Caroline, her parents left us alone in the parlor after an obligatory ten-minute chat. They would not ever show their faces again, even into the wee hours of the morning, which surprised me, as it seemed highly improper that they were not chaperoning. As the weeks went by, I started taking liberties with her. I am not proud of it, but temptation got the better hand of me. At first, we only sat close and kissed for hours. One night, after drinking too much whiskey, I lost my mind. Caroline and I started socializing with our ritual of small talk, and then we proceeded to kissing and touching. Unfortunately, my passions were uncontrollable, and I asked her to raise her skirts. She willingly did as I asked, while on her back on the sofa. I had my way with her. I did not love her, and never told her that I loved her. I have always regretted my actions of that night. She, on the other hand, seemed unaffected, and happily assumed our marriage would be very soon. I left that night with a heavy heart."

At this point, I wept, tears running down my face. Major Willard handed me a handkerchief and said, "You will see that I am entirely honest with you, Antonia. To continue my story, Caroline found within a few weeks that she was 'with child.' We had a swift marriage, although loveless from my perspective. Shortly after our wedding, Caroline miscarried the baby. She went into a deep depression that the physician said sometimes happened after childbirth. He prescribed some pills to help with her emotions, but the pills did not work. Caroline probably knew that I did not love her. She refused conjugal rights to me. She slept half the day, and did not groom or wash herself. I almost considered institutionalizing her."

"My brother, Henry, my best friend and confidant during this stressful period, helped me. Slowly, Caroline regained her mind. She never laughed, did not socialize with friends, and kept a separate bedroom from mine. Five years went by."

"How awful for both of you," I sympathized.

"In 1850, I had an opportunity to be a cashier for the Aspinwall and

Company, in San Francisco, California. The sense of adventure appealed to me, and the idea of striking gold was enticing. Caroline refused to go with me, however, and moved in with some relatives. I spent two years in California, then returned to Washington City, and with my brother, Henry, purchased our hotel in 1853. Caroline and I lived at the hotel for a while, as she liked having everything done for her."

"Did you correspond with her while you were in California?"

"I'm ashamed to say that I did not. Henry then married the former Sarah Kellogg in 1855. We thought it time to have a real home, so Henry and I jointly purchased one that was one block from the hotel. Henry, Sarah, and I settled in quickly, but Caroline remained at the hotel, refusing to move with me. I saw Caroline now and then, because I frequented the hotel, but she asked nothing of me. On the other hand, she lacked for nothing. She had her family nearby, and enough money to maintain an elegant and carefree lifestyle in the hotel. We had slaves that did all the cooking and housework in our own house, of course, but that did not entice her.

"Caroline certainly did not object when I was commissioned in the Union army. I have broached the idea of divorce with her, but it is still socially stigmatizing. She has no objection, otherwise."

At this point, the guard, whom I am sure listened raptly, announced that the visiting time was over.

"Major Willard," I said sadly, "I will prayerfully consider what you have told me. I do not know if I will agree to see you again. If not—farewell and thank you for all you have done for me thus far."

I left the room, went back to my cell, and cried, inconsolably.

Abigail asked, "Whatever is wrong?"

"My heart is broken, and I cannot talk about it now."

Shortly, a powerful migraine attacked me. I knew that besides my monthly mood swings, stress also greatly triggered my attacks. I asked a servant to bring me a strong pot of tea because this remedy helped to alleviate my pain. In addition, I had on hand some opiates to dull the ache. After drinking the tea, Abigail put a cold, wet rag over my eyes and forehead, and I lay down to wait out the attack. I must have slept, because it approached two o'clock when I awoke. I sat at the table and tried to force down a little bread. My head did not hurt anymore, but I felt a bit woozy from the painkiller. The door suddenly crashed open. Hands raised me from my chair and held onto me.

"Unhand me sir!" I said.

The guard did as I asked, but did not speak and escorted me out. Abigail watched with a look of horror on her face.

My destination was Mr. Wood's office.

Mr. Wood abruptly said, "You are to be sent for exchange to Fortress Monroe, then to City Point, Virginia. Pack everything as quickly as possible, as you are being transported today, by train to Baltimore, Maryland."

"Why Baltimore?" I asked.

"Navigating the Potomac to the Chesapeake from the Sixth Street wharf here in town is an option, but is time-consuming and tricky. It is far easier to transport prisoners by railway to Baltimore, then by steamer traveling on the Patapsco River into the Bay, then down to Virginia on the Chesapeake Bay."

"Will you get word to my family about my exchange?"

"Yes. I'm sure that Major Willard will find out tomorrow."

"Oh … him. It doesn't matter about him," I said angrily.

Mr. Wood gave me a puzzled look and wished me well.

I went back to my cell, packed quickly, kissed sickly Abigail goodbye, and waited in the front hall for the carriage that would take me the few blocks to the Washington depot at New Jersey Avenue and "C" Street. From there, I would begin my journey by riding the Baltimore and Ohio train to Baltimore, a distance of thirty-eight miles.

Chapter Twenty-nine

Being Sent South, May 14-17, 1863

I awaited my carriage from the hallway of the Carroll along with thirteen other women being exchanged. Among them waited Mrs. Mitchell and her two grown-up daughters, Claire and Melanie. I had passed notes back and forth to them a few times and had seen them in the exercise yard, and felt comforted that I would not be traveling alone.

Obviously, sisters, both Claire and Melanie had long brown hair, and oval faces framed by big expressive eyes. Melanie, the shyer of the two, had an inner kindness and gentle spirit that would make her a friend to anyone.

I asked her, "Why do you wear your hair long?"

She answered, "I like the way it feels sheltering my shoulders."

Claire added, "We've never been compelled to follow dictates of society by putting our hair up."

Mrs. Mitchell said, "General Rosecrans arrested my daughters and me for aiding and abetting the escape of Rebel prisoners. What is your story?"

"I am said to be a spy," I replied succinctly.

We did not have long to wait before the guarded carriages arrived. The driver loaded our belongings and drove us the few blocks to the railroad depot. At the depot, mostly uniformed men lingered, while others, more active, held off a group of Southern sympathizers. The train arrived, we entered our own compartment and settled down for the hour and one-half ride to Baltimore.

Mrs. Mitchell said, "This is quite an adventure, isn't it?"

I replied, "I like to travel, but not under these circumstances. The only place I've been to is college in Gravel Hill, Virginia."

"That must be the Buckingham Female Collegiate Institute," she responded.

"Yes, I graduated in 1857 with an English Literature degree."

We continued our small talk until we pulled into the depot at Baltimore.

A gang of young men walked quickly by our group. One of the boys threw a rock at our guard and hit him on the boot. The group laughed and made jeers and derogatory remarks about the Federals as they ran off.

The guard muttered, "These plug-uglies are asking for trouble. They need to be jailed, with the key thrown away forever!"

From the depot, carriages took us to the Gilmore House to spend the night. This residence, converted into a comfortable boarding establishment, housed two or three women to a room. At last, I luxuriated in the thought that I would sleep on a real bed once again with real sheets. A washbowl, chamber pot, towels, and soap were visible, so the first thing I did was to take a sponge bath. It did wonders for my body and soul.

I felt famished, and was relieved to hear that the proprietor would serve supper in a dining room in the house. Although simple, the food was plentiful and delicious. After supper, a group of us gathered in the parlor to play cards. As night fell, the servants lit the oil lamps. The guard remained with us, and would do so until we stepped onto the steamer in the morning.

"I hear a commotion outside," I said to Mrs. Mitchell.

We went to the window overlooking the street and saw a large group of young men, marching with torches in their hands. They were clad in oilcloths and caps, and had a flag that said "Wide Awake" with an eye symbol.

Our guard also came to the window and commented, "These 'Wide Awakes' originally formed during the 1860 election and gathered to sing political songs and rally the 'party faithful' to the polls to vote for Lincoln. Fights broke out when they met up with Democratic squadrons and other rivals. Now, they are just Republicans who gather for social and recreational activities."

"I'm surprised to see so many of them. Why are they not fighting in the war?"

"Some of them are too young. Others are veterans."

As they passed by, singing the "Battle Hymn of the Republic," I wondered where my brother, Charlie, was at that very moment.

That night, I slept soundly in spite of the revelation that Major Willard had shared with me, which I was trying not to think about, just yet. I had to conserve my energy for what lay ahead of me. Father and I had discussed contingency plans in case I was sent South, and I knew I would be staying for periods in Culpeper and Warrenton, before returning home.

The next morning, early, after a hearty breakfast, the conveyances again came for all thirteen of us. I managed to obtain a copy of the previous day's *Washington Star*. I read an article entitled "Females Sent South" with growing dismay to see my own name published:

> *The last lot of Rebel prisoners sent south from this city were accompanied by fourteen females, who had been in confinement in the Old Capitol. Among them were Mrs. Mitchell and her two daughters, arrested by General Rosecrans for persistently aiding and abetting the escape of Rebel prisoners, most intensely vituperative traitors as they proved to be while here. Also, a woman who had served for some months as a Rebel sergeant of cavalry, a regular bruiser. Also, the noted Miss Ford, of Fairfax County, Virginia, arrested for participation in Moseby's abduction of General Stoughton, &c. It is due to Miss Ford that we should state that her behavior while a prisoner here was so entirely modest and correct as to make friends for her all whose duties were about the Old Capitol, and to impress them with the conviction that General Stuart's commission appointing*

her as one of his aides-de-camp, which was found with her when
arrested, was but a joke on the part of all concerned in it.

I shared the article with Mrs. Mitchell and her daughters. Mrs. Mitchell just laughed uproariously.

As we walked toward the steamer, escorted by an orderly-sergeant, Baltimore secessionists gave us gifts of food tied in colorful handkerchiefs. They called "God bless you" and offered to mail any letters that we had written the previous evening. We embarked the Juanita steamer.

I asked a courteous-looking man with a nametag of Captain Mix, "How soon will we leave?"

Captain Mix laughed and said, "No one told you that we journey by night? We will lie offshore most of the day."

I digested the bad news, feeling impatient about anything that would prolong my journey. Men for prisoner exchange came on the steamer during the next few hours. Soon, with a full ship, we went a little ways offshore and dropped anchor. Boredom caused by inactivity was prevalent on the ship, but thankfully, the men, being political prisoners, were for the most part refined. I did find out that Confederate General Hays and several other officers on the ship with us were to be exchanged. At noon, the captain requested all the ladies to follow him. Not knowing why, I expected the worst, but was pleasantly surprised to be led to the "officers' mess." There the captain arranged for a nice luncheon, including iced champagne. The captain told us that the men's meal consisted of stew and water, elsewhere.

I whiled away the hours reading local newspapers and chatting with the other passengers. We had no beds to sleep on that night, or the night after, but I managed to sleep sitting up as we traveled over the waters. It took us two days to get to Fortress Monroe. We arrived at Old Point Comfort. A lighthouse faced the Chesapeake Bay. I could see the fort in the distance through the fading light. A transport pulled up to our steamer, and to my dismay, Lafayette C. Baker, now a colonel, came aboard.

"We meet again," Colonel Baker said to me.

I only nodded my head, as I did not like the man.

"I will escort you and the other prisoners from this point forward," he said to me.

Our steamer went further and docked at the wharf. A small, white, wooden building with a slanted roof whose sign read "Captain of the Port's Office" stood at the end of the wharf. A Union flag flew in front of the structure. Next door to it stood a relatively fancy building with decorative posts in the front and a two-tiered roof with shingles. Two dormer windows with a sign stating "Hygeia Dining Saloon" appeared in the top part of the roof. The ladies were given permission to partake of food in the dining saloon before proceeding to Fortress Monroe. The men, not given that opportunity, were whisked away in waiting carriages.

After our meal, Mrs. Mitchell, her daughters, and I sat on benches on the wharf, awaiting our coaches. I paid little attention to the comings and goings of steamers, while we waited. I basked, half-asleep, in the warmth of this spring day, but roused as a shadow fell over me. I looked up—into the face of Major Willard.

He bowed to me, and then said, "Antonia, how happy I am to see that you are safe. When I found out what had happened to you, I came as swiftly as I could to take you back the same route that I took to get here. Your mother seemed quite relieved when I told her my plan."

"You don't mean you came to rescue me!" I exclaimed indignantly.

"Don't you need to be rescued?" he asked, somewhat hurt.

"I take care of myself, sir, as you can plainly see."

At that point Colonel Baker came up to Major Willard. "I see you have an interest in this woman. Unfortunately, so do I—as an officer of the Union army. She may only be released at the time and place that is appropriate."

Major Willard said, "Just give the oath, Antonia. Then I will be able to take you north. Do not despair. I have some money for you that your father sent."

"My father! Does that mean he obtained his freedom?"

"Yes. Mr. Wood liberated your father from prison soon after you left Carroll because of insufficient evidence."

I imagined that he had released the other townspeople also.

"May I escort you home by water when the exchange is complete?" he asked.

Melanie Mitchell stared in awe at the handsome rescuer-to-be.

"He might be of some use to us as an escort to keep the ruffians away," Mrs. Mitchell said in an aside to me.

I turned to Mrs. Mitchell. "That might be true if we were going by the water route, but we are going north by rail," I said stubbornly. "Besides, it is not safe for me to go home right now. He wouldn't be able to go very far in the Confederate cities through which we will be traveling wearing his charming blue suit."

"As you wish," Major Willard replied. "I am partaking of food in the dining saloon, but will be back before you leave," he said as he walked away.

Mrs. Mitchell remarked, "Whatever did he do to you? Is it because he is a Union officer that you are so rude to him?"

"No, there is more to it than that, but I would rather not discuss the details."

He did return, and I explained to him our plan of action to travel north via railway. He agreed that it would be the best route to go. He pulled me aside and asked me, "Have you thought about my marital predicament and whether there is any hope for my courting you?"

"I have not had time to think, since you told me. When I get back home, I will consider what you discussed with me. Right now, I have other matters on my mind. Have you heard any news about my brother?"

"No, I haven't. I see your coaches have arrived. I am also going to Fortress Monroe to handle some business with Captain Butler. I know this area well, as my brother Caleb used to manage the Hygeia Hotel here. I will strive to see you off at the railway depot whenever you are exchanged."

"Goodbye, sir," I said as I entered the coach with my traveling companions.

We passed the Hygeia Hotel, now a hospital, on the way to the fort. Fortress Monroe claimed to be America's largest garrison and I could see why as we approached it. A moat surrounded the fort, reminding me of medieval England. The stone walls at the moat's edge exhibited small windows every few feet, whose purpose was to shoot weapons through. A long, narrow bridge with guardrails spanned the moat. A massive squared-off entrance that cut through the stone wall was just wide enough for one carriage to fit. Of course, a guard stood at attention. Areas of stately oak trees decorated the fort, and as we entered, I saw a large red brick building to my left. I presumed that the numerous two- and three-story brick buildings in this huge complex housed the army personnel. The driver acted as an unofficial tour guide and showed us the officer's quarters. Simple and well groomed, they faced a large grassy area with the water's edge just beyond. Altogether, I found the fort to be picturesque and lovely. We headed toward the Prison House, known as a casemate. We left the carriage and entered the building. Colonel Baker escorted my group of traveling companions through a maze of corridors to a room designated "Prisoner Exchange." Captain Cassels, the provost marshal, sat behind a desk. We crowded into the room and he asked each of us to sign the Oath of Allegiance. Most of my lady friends agreed, but I could not conscientiously do so.

Colonel Baker remarked, "You are not making life easier for yourself."

I scornfully replied, "Sometimes the right way is not the easy way, Colonel!"

"As you wish, miss," interjected Captain Cassels. "I am immediately releasing those who sign, with travel passes, in order that they may make their way back to their homes. The rest of you will have to stay here until I properly document the exchanges. You will be paroled—that is, you will promise to stay out of Federal territory and not interfere in military affairs of any kind."

"Do you anticipate that our exchange will occur soon?" I asked.

"Probably tomorrow," he replied. "Basic quarters are available here for your overnight stay."

I located my luggage, and discussed with Mrs. Mitchell the best way to proceed. A guard showed us the way to a stark, but adequate room. After some conversation and Bible reading, we blew out the candles and went to bed, hoping for release the next day.

Chapter Thirty

Traveling to Culpeper, May 18-22, 1863

The next morning, Colonel Baker ordered all of us to Captain Cassels' office once again.

"Your exchange is now complete," Captain Cassels said. "I request once more that you take the Oath of Allegiance."

All four of us refused. With a sigh and a scowl, Colonel Baker handed us our travel passes, and gruffly told us to pack, as we were going to the wharf to get the steamer Belvidere to take us to City Point.

A coach took Colonel Baker and us to the wharf, where a large crowd of soldiers awaited the transport and their subsequent exchanges.

Mrs. Mitchell nudged me and said, "Pray tell me, Antonia, isn't that Major Willard coming toward us?"

"Yes it is," I replied. I walked away to meet him and to have some privacy in our conversation.

"I can only wish you safe travels, my dear," he said to me as he looked tenderly into my eyes. "I will find out from your parents where you are residing through the summer. I will write to you with whatever news of your friends and relatives that I am able to ascertain. I care deeply for you."

I looked at him, I heard the sincerity in his voice, and my stoicism broke down. My voice faltered and quivered as I said simply, "I would like that very much. I need a friend."

The gesture occurred spontaneously on both our parts. I did not intend for it to happen, but the brief hug occurred. I backed away, ashamed of my public display of affection. Gasps escaped from the people and soldiers who realized that a Southern lady had just consorted with a Federal officer.

Our large group of exchange prisoners slowly embarked the steamer Belvidere and we cast off. Major Mulford received us aboard and showed us to the saloon. He introduced us to his wife, who treated us with kindness and gentility. We spent the day there, and enjoyed a delicious and delightful midday meal. To pass the time away, we played cards, read the newspapers, had our evening meal, and simply waited all night in the saloon. I enjoyed discussing about various authors and books with Melanie, Mrs. Mitchell's eldest daughter.

The steamer got under way at seven o'clock the next morning. We steamed forward all day and finally reached the mouth of the James River, where the water became slightly yellow and streaky on the surface. Our travels took us two days. Finally, we saw Confederate signal officers signaling our approach to City Point. We observed mounted Confederates on the shoreline.

As we approached City Point, a village just northeast of Petersburg, I saw a long wharf lined with artillery and many anchored schooners and supply boats nearby. At the end of the wharf, a wooden building displayed a Confederate flag, flying proudly. The Confederate exchange agent, Colonel Robert Ould, and his assistant, Mr. Watson, came out of that building to meet us. The two of them directed some of the soldiers and civilians off the ship and onto shore. The Mitchells and I, along with some other passengers remained on board and awaited the flag-of-truce tugboat from Richmond, due to arrive during the night. The next morning, I awoke to find a man named Captain Hatch calling to my traveling friends and me.

"Rise and shine," he boomed at us. The heavy-set, jolly man, with blond hair and mustache, asked a porter to bring our luggage on board, and then escorted us onto his tugboat. We continued our journey to Richmond, which would take another twelve hours. Captain Hatch acted pleased to play the tour guide.

"Why are we on a tugboat and not a steamer?" I asked curiously.

"The area around Drewry's Bluff is treacherous to larger ships. We would not want to run aground."

The untamed scenery varied, yet remained essentially the same, with trees and other wildlife in their springtime blooms. I was pleased to find out that I was not at all seasick, and could stand on deck and enjoy nature's bounty. Claire Mitchell felt rather queasy and I instructed her to stand in the middle of the tugboat, look into the distance, and allow the wind to blow on her face. I obtained some ginger root from the captain for her to suck on. I think it helped her a bit.

Captain Hatch announced, "We have just passed Chapin's Bluff. Two miles ahead, we will make a sharp turn due west and come to Drewry's Bluff on your left. This bluff rises abruptly some ninety feet above the James River. You can see the fort on the bluff. I am proud to say that one year ago, Commander Ebeneezer Farrand and his men in the fort kept the Union flotilla from advancing to Richmond. Captain Sydney Smith Lee, General Robert E. Lee's brother, has since taken command of the site and supervised its expansion and strengthening into a permanent fort."

Finally, we arrived at Shockhoe Slip in Richmond and found a carriage to take us for the night to the Exchange Hotel, located conveniently close to the train depot.

The next morning, we met at the depot at Broad and Seventeenth Streets, and from there, traveled on the Virginia Central, which connected with the O&A at Gordonsville. The O&A, originally designed as a freight line, became, out of necessity and convenience, a passenger train. Culpeper Courthouse was my immediate destination, while the Mitchells were traveling a bit further to Warrenton. We exchanged information on how to reach each other. The train rolled through several hills, and arrived in a valley. Through my window, I could see some church steeples in the distance. Farms with picket fences dominated the landscape. A few farm animals milled about. As the train stopped at the Culpeper depot, I tearfully wished my traveling companions, Mrs. Mitchell, Claire, and Melanie, goodbye and left the train, frail and weary. Both hungry and thirsty, I needed to decide on a plan of action.

Chapter Thirty-one

Culpeper Courthouse, May 22, 1863

Culpeper Courthouse, with just over a thousand residents, and sixty merchants and shopkeepers, proved to be a gigantic community compared to Fairfax Courthouse. The Orange & Alexandria Railroad had much to do with the town's wealth. The depot in town, a rough wooden rectangular building with a steep pitched roof, was the largest of Culpeper County's five depots. After stepping off the train, I saw across the track a discolored picket fence with white camp tents pitched haphazardly. I left my luggage at the depot, and set off on foot to obtain information and to investigate the town. I walked on the main street and came to a pump where some residents were drawing their water into buckets. I viewed the courthouse with its weather vane on top. Trees lined the road and provided some shade for me. The dust from the street quickly soiled my dress and shoes—not that they were that clean anyway from my travels. A few civilians and infrequent uniformed soldiers dressed in gray meandered in the street. A year ago, the Federals had occupied the town, but it was currently under Southern control. Finally, I came to the Old Virginia Hotel at 202 Main Street. A two-story frame building with an exterior cornice loomed in front of me. Although I had three to choose from, this hotel was the place that my father recommended to me. He knew the Paynes and their reputation as kind people. Outside the hotel, a horse tied to a tree looked skinny and sick. A red hospital flag hung from a pole attached to the front of the house. I knocked on the door and a middle-aged woman, dressed in widow's weeds, answered. I guessed her to be Mary Payne. Her husband, William, had just passed away in March, so she ran the hotel with her four daughters.

"Good day," she said to me. "I am Mary Payne. How can I help you?"

"My name is Antonia Ford. My father told me to come here as a safe haven."

"Come in, child," she said swiftly as she ushered me inside. "I have been expecting you. Where is your luggage?"

"I left it at the depot."

"I will send a servant for it."

She rang a bell and a Negro servant appeared.

"Please go to the depot and retrieve Miss Ford's luggage," she instructed the servant.

"Right away, ma'am," he replied.

"Your father has stayed here in better days, when he had business to transact in Culpeper Courthouse. As you could probably see from the red hospital flag, my hotel is now being used as a hospital. The Federals stripped the hotel of all furnishings in the eighteen guest rooms save for beds and mattresses. Only the barroom and my family's living quarters and rooms remain preserved. Of course, we have room for you, dear. You may stay with my four daughters."

Mrs. Payne showed me to the parlor where a fine piano stood. A woman played "When Johnny Comes Marching Home Again." She stopped when she saw us.

"Antonia, this is my daughter, Millie."

"Pleased to meet you," I said. "I've heard accounts of you and your sisters from my father over the years." Millie, twenty years old, looked lovely, with long, loose dark hair, sparkling eyes, and a slim build.

"Hello, Antonia," she said warmly. "My other sisters are in the dining room. Come with me and we will have tea. You must be weary after your journey."

I followed Millie into the dining room. A large fireplace with an intricately carved mantelpiece displayed china plates. Her sisters, Josephine, thirty-two, Charlene, twenty-six, and Amanda, twenty-four, sat at the table, drinking tea, and eating biscuits and jam. The family resemblance to their mother was unmistakable, but Millie looked to be the beauty of the family. I sat down and could barely contain my ravenous appetite. The sisters must have thought me uncivilized the way I gulped my food down. Mrs. Payne took pity on me, for she brought me a bowl of soup.

Millie said, "I am so glad that the awful Yankees are gone from our town. They used this hotel as their command center. The men ate like pigs, and expected us to be polite and entertain them. We made a show of sitting apart from the soldiers. They did not dare hang a national flag from our hotel, as we scorned it so terribly."

Mary said sharply, "Millie it was only due to our playing along with them that we still have a hotel standing in one piece. Anyone in town known to be Southern supporters were arrested and their homes practically torn down."

"Your barroom was also a big draw, Mother," said Josephine.

"You're right, until Colonel Taylor closed the hotel last year because he said that my bar keeper showed no patriotic restraint in trade with the soldiers."

Millie said with a smirk, "Too many drunken soldiers running around, I suppose."

After tea, Millie took me by the arm and led me to the room where she and her sisters slept. I saw my luggage against the wall.

Millie pointed to a bed and said, "Nap time for you. No arguments."

As soon as my head hit the pillow, I fell asleep.

Chapter Thirty-two

Life in Culpeper, May-June 1863

T he first thing I did upon awakening was write a letter to my parents in Fairfax Courthouse to tell them of my whereabouts. I gave the letter to Mrs. Payne and she assured me that it would arrive safely in my hometown in the next few days.

Millie and her sisters proved to be good companions for me and my spirits lifted every day that I was with that good family. Millie had a beau, named John, who fought in the war. She wrote him steamy love letters. She showed one of them to me:

My love, I cannot wait to gaze into your soulful eyes. My heart yearns for your embrace . . .

I lightly admonished her for writing so intimately to her suitor.

"This war has taken so many young lives," she said. "Restraint and formality seem inconsequential compared to life and death. If my words are the last things he will ever see, I want them to mean something and to give him some comfort and peace. I want him to fight to come home to me, my dear beloved John."

Millie verbalized to me what love could be like. I wondered if I would ever have such a depth of feeling towards a man. Sometimes I feared and worried that I would become an old maid because the right man had not come along.

Mrs. Payne related to me the last few months of her dearly departed husband's life.

"He had a slow decline and was partially paralyzed for a number of years. He could neither walk nor speak in his final weeks. I think the war was the final blow to his weakened condition. Even though he has been gone for only two months, it really has been several years that we have been running the hotel without him."

Millie said, "Jeb Stuart and Major John Pelham dined with us in March right before Father died. I know that Jeb is an acquaintance of yours, Antonia. Is it true that you are an aide-de-camp to him?"

I grimaced, and then said, "That was simply a parlor game gone bad, I'm afraid. That silly document is in part what put me in jail!"

T wo days after I arrived, General Jeb Stuart and his cavalry and horse artillery arrived in town and headquartered at the Samuel Bradford farm, near Brandy. General Lee's instructions were to guard the upper

Rappahannock and monitor Federal movements in the area. Jeb stopped by the hotel to pay his respects to Mrs. Payne, but when he saw me, a look of surprise and happiness crossed his face.

"I had heard you were sent South, but I am so pleased to see you are almost home again. I did what I could to exonerate you, but my appeals were to no avail."

"That is all behind me now. How are your wife, Flora, and your son, James?" I asked.

"My precious Flora is coping well with her third pregnancy. We expect another child in October. James Jr. is almost three now and is a real rapscallion."

"Just like his father!" I replied.

"Such disrespect from a lady," he murmured with a laugh. "I hope you will be here in two days for the grand review of my cavalry and horse artillery—some four thousand men?"

"I would not miss it! It has been such a long time since any gaiety has passed before me."

On May 22, near the courthouse, the grand review took place with General Stuart looking on carefully. Most of the townspeople attended, wearing their best clothes. Stuart's men looked as clean as possible, and they even bathed and brushed their horses. Metal adornments gleamed, boots and saddles were polished, and the soldiers displayed weapons proudly. A little drummer boy, not more than twelve years old, walked to the side of the line of horses, beating a cadence.

The Paynes, Mrs. Ashby, and I received an invitation from the Bradfords for an evening of entertainment that same night.

After our sponge baths, the Payne sisters and I planned our outfits for the soiree. I bemoaned the fact that I did not have any fancy dresses with me, appropriate for an evening gala.

"You're my size," said Amanda. "Why don't you pick out something that takes your fancy from my wardrobe?"

I gratefully did as she offered and found a lovely light pink silk dress. It had a satin bow around the waist, scoop neck with embroidered flowers on the bodice and puffed sleeves. Because of my imprisonment and traveling, I was too thin for the dress, but one of the Payne servants was handy with needle and thread and made some temporary alterations for me. She pinned my hair up and I pinched my cheeks to bring some color to them. I thought my looks were passable.

Mrs. Payne sent for a carriage to take us to Brandy. We picked up Mrs. Ashby on the way. Dr. John Ashby closed his medical practice in Culpeper near the beginning of the war to enlist in the Hazelwood Volunteers, and became an army surgeon. My father knew the Ashbys, and would be happy to get news about them.

We arrived at the Bradford farm, Afton, at eight o'clock. Samuel and his wife "Aunt Sally" welcomed us to their fine home. Samuel introduced us to Mrs. Myrta Grey, who boarded with the Bradfords. Myrta, the nineteen-year-old wife of one of Stuart's men, Major Daniel Grey, was five months pregnant. Captain John Esten Cooke and Jeb Stuart were there, too.

I greeted John warmly, "What a surprise. I did not realize that you were stationed nearby."

"I heard that you were in town. I'm pleased to finally catch up with you," he replied. In an aside to me he whispered, "I'm sure I was invited because of our friendship and the fact that Jeb's wife and I are cousins!"

"Whatever the reason, you are my oasis in the storm."

That night, at dinner, Jeb remarked, "You must really miss your husband, Mrs. Grey. He is so important, that I could not spare him from his duties at camp. And here I am, all alone, missing my wife . . ." He gave her a pouty, sad look.

"Enough of that!" exclaimed Aunt Sally. "There will be no hanky panky at my table!"

Just then, a knock at the door interrupted us, and who should enter the room, but Major Dan Grey, Myrta's husband. Jeb had arranged the rendezvous in his typical, devilish manner. Such joyous glances went between the two, that it became contagious. To keep the dinnertime atmosphere light and gay, we discussed war events only lightly.

Major Grey said, "We sure could use more men for the artillery and infantry."

Myrta glanced down at her swelling abdomen and said shyly, "I do not know anything about artillery, but if it is more men for the infant-ry that you want, you'd better send our boys back home to their wives!"

We laughed uproariously, especially Jeb. I thought to myself that surely Myrta knew she was jesting when she made that comment.

After dinner, Sam Sweeney, Jeb's banjo-playing companion, entertained us all with the songs of the day. He led us while his nimble fingers plucked and picked and stroked the strings in a display of artistic brilliance. Jeb led us in singing "Old Joe Hooker, Won't You Come Out of the Wilderness?" It was the song that he had sung while leading the troops after the fall of General Stonewall Jackson at the battle of Chancellorsville. We all thought the song a fitting end for such a glorious spring evening.

My father must have given Major Willard my address, because Major faithfully kept his word. He sent me a letter every week. I did not feel the urge to write back to him yet, but I read his letters with some interest, as my days were much the same, day after day, week after week. He sent me books to read and gave me encouragement on returning home soon. Unfortunately, even he had not the power to make it safe for my return as soon as he wished it.

In early June, Commander Lee decided to relocate most of his remaining army to Culpeper. On occasion, riding close to the river, Millie and I could hear the Yankee and Rebel soldiers talking to each other across the river. They traded goods, such as tobacco for coffee. We kept a wide berth of them, for fear of stray bullets. The soldiers displaced most of the farmers from their lands. They had no surplus crops to sell and barely enough for their families to live on. Somehow, we managed to get enough to eat, as did our army.

On the evening of June 4, Jeb organized a grand ball at the courthouse building. The entire town decked out in their best clothes for a festive evening. Even gentry from surrounding counties came. Jeb's band provided music for waltzes, the Virginia reel, and quadrilles, and I did not lack for dance partners. The festivity continued until midnight.

The next day, Jeb held a second review of his cavalry. The Payne family and I went by carriage to the review site, which was in reality, a cornfield, midway between Brandy Station and the courthouse on the northern side of the O & A Railroad. The Payne sisters and I threw flowers at the troops as they passed by our reviewing spot—our carriage on the high ground surrounding the plain. We cheered until our throats became hoarse. Jeb looked dashing in a short gray jacket and a wide-brimmed whitish hat with a long black plume. He rode astride his favorite horse and was the most colorful character in town that day. After the review, we watched as the soldiers enacted a sham battle that lasted until late afternoon. Jeb invited us to attend an impromptu outdoor ball near his Brandy camp that evening. We returned to the hotel and rested before the seven-mile carriage ride to Brandy.

That night, our dance floor was grass, and bonfires provided the lights. Again, we set aside our daily war worries to relax with music, dancing, and gaiety. Jeb came up to me and pulled me aside. "There is someone I wish you to meet."

Thinking that he meant to set me up with some dashing young lieutenant, I trailed along with him to a nearby campfire.

"Now close your eyes," he said.

I did so, and before I could open them, my brother Charlie had hold of me, hugging me so hard it almost took my breath away.

"Charlie!" I screamed in joy.

We pointed at each other's physique, as we both looked so much thinner than when we last had seen each other.

"I've heard about your ordeal," Charlie said. "Now I want to hear your account of what happened."

I proceeded to tell him everything that happened to me since my arrest.

He caught me up on some of the battles he had fought. By some miracle, he remained unscathed.

"I have found peace with the Lord. Jesus said that 'With God all things are possible.' I believe this—even in relation to the horrible war that I am fighting. Are you a follower of Jesus, Antonia?"

"I have not given my full heart to Him, no. I am seeking the truth, however."

"Faith is believing the unbelievable. I will pray for you, and I hope you will pray for my safekeeping. If it is not to be, however, have no fear, for I will be in a better place."

We kissed and hugged each other before departing, and I made sure that Charlie had my current address. I left that evening, truly happy.

Chapter Thirty-three

In the Middle of It All, June 1863

Robert E. Lee established his camp near the courthouse on June 7. On June 8, Stuart staged another review, but this time for General Lee's eyes only. Later, I learned that nearly nine thousand mounted troopers passed Lee's reviewing stand, first at a walk, then in full gallop as sabers glistened in the sun and twenty-two batteries of horse artillery rode past.

My fleeting happiness turned to worry when on June 9, fighting occurred at Beverly's Ford and Kelly's Ford. Skirmishing at St. James and fighting at Brandy Station made me feel vulnerable. With fire action only six miles to the east, I felt that the sounds of gunfire, cannons, and galloping horses bombarded me. I knew that Charlie was somewhere out there in the midst of battle.

Orderlies brought wounded men to the hotel, as they could not make it to the hospitals in Richmond. We even had a dying Federal boy amongst us. We tenderly stayed by his side during his last hours and wrote his mother his goodbyes. Stuart lost seventy-five men, with three hundred wounded. General McClellan's Federal losses were slightly over 450 killed and wounded. The hotel filled, and we all worked as nurses, as best we could. We tried to make the men comfortable, wrote letters home for them, and even final wills for the dying. And die they did. Since we got only the worst cases, the majority did die. Occasionally, a particularly hearty boy would pull through, but that proved to be the exception. Myrta Grey found out that her major was safe. I heard that Charlie pulled through without injury. On Saturday, June 13, the church bells in town rang for services and the churches overflowed with praying soldiers and families. I went on Saturday to pray for my loved ones and saw General Lee in attendance at the Episcopal Church that I attended on Sunday.

On June 15, Stuart's cavalry left town, heading toward the Blue Ridge and the trail north. I found out later from Myrta Grey that John Esten Cooke was one of the last soldiers remaining. While in the Bradford parlor finishing some reports for his commanding officer and writing some personal correspondence, he advised Myrta to wait out the war in Richmond and she decided to take his advice.

"Perhaps you should come with me Antonia," Myrta pleaded.

"Now that I am so close to home, I cannot backtrack," I replied. "If I go anywhere, it will be closer to home—to Warrenton."

Major Willard wrote me a sad letter to tell me that his brother, Edwin, had died at the battle of Brandy Station. I felt horrified to think that my brother, doing his duty and fighting for his homeland, could have been the cause of the major's anguish. Selfishly, I sent a small prayer of thanks to God—better his brother dead, than mine.

On June 18, I received a letter from Dabney Ball, stationed near Middleburg. He was a chaplain on the staff of General Stuart, and known for his bravery and courage. Our families had socialized prior to the war. He advised me not to come to Middleburg yet. He said it would be "unhealthy." He especially warned me:

> *Don't attempt to go to Fairfax. Do not become impatient or depressed, be a heroine as you are. My Dear Antonia please do me the favor to write, for me, to my wife—embody anything in this you think proper. I can't possibly mail a letter to her from here.*
>
> *I haven't seen Charlie since I left Culpeper. He has not been near our Brigade. He is well, however, and I expect to see him soon. How much I would like to see you. You can't guess. Love to Mrs. Ashby's family—and Mrs. Payne's. Kiss Millie for me.*
>
> *Your devoted friend, Dabney Ball.*

Father, now in Warrenton at the home of Joseph B. Hunton, wrote to me:

At Mr. Joseph B. Hunton
Monday morning, June 28, 1863
My dear Antonia,

> *I left Warrenton yesterday evening very hurriedly. I had not intended leaving before morning but seeing a person from Fairfax who informed me there was certainly no Yanks at Fairfax C.H. you may imagine my impatience to be off. I had hoped you would have come before I left. I wrote you a short note saying I wish you to stay at the home of Mr. William H. Gaines until you hear from me. Should you succeed in getting thru try and drop me a line immediately and if it's safe for you to come home will come after you. Will come and see you anyway. I think you had better stay in Warrenton for this present. Mr. Gaines and family have been exceedingly kind and in fact, I had so many invitations I could not call on all. I spoke to Mr. Gaines about getting me some Confederate Stock. I wish you to give him a check for $1,500 but if I can get up will get more. I should have given him a check myself for $2,000 but as I left on Sunday did not like to do it. I hope to be up soon. Mr. John Bronaugh, formerly of our county, gave you a standing invitation to stay with them. He has no children. Mr. Helm also invited you, but I should prefer your making Mr. Gaines your headquarters to visit the others. I know you will like Mr. and Mrs. Gaines. Mr. Tavenner, the hotelkeeper, saw Charley on*

Wednesday or Thursday between Paris and Winchester since all the fighting is up there. I saw Tom Love last night—he said Charley was with Gen. Stuart on his move on Fairfax and I think he said Bud saw him on Friday. He was well—if we could all get home once more how very pleasant it would be. This is a very uncomfortable morning— heavy mist will wet a person in a little while. I am for trying it. We are 22 miles from home to walk through the rain, and carry our luggage is no easy task, but I am so afraid if we defer it something will prevent our getting home. I hope and pray you may keep well and be comfortable. Try to keep up your spirits. We expect to reach home tomorrow if we have good luck and meet with no Yankees. Goodbye my Dear Child. May every blessing attend you.

Your affectionate father, E.R. Ford

I wondered whom the "we" meant in the letter. It was possible that Clanie accompanied Father, or perhaps one of our servants was with him.

Although hesitant to relocate, I rejoiced that Warrenton was closer to home. I also wanted to get away from the sounds of battle. My father thought highly of Mr. Gaines, a former mayor, retired merchant and wealthy landowner. He now held the title of Justice in Warrenton. It would not be a quiet household to stay in, with four small children running around. Father said that Mr. Gaines' young wife, Mary, was pleasant and engaging. In addition, Susan Foster, aged twenty-six, and her father, Thomas, boarded at that household. Susan sewed for a living and her father was formerly a merchant. I decided to make my way to Warrenton as my father wished, even though I was safe, snug, and comfortable where I was. Since the Gaines family expected me, I saw no need to write them a letter saying I was coming, because I would get there before any letter.

The next morning, after bidding my kind hosts goodbye, I rode on the Orange & Alexandria train to Warrenton.

Chapter Thirty-four

My Arrival in Warrenton, July 1863

I arrived on July 1, with no mishaps, at the Warrenton Branch station, consisting of two wooden platforms. I spied several stores and warehouses nearby, as well as some empty stockyards and a few dwellings. Along the single railroad track dangled the county's only overhead telegraph wire. Looking around, I saw no one to hire to carry my luggage but an unkempt man. He came close to me to peer in my face as if he was half-blind.

"I can assist with your luggage," he said while picking up my bags. "My name is Joe Smith. Too old to fight, I reckon, but not to carry," he said slowly.

Feeling relieved that he was not a ruffian, I nodded.

"You can see the courthouse spiral and St. James steeple over that a-ways, miss," he pointed. "We have three hostelries in town; the Warren Green, owned by Mr. Tavenner, Warrenton House, and Farmers' Hotel. Will you be going to one of them?"

"No, I am going to the home of William H. Gaines."

"Ah, yes indeedy, our former mayor—a fine man he be. Follow me."

Joe felt it his duty to give me the visitor's tour of Warrenton.

"Our population used to be 'bout twelve hundred, including 564 whites and forty-three blacks. We have five doctors, fifteen lawyers, five schools, and a boomin' library. Our businesses consist of fifteen stores, including three bakeries, three tailors, two boot makers, a druggist, a jeweler, and two coach and carriage makers. People also call Warrenton 'Warrenton Springs' or 'Fauquier White Sulphur Springs.' Locally, we call it 'The Springs.' Last winter, most of the folk who could afford it, moved away. The folk left behind are the stubborn independents, plum sure to guard their home and property."

We walked up the stepping-stone path to Main Street. Board sidewalks lined the street. Main Street appeared to be only six compact blocks from Main to Lee, and from Ashby to Sixth. I saw some fine brick and frame buildings along the road and many former businesses, now abandoned.

Opposite us, I saw a deserted clock and watchmaker shop, and a post office. We passed a grocery store with bare shelves and a bakery. The street, shady with trees alongside for tethering horses, was horseless. A few residents were out and about, but I noticed the lack of women and remarked on that.

Joe said, "With all the young men folk gone, the women do not feel safe in the streets. They only go out if forced to do so. Nearly every single girl dresses in mourning rags."

We came to the public square where the courthouse stood. The tower of the building held a clock, still in remarkably good shape. The Warren Green Hotel stood directly across from the courthouse. The lovely structure had a second floor porch along the entire side of the building. This square was the center of town and from here were the main roads to Washington, Winchester, Fredericksburg, and The Springs Resort.

"This area is where the hotels are located. You can see the Farmers Hotel straight ahead."

I commented about the burned lot in front of me.

"That empty lot is where Bronough & Fant's Hotel once stood. Two of our large hotels burned to the ground in 1862."

We turned left onto Culpeper Street.

Joe said, "This home on the corner is named 'Chestnut Grove.' It is the home of attorney Berkeley Ward. He has two daughters. His wife, Harriet, died a few years back."

We walked to the fourth home on the left. The large brick home reminded me of my own, with a porch and two fireplaces, one on either side of the house. Immediately, I noticed the absence of fences around this yard, or any yard, for that matter. I supposed they had been burned for fuel.

Joe said, "Here we are at William H. Gaines' home."

We went to the front door and knocked. A servant opened the door and smiled when she saw Joe.

"Miss Ford has just arrived on the train and would like to see Mr. Gaines."

I thanked Joe, paid him for his assistance, and entered the hallway.

Mr. Gaines came from the parlor to greet me. He was of average height, with black hair and a dark beard and mustache. His intelligent eyes softened when he looked into my eyes.

"You must be Antonia Ford. I have been expecting you."

"I am so pleased to meet you, Mr. Gaines. My father speaks highly of you."

"And I of him. There is no finer man than your father. How was the train ride from Culpeper?"

"Uneventful. I like your town. It is picturesque."

"So far it is. We have had no fighting here yet. You do know that our town is occupied by the Yankees?"

"Yes. Will there be trouble for me here?"

"No. Hopefully, none of the officers will know who you are."

"Do you ever see any of our men?" I asked.

"I have heard that there are small scouting parties between here and Culpeper. Probably Mosby's men."

By this time, Mrs. Gaines and her children had entered the parlor. Mary appeared to be quite a bit younger than her husband was. Barely over five feet tall, her petite figure made her look like a child.

She smiled and said to me, "We are very happy to provide shelter for you, Antonia. These are my children: Lizzie, eleven; Grenville, nine; William, seven; and Lena, five."

They all bowed or gave curtsies. I adored them, because they were so innocent and oblivious of the tragedy of our nation.

"I have a younger brother named Frank who is almost your age, William," I said.

"Can I play with him?" William asked eagerly.

"No, he is back in my town called Fairfax Courthouse. But maybe someday you will meet him."

Susan Foster and her father Thomas also came to greet me. Susan looked about my age and acted a bit prim and weary. At least I would have some female companionship, I thought.

Mary Gaines said, "You will be sharing a room with Susan. One of the servants will take your luggage there. May I serve you some coffee?"

"That would be lovely," I said. I followed Mary into the kitchen.

"You probably know that coffee, tea, sugar, and salt are simply not available anymore. We drink a coffee substitute consisting of water flavored with burnt rye, corn cake, and bacon. Give it a try before you pass judgment."

We went back to the parlor where Susan sat sewing a tan and beige star quilt. Her bag of rags stood beside her, and she meticulously pieced the star blocks together. The children played outside while the three of us drank our mock coffee and ate some fresh berries.

Susan said to me, "Our town is known as a 'hotbed of disloyalty.' Most of us are secessionists, and proud of it. It is difficult for us to be civil to the Yankees occupying our town."

"I've always found that I get along better in life with insincere sweetness," I laughed.

"You actually talk to the Yankees?" Susan queried.

"I not only talk to them and find out military information; I actually correspond with a Union major named Joseph Willard."

Silence filled the room. Finally Mary spoke.

"Was being sent South too horrible for words?"

"To me it was an adventure, although a bad, tiring one. There were some unpleasant aspects and hardships, certainly, but for the most part, I was treated civilly. Do you know if Mrs. Mitchell and her two daughters are still here? They were also making their way home, and I got to know them."

"They have left already," said Mary.

"You look so terribly thin, dear," said Susan.

"My nutrition has not been too good," I admitted. "I recovered somewhat during my stay with the Paynes in Culpeper. I am still not back to my normal weight, and I feel weak."

Mary said, "We have no fresh vegetables from the grocer, as planting was not done in the spring. Our servants maintain a small vegetable garden in the back, and that is for our household only. We will harvest some fruit trees and berries, but few edible livestock are left. We have a few laying chickens, so we can have eggs as a source of protein. Our town is very much devastated. I hope this does not sound too miserable to endure."

"Not at all. I will assist in any food gathering or preparation that you need me to do. What choice do I have? I cannot go home yet."

"Your father told me that you went to a women's college in Gravel Hill, Virginia. Did you know that in 1857 a three-story girl's boarding school existed on Lee Street called Fauquier Female Institute? My husband contracted for the seminary to be built and was on the Board of Visitors several years ago."

"I did hear about the school, but it was too late for me, as I graduated in 1857."

"Perhaps my girls will go there someday. It was always pleasant to be part of the social scene, including dances held at the school. Of course, the school is closed now because of the war."

After our snack, the servant showed me to my room. I collapsed on the bed, grateful for a brief rest.

Chapter Thirty-five

A Surprise Visit, July 1863

Isettled in quickly to my life in Warrenton. I wrote to my parents right away to let them know that I had arrived safely. I asked them to give Major my address.

My mother wrote that Charlie had fought in the battle of Rector's Cross Roads, also known as Hanover, on June 30. Could his luck in staying alive really hold out until the war ended?

I attended the Presbyterian Church when it was open for services and prayed for his safety and for the war to be over soon. The church was available now, but not in 1862 when the sanctuary was a hospital for Federal troops with the basement as a stable.

I had always loved to read, and with all the free time on my hands, I was reading *The Woman in White* by Wilkie Collins. I devoured the 1860 book, reveling in the suspense, and relating to the character Marian, who, as a resourceful, intelligent woman, used her wiles to exist in a male-dominated society. I dozed off while reading, dreaming of my own true love. I roused myself to rejoin the rest of the family downstairs for our evening meal, then played cards with the group and then to bed. My existence, although mundane, proved peaceful.

On July 15, at three o'clock, I sat on the front porch of our house with Susan, sewing. We heard an equestrian coming, and looked up to see an officer dressed in blue riding towards us. He dismounted, tied his horse to a tree, and strode up the walkway. Major Willard looked dashing!

Susan glanced at me, noticed my startled expression, and soothed me by saying, "Do not worry. I am sure he will not harm us."

She totally misunderstood my expression to be one of fear.

"Good afternoon, ladies," he said. He walked up the steps.

"Major Willard, I would like to introduce you to Miss Susan Foster. Susan, this is Major Willard, an acquaintance of mine."

"Pleased to meet you," he said to Susan.

Susan looked at each of us, and saw something that made her gather up her sewing and tactfully retreat inside the house.

"Perhaps you would like a beverage, Major," I said.

"Riding these dusty roads does make a man thirsty. Water would be fine."

I went inside to fetch some water and biscuits, and found Susan whispering to Mrs. Gaines in the kitchen.

"Is my friend welcome to visit with me here?" I asked Mrs. Gaines.

"He is, but I would be hard pressed to house Federals here."

"There is no chance of that," I said quickly. "He is on General

Heintzelman's staff and is usually in or around Washington City."

I left them and returned to the major. He took the glass of water from me, our fingers briefly touching.

"You look well," he lied.

"You flatter me. I have a tattered old dress on, and have not quite regained my strength yet."

"You are a fine sight for this man's eyes. I see a glow in your cheeks that presumes nutrition of an adequate amount."

"We do what we can to forage for food. Most of the townsfolk are gone, and those left must appeal to the 'tender mercies' of their friends."

"How long do you think you will be housed here?"

"Perhaps that answer should come from you, Major. My parents and friends warn me not to return to Fairfax Courthouse at this time. Do you know otherwise?"

"I know that Federals still occupy your town and are vigilant in sending suspected Southern collaborators to prison."

"You see then, I have no choice but to remain here. Nevertheless, enough about me. Are you and your relatives staying out of harm's way?"

"My duties are mostly administrative now. I had my turn in the field. The overseer is running the hotel on a day-to-day basis. Henry and his wife, Sarah, and their seven-year-old son, little Henry, are faring well in New York. My wife is no better or worse than usual."

"When will you be divorced?"

"As you know, divorce is not an easy matter, because Congress only authorized them in Washington in 1860. Vermont has some of the most lenient grounds for divorce, but it seems that a local decree would be easiest. I need to establish grounds for divorce."

"What are some grounds for an absolute divorce?"

"Adultery, bigamy, lunacy, or impotence."

"I suppose then, that you would be divorcing on the grounds of lunacy."

"Yes, that is the only logical course to take. I am starting the process and have hired a lawyer to assist me."

"I feel that you are in a tragic situation. Does Caroline know what you are doing?"

"I will wait on that. No time is a good time to tell her. I doubt that being divorced from me will make any difference to her, so long as she is provided for in the manner to which she is accustomed."

"Enough of these serious topics," I said. "Let's walk. I do not often stroll around town, as it is not recommended for any woman to take the chance of being accosted by a scoundrel."

"Are you sure I'm not a scoundrel?" Major teased.

"I know you are a scoundrel, but I like you anyway."

By this time, we had reached the public square and approached the courthouse. We turned left on Main Street and wondered at the lack of activity going on around us. Most of the shopkeepers looked middle-aged or older. There might be a young son assisting his father in stocking or waiting on customers. The fragrant scent of baked goods accosted my senses as we came to the only open bakery in town. The major escorted me through the open door and approached the baker. Only two sweet rolls remained in his bare display case.

"I'll take the sweet rolls, please," he said, as he withdrew bills from his pocket.

The baker handed me one, and my mouth watered even before the delicacy could reach it. A sweet roll made with real sugar was a treat, but it cost Major plenty.

"Where did you get the ingredients to make this wonderful pastry?" he asked.

"Here and there," the baker said evasively. Obviously, the supplies had either been smuggled into town, or stolen from the Federals.

We left the bakery, passed Mr. Bragg's livery stable, and continued walking until we reached a dry goods store. Major and I entered the shop.

"You wait right here," he told me. "I want to get you a gift."

After several minutes passed, he came to me with his hand behind his back.

"Close your eyes," he ordered me.

I did so, holding out my hands, barely controlling my excitement. Such a small thing to receive a gift, but I had limited experience in that realm. I opened my eyes to find some writing paper and a pen.

"This is so you will have no excuse to not write me, my dear," he said with a smile.

"Thank you! I will cherish the pen. You are good to me, Joseph."

Although I customarily called him "Major," I slipped in a Joseph every now and then just to keep him off guard.

"General Meade's headquarters are going to be here in Warrenton. I'm sure you know that he is now the Commander of the Army of the Potomac," said Major.

"Yes, and I am relieved to hear that he has commandeered some other house than where I am staying."

"The tide of the war has turned against the South after the terrible battle at Gettysburg and the surrender of Vicksburg earlier this month. I am hopeful that the war is almost over," Major said.

"Oh, for life to get back to normal," I sighed. "I just want to do what Southern girls do at my age without worries."

"Tell me, what are Southern girls supposed to do?"

"We are supposed to be well-versed in etiquette and have a stylish wardrobe. The mastering of a musical instrument is admirable. Medical remedies are helpful to know and some culinary skills are a plus. In addition, home management skills are essential for undertaking the role of 'lady of the house.'"

"Do you desire to be 'lady of the house' soon?" he queried with a smile.

"I am twenty-five and look forward to a happy future with a husband and children," I said simply.

Chapter Thirty-six

A Quilting Bee, July 23, 1863

The other women in town were friendly, and I grew especially fond of the Lucas sisters, Annie, Fanny and Peggy. Since it was my birthday, July 23, we decided to celebrate by having a quilting bee together and sharing some refreshments. I walked through town to the Lucas home with a small embroidery project, pincushion, needle, and thread in a small satchel. The Weaver sisters, Janet and Elizabeth, were already in the parlor when I arrived.

"Happy Birthday, Antonia!" Janet exclaimed when she saw me.

"It is sure to be happy in the company of all of you," I said while giving a small curtsey.

Roberta "Bert" Pollock, and Mary Ann and Grace Ward arrived at that moment and the nine of us noisily chattered, moving about with a flurry of skirts rustling, as we organized our quilt.

Mrs. Lucas set up a large frame for us. We carefully rolled the quilt top, middle layer and backing on the frame, pinning where necessary. All nine of us could not fit around the frame at once, so we took shifts, doing embroidery or knitting while we waited our turn. We quilted lines one-eighth of an inch outside of all the stitching lines. The quilt looked stunning, with homespun and dyed cottons in shades of brown, Turkey red, beige, dotted yellow, and an occasional sky blue. The pattern called for a central medallion, with a row of nine-patch squares around it and a border of thin stripes. We had not decided what the purpose of this particular quilt might be. Perhaps we would give it to the next girl to be married as a wedding present. Our goal was to make two quilts in the next month.

Mary Ann and Grace's mother had passed away two years earlier, and their father, attorney Berkeley Ward, was doing his best to raise them. As intelligent and attractive as they were, I had no doubts that they would find husbands, that is, if there were any young men left after the war.

Janet and Elizabeth Weaver and six other family members lived at the corner of Diagonal and Winchester Streets, at Carter Hall. Their raven hair and dark eyes gave them a gypsy appearance. I thought that perhaps they were not getting enough to eat, as their clothes fit them too loosely and they looked very thin.

Janet said, "I am nervous all the time living in the middle of a war. I cannot sleep well at night for all the noises coming through my bedroom window, as it faces the street."

"I'm not as light a sleeper as you, Janet, but I know what you mean," said Elizabeth. "If I hear a noisy horse carrying a loud, boisterous rider, with sounds of metal clanking, I know that a Union soldier is passing through.

Since our town is Union occupied, stealth and cautiousness on the part of our own Southern men is necessary. They silently guide their horses through town. I sleep better when I hear the quiet ones."

I could attest to Janet's observation, as my own window was not too far from Main Street. "Compared to Fairfax Courthouse, I find this town quiet."

"That is because, for the most part, Union pickets and scouts keep to the main roads outside of town," said Janet.

Annie Lucas' face glowed, and she stood up and walked around as she spoke about her Confederate fiancé. "Last Christmas, my fiancé planned to visit me at a party here. I overheard that there was a trap on the roads leading into town, and I managed to get word to him in time. In the last six months, he has come here clandestinely now and then to visit me when his unit is nearby."

"What we do for the men we love," I said to her.

"Do you love someone, Antonia?" Annie asked me.

"My heart says yes, but my mind says no. You see, he is a Federal. His name is Major Joseph Willard. We have been corresponding and he visited me here recently."

Bert, a first cousin of General Lee, lived at Leeton Forest, just outside of Warrenton on the Springs Road. She said, "We do not condemn you for loving the enemy." She looked at me, smiled, then said, "Perhaps we will all get to meet him some day."

Fanny Lucas changed the subject. "Our mother, Peggy, received a fine in 1853 for allowing our slaves to trade as free persons in the marketplace."

"She was a woman ahead of her time," I said.

"Yes, certainly," said Annie Lucas. "We treat our servants well, and did so when they were slaves. It is surprising to me that one of our male servants just left our house to settle farther north."

I said, "Even though he was freed by the Emancipation Proclamation, lingering remembrances of servitude must run through his head. He probably wants to make a fresh start and be his own boss wherever he settles. I can relate to feelings of imprisonment against my will because of my two months of incarceration in Washington City. As kind as one of my captors, Mr. Wood, treated me at prison, I hope to never see his face again."

"How was Mr. Wood especially kind to you, Antonia?" asked Annie.

"He gave me special privileges because of his friendly ties to my family prior to the war, and also because I had someone high up watching out for me."

"You mean God?" Fanny innocently asked.

I laughed, and soon everyone joined me. "I really meant Major Willard, but, yes, God is watching out for me too."

Bert Pollock spoke. "Speaking of watching out, last winter while in the dry goods store I overheard a Negro telling Union soldiers where they could find Mosby and his rangers hiding near Marshall."

"Colonel Mosby is a friend of mine!" I exclaimed. "What did you do?"

"My servant and I mounted our horses and found one of Mosby's pickets stationed outside of town. The picket warned Colonel Mosby in time and they all escaped."

Not surprisingly, these women did what they could to help the South. Both the Weaver and Lucas families had already suffered losses of family members during this cruel conflict.

Annie Weaver opined, "Oh, for the grand balls we used to attend at the Warren Green. There is no one left in town to even hold a ball, much less go to one."

I remarked, "I heard the provost marshal has his headquarters there now."

Mrs. Lucas served us a small cake made with molasses. Her servant concocted a delicious blackberry drink that quenched our thirst. After our little break, we were ready to continue quilting. My hand accidentally knocked a pair of scissors to the floor. I looked down to see one point sticking in the wooden floor, in a crack.

Mrs. Lucas said, "You are sure to receive a visitor, Antonia. The visitor will come in the direction of the point that is not stuck in the floor."

"That is north," said Annie. "Are you expecting someone from the north?" she said innocently with a smile on her face.

"Be careful when you pick up the scissors, Antonia," warned Fanny. "If you see the underside of the unfinished quilt, you will never marry!"

"Are there any more superstitions you think I should know?" I asked.

"If a girl shakes a new quilt out the front door, the first man who enters will be her husband," said Fanny.

"If you break a thread, it will bring bad fortune," chimed in Peggy.

"Goodness, I thought I was superstitious, but my knowledge is nothing compared to yours," I said. "Have you heard the one about shaking the cat?"

"Tell us," said Fanny.

"You put a cat on the finished quilt, and gather round to shake the quilt. The girl closest to the cat when it jumps out will be the next one to marry."

We all laughed at the picture that evoked.

"Just be sure you don't put the last stitch in a quilt, or you'll be an old maid," said Bert. "And never, ever, begin a quilt on a Friday."

We resumed our quilting for several more hours, relating our tribulations to each other. Although practically strangers, we were all more alike than different. We believed in God, our country, and the rights of fellow human beings. We nursed the wounded, grieved with those who lost loved ones, tenderly cared for new brothers and sisters in the family, and looked to the future with hope. Our quilting bee ended, a great success, with the quilt finished except for the binding. We formed bonds that day between us that would last our entire lives.

Chapter Thirty-seven

Life in Warrenton, August 1863

I received a few letters from home and from the major during my stay in Warrenton. Mother wrote that the provost marshal arrested Uncle Brower and sent him to Old Capitol Prison.

My family knew the crisis that we were in, with such limited food and fuel available. The food supply, although better in Fairfax, was not plentiful. My father recommended that I stay here through August, as too much of a Federal presence remained in Fairfax Courthouse. I still had not regained my former strength and vitality. Occasionally, Union soldiers came into town to buy supplies and to visit. The "Secession Ladies" here spit on the men if they passed close by. The population acted far more anti-Yankee than Fairfax Courthouse residents did.

Mr. and Mrs. Gaines, and the Fosters and I spent much of the day inside in the parlor, trying to keep cool. I shared a letter with them that my friend, John Mosby, wrote to me. He gave me an account of a daring raid that he successfully executed on August 4, 1863:

> *At Fairfax Court House a few nights ago I captured 29 loaded sutlers' wagons, about 100 prisoners and 140 horses. I had brought all off safely near Aldie, where I fell in with a large force of the enemy's cavalry, who recaptured them. The enemy had several hundred. I had only 27 men. We killed and captured several. My loss: one wounded and captured.*

As it was mealtime, we sat down at the dining room table. Supper consisted of hominy and carrots today, washed down by some weak tea. Yesterday's main meal was fried mush. The only vegetables available were those that came back annually, as planting was not done for the season. Last week, Mr. Gaines and Mr. Foster went to Baltimore to buy clothes for the family and servants, but could find no groceries to purchase.

Mrs. Gaines said, "Thank God that you traveled to Harper's Ferry yesterday for groceries, even though you only found some brown sugar, tea, and salt pork. What we really need though is assistance from Lincoln's Government to prevent the whole town from starving!"

Mr. Gaines added, "We heard from a shop keeper in Harper's Ferry that the prices in Richmond are high: seventy-five dollars for a cord of wood, eight dollars for a small turkey, two hundred dollars for a horse, three dollars a yard for cotton and calico, thirty dollars for a pair of lady's shoes, and fifty dollars for four barrels of flour."

"What I would do for a new pair of shoes!" I said. I looked down at my dusty, worn shoes, with holes in the soles.

"What I would do for flour," said Mrs. Gaines. "Speaking of food, you missed our delicacy of asparagus in the spring, Antonia."

"I had some in Culpeper, and appreciated it as a real treat," I said.

Our conversations generally went this way: either reminiscing about past days, food, or talk of the war and politics.

I said, "General Meade sure is protective of his railroad. What do you think of his proclamation that if the railroad were damaged by civilians in any way, they will be impressed as laborers to repair all damages?"

Mr. Gaines replied, "He is bullying us, but feels he has to. Did you know that General Birney has his headquarters at Warrenton White Springs now? I hope he enjoys the water, as the accommodations are non-existent since the main hotel burned down last year."

That provoked laughter from all of us.

Mr. Foster joined the conversation by remarking on the work that Major General Irvin McDowell's engineer corps was doing.

"They are re-laying The Springs Bridge. I remember when it consisted of a riverside building, previously a cheese factory, and then a brewery. I had my share of whiskey there!"

Susan told me what happened about nine months ago when the Irish Brigade passed through town: "As the Irish Brigade marched down Main Street, the women and children standing in doorways and windows hissed and yelled at the men as they passed. I was at the Public Square and witnessed women throwing any expendable object available towards the men. The men's commanders had instructed them not to fight back unless ordered by their general to do so. They were mad, I can tell you that!"

Mrs. Gaines added, "They retaliated by stealing meal from our local mill. Then the soldiers killed a neighbor's hogs, and stole the remaining horses and cattle that were not hidden in the woods."

One of the Gaines' servants came in hurriedly from outside, with a wild look in her eyes.

"Two Union officers are coming this way!"

We jumped to action. Any valuable objects, such as silver, money, and jewelry we either hid in the house, or secreted under our hoopskirts. The servants grabbed the chickens and available food, and ran out the back door with them to hide near the end of our lot, with an escape to the street, if it proved necessary.

Mr. Gaines answered the knock on the door and spoke a few minutes to the officers before rejoining us.

"That was Major Hitchcock, an acquaintance during friendlier times. He is a decent man and is regretful for the incident that occurred last week to a neighboring family. It seems that some of the troops helped themselves to the family's food supplies, and were about to become indecent with the lone women in the house when they were caught red-handed by him. He came personally to apologize to that family. He is safeguarding our house the same way that he did theirs. We will take a United States flag and put it at an angle between the house and a wing. As long as it remains there, we will not be molested."

The rest of August passed in a swelter. The food situation, critical now, had created a ghost town, and it was time for me to go home.

Chapter Thirty-eight

Home, September 1863

My journey home occurred on Saturday, September 12. Major Willard escorted me by rail, from Warrenton Junction to the rebuilt depot at Fairfax Station. It was pleasant to be able to sit by him, even for that brief journey. From there, we hired a carriage to bring me to my residence. We spoke of everything except his wife, agreeing between us, the less said about her, the better. I still had not told my parents of his marital status.

We came to Payne Street and my beloved abode. It had been six months since I had seen it. I stifled a sob, but Major heard me.

"My dearest, you are overcome!" he said as he put a comforting arm around my shoulder.

"I am emotional, but can you blame me?" I said.

My parents, who must have been looking eagerly through the parlor windows, rushed out to the street to meet us.

As I alighted from the carriage, Mother rushed forward and hugged me tightly to her bosom. "My child, how I have missed you. You are all skin and bones!"

Father also clung to me and I heard some sobs coming from him. "Major Willard, I can not thank you enough for bringing my child home, safely," said Father.

By this time, Clanie, Pattie, and Frank had joined the happy group.

"Frank! How you have grown up!" I exclaimed. He was now a rambunctious boy of five. I hugged and kissed him.

"Is there any word of Charlie?" I asked.

"The last we heard he is nearby, and safe," said Father.

We entered our home and settled in the parlor. The house looked a bit more shopworn than when I had left. Mother said the wear and tear from the military using our home as headquarters caused the mess. Otherwise, it was such a welcome sight.

"I need to depart now, Antonia," said Major Willard.

"Not before we serve you some tea and refreshments," said Mathilde, who had overheard the major and came towards us in the parlor.

I rushed over to her and gave her a warm hug.

After our tea and tiny biscuits, the major left.

I proceeded to tell my family everything that had happened to me that they had not already heard from my letters. Amazingly, most of my letters had arrived safely. I supposed that was because they were hand-carried, the mail service being so irregular.

I took a deep breath and blurted out, "Major Willard is a married man."

Mother sighed and covered her face with her hands. Father looked at me sternly.

"What is going on with you two? Should I be alarmed?" he asked.

"Yes, as alarmed as I am. I have fallen in love with him." I told them the story of Major Willard's sad marriage and the steps he was taking to extricate himself.

"I am disappointed and somewhat ashamed of you," said Father.

This harsh statement provoked a rush of tears and I stuttered, "I cannot bear your anger at me."

"I cannot forbid you to see him," Father said. "You have reached your majority and have a mind of your own. I must point out, however, the obstacles that you face. Divorces are not easy to obtain, despite the divorce reform that occurred in Washington in 1860, and he is a Union officer and you hold your allegiance toward the South."

"You are blighting my life."

Father's tone became softer as he relented by saying, "No child of mine shall ever truthfully bring that charge against me. I reluctantly withdraw my opposition."

"You won't be sorry. He is a good man. If he cannot obtain a divorce, there is no hope for me," I said sadly. "The other obstacles are surmountable. He intends on resigning his commission, and I will sign the oath."

Mother chimed in, "Whether we sign the oath now, or later, is of no consequence, I'm afraid. The South is losing the war."

I went upstairs to my old room and started unpacking my few, threadbare belongings. I could hear my parents talking in low voices, no doubt, about me. Mathilde gathered up an armful of my clothes to wash as Pattie, thirteen, watched. I had lost so much weight that I could now fit into some of her clothes. She maturely and generously shared all that she had with me. I loved her so much!

After taking a sponge bath, she and I decided to walk. I missed regular exercise, as it was not common to walk about town in Warrenton.

"Not much has changed, Sister," she said as we walked to Fairfax Street and turned right. The only scene of activity seemed to be at the courthouse and jail area, with Union soldiers out and about. We turned around and walked the other way, past Father's store, which had a "closed" sign on it.

"Who minds the shop?" I asked.

"When Father and Clanie are not there, we close it. You understand that we have a dearth of young men around to help."

"I can tell that Fairfax Courthouse is not in desperate straits the way Warrenton is for food and fuel."

"That's only because the Federals make sure that there is enough for them, and thus allow our shops to remain well-stocked with food shipped from Baltimore and cities farther north. We will miss fresh vegetables as fall and winter approach."

"Are there many villagers locked up in Old Capitol?" I asked.

"Villagers, no, but last week I read in *The Alexandria Gazette* that Annie Jones was sent there on the allegation that she had papers containing the location and force of the Federal army! Since her commitment, she eats nothing. She wears a cross around her neck."

"Maybe my evangelism touched her heart," I said.

After our stroll, we returned home. Mathilde took it upon herself as her personal mission to "fatten me up." At every opportunity, she offered me enticing tidbits. My appetite had changed, though, and I found I could not eat as much as I used to, even though desiring it.

I slept well that first night home, in my own bed, with my loving family close by. I thanked God and his mercy for these small comforts.

The next day, Sunday, we all went to church services in the courthouse. We sat amidst Union soldiers and other townspeople. I looked around and saw an abundance of women, children and elderly folks; and then the soldiers, dressed all in blue. I saw our neighbors, the Loves, Grigsbys, Chichesters, and Moores. The Gunnells had fled to "safer pastures." I could not help but notice the Union flag displayed near the makeshift pulpit. Many of the buildings and houses had them flying outside the doors. We had no flag flying from our house.

The next afternoon, while quilting in the parlor, I glanced through the window to see two ambulances outside our home. Two officers walked to our door and knocked. Father answered the door and I heard voices, becoming louder and angrier as the seconds went by. Finally, Father let the men enter our home and brought them to the parlor.

"I, Captain Dennis, from the Centreville district, along with Colonel Lowell, military commander here at Fairfax Courthouse, arrest you, Miss Ford, on the charge of disloyalty. Pack your things and get ready to go immediately."

"What has she done?" asked Father. "She only arrived home from being sent South last week. It proved necessary that she come home, as she was subjected to starvation rations in Warrenton."

"I do not see a Federal flag flying from your house, sir. Have you taken the Oath of Allegiance?"

"I have not," answered Father angrily.

"You, too, will come with us, sir," said Colonel Lowell.

"Where are you taking us?" asked Father.

Colonel Lowell said, "First you will be sent to Colonel H.H. Wells, the Department of the Potomac's provost general, in Alexandria. His job is to take charge of all prisoners. From there, I do not know your disposition, but it will probably be Old Capitol."

Clanie observed this entire incident. "Do you have an arrest warrant?" he asked angrily.

"One is not necessary. Would you like to come along?" Captain Dennis sarcastically replied.

"Stay out of this, Clanie," Father said.

We each packed a small bag and went to the second ambulance. Inside the first ambulance sat Thomas N. Williams, Amos Fox, and William F. Moore. Father and I joined William R. Chapman in our conveyance. The men were charged with being sympathizers to the Confederacy.

We traveled quickly to Alexandria, passing guards and pickets who waved us through without requiring us to stop. When we had reached the provost general's headquarters, we alighted and armed soldiers escorted us to his office.

Captain Dennis spoke, "Colonel Wells, I present these disloyal citizens for such disposition as you may deem proper in the case."

"I will review the matter," said Colonel Wells. "For now, take them to the waiting area."

We went outside to use the privies, and then guards escorted us to our rooms in the house next door. When I saw that the guard was going to separate me from my father, I hugged Father with all my might. He assured me that this matter would be cleared up speedily.

A servant brought me food and water, and I spent the night on the floor with no further communication from anyone.

The next morning, we reconvened in Colonel Wells' room.

"I am sending all of you to Lieutenant Colonel J.H. Taylor, Chief of Staff in Washington, for his disposition."

Father said angrily, "Do you not have the guts to let us go of your own accord? We innocent citizens, patiently awaiting the end of the war, are causing no trouble to anyone and want to get back to our families. If not for my sake, have pity on my daughter, Antonia. She has been through so much already, and is as innocent and pure as the driven snow. Look at how frail she appears."

A murmur of assent issued from the other men in the room.

"I take my orders from the Chief of Staff, and it is his wish that you be brought to him. All of you," he replied curtly.

Chapter Thirty-nine

Prison Again, September 15-18, 1863

Nothing had changed much at the Carroll. Colonel Taylor met with me when I arrived.

"Will you take the oath?" he asked me.

"No, I cannot in good conscience do so," I said stubbornly.

"Then you will remain here a sufficient length of time to reflect upon your evil ways."

I returned to my cell in Carroll for the night.

The next morning, I eagerly asked to go to the exercise yard to see if my father and other acquaintances were there. I received permission to do so and followed the well-known path to the yard.

Immediately I spied my father. I went up to him as unobtrusively as possible.

"Antonia, you must take the oath, even if you do not believe in it. My compatriots and I are going to do the same."

I had a guilty conscience even thinking of my intended lie, but I had to be pragmatic. A potential new and wonderful life with Major Willard was available to me, and why should I sacrifice it all for the Confederate cause?

I agreed to the plan, and then left him, head up and back straight as I walked. I looked for Annie Jones, but did not see her. Perhaps she had been released, I thought.

After my brief visit to the exercise yard, a guard summoned me from my room to the visitors' room.

Major Willard came forward and briefly embraced me, ignoring the flabbergasted expression of the guard.

"I am prevailing on Major General Samuel Heintzelman to release you. He tells me that he can accomplish that if you take the oath. Will you do so, my dear?"

I had already made up my mind to acquiesce, but saw this as an excellent opportunity to gain a concession from my beloved as well.

"I will do so if you promise on your honor to resign your commission."

A brief leaden moment of silence lay in the air.

"I have been thinking of doing so. I will start the process immediately. I have a document to show you."

He handed me the paper:

Headquarters, Dept. of Washington
September 16, 1863

    Major Willard, ADC, will administer in accordance with

instructions from the Secretary of War the Oath of Allegiance to Miss Antonia Ford who will afterwards at proper time be transferred to her home at Fairfax Courthouse, receiving a written authority to remain at that place with her family.

By Command of Major General Heintzelman
(Signed: J. H. Taylor, Chief of Staff, AAG)

The major sat with me at a table and gave me paper and a pen. He dictated the standard oath for me to write:

On being released from my arrest, I, Antonia Ford of Fairfax Co. Va., do solemnly affirm that I will support, protect and defend the Constitution and Government of the United States against all enemies whether domestic or foreign; that I will bear true faith, allegiance and loyalty to the same, any ordinance, resolution or law of any State convention or legislative to the contrary notwithstanding, that I will not give aid, comfort or information to its enemies, and further, that I do this with a full determination pledge and purpose without any mental reservation or evasion whatsoever. So help me God.

Antonia Ford
Sworn and subscribed to before me this 16th day of September 1863,
J.C. Willard
Headquarters Department of Washington

Major signed his name as witness at the bottom of the document. He wished me well, handed me today's *Gazette,* kissed me lightly on the cheek, and departed, document in hand.

Back in my cell, I stared at nothing for a while, and then started reading today's paper to keep my mind from wandering. I saw immediately on page one a brief article about the arrest of my father and the others. No mention was made of me, until I turned the page:

Miss Ford, of Fairfax, who was some time ago arrested by the Federal authorities, taken to Washington and thence sent south, last week returned to her home, when she was again arrested by the U. S. military commander, at Fairfax C. H. and sent to this place Monday night, and yesterday she was sent on to Washington.

So much for the convention of keeping ladies' names out of the paper! I read on page three:

> *The subject of feeding disloyal citizens within the lines of the army is engaging the attention of the President and Cabinet. In the region now occupied by the Army of the Potomac, between the Potomac and Rappahannock rivers there are at least 2,500 to 3,000 persons who are destitute of the necessaries of life, and who are now living, as it were, upon donations from the officers and soldiers.*
>
> *Heretofore, sales of Commissary stores, coffee, sugar, tea, &c., have been made to those would take the Oath of Allegiance, and pay the Government prices for the articles. Many of these people, however, refuse to take the Oath of Allegiance, particularly the citizens of the village of Warrenton, who are bitter Secessionists in feeling.*
>
> *These people are mostly females and aged persons, and their very helplessness excites sympathy among the officers and soldiers. Some settled policy will be decided on in relation to these citizens, and it is not improbable they will be sent through the lines to their friends in Dixie.*

I could attest to the truth in that article.

Two uneventful days went by. On September 18, Mr. Wood issued a pass to me to allow me greater freedom in roaming the prison:

September 18, 1863

> *Antonia Ford may visit the room of Mrs. Smithson—the kitchen, either privy, and yard, at all times, during the day.*

William P. Wood

The pass proved unnecessary, as General Heintzelman kept his word— Major Willard came to fetch me that very same day. He carried a letter from the general:

September 18, 1863

> *The bearer Antonia Ford having taken the Oath of Allegiance to the United States is hereby permitted by direct authority from the Secretary of War to return to her home Fairfax Courthouse—there to remain subject to orders from these Headquarters. Excepting under instructions from Headquarters, Washington she will in no case be molested or interfered with by any military authority—The Provost Marshal of "Rug's Division" will see that this order is carried out.*

By concurrence of
Major General Heintzelman
J. H. Taylor
Chief of Staff, AAG

By this point, I felt so beholden to Major Willard, that if he had said, "Let's commit bigamy," I probably would have agreed to it. He carried my small suitcase to the waiting carriage and we traveled home, once again.

Chapter Forty

Fall 1863

My father and neighbors were also released from Old Capitol, after taking the oath. A Union flag now sailed from one of our front windows. I do not know how he did it, but Major obtained an official pass on September 19 for me to travel on the Orange and Alexandria Railroad between Fairfax and Washington, "on family business."

On October 19, at eight o'clock in the evening, I heard a knock on our door. Father called through the door, "Who is it?"

"It is John Mosby. Quickly let me in."

Father opened the door, and he and John came into the parlor.

"You are in great peril, John, by coming here," said Father. "In addition, we are vulnerable to punishment, as a family, because we have taken the Oath of Allegiance."

"I will make it quick then. Do you have any medical supplies and ammunition I can take with me? It is very much needed."

Mother went to get the medical supplies, but we had no ammunition to spare.

Father asked, "What happened?"

"On Thursday, the 15th, we came here to the outskirts of Fairfax Courthouse, where I have set up surveillance of the enemy's rear guard. I have captured over one hundred horses and mules, several wagons loaded with valuable stores, and between seventy-five and one hundred prisoners, arms, equipments, etc. Among the prisoners—three captains and one lieutenant."

"I heard about a skirmish yesterday near Annandale. Were you part of that?" I asked.

"Yes, I had more than my usual number of cavalry and I routed the Yankees, capturing the commanding captain and seven men and horses."

"Have you any losses?" asked Father.

"Thus far, no. It has been my object to detain the troops that are occupying Fairfax by waylaying their communications and preventing them from operating. I contemplate attacking a cavalry camp at Falls Church tomorrow night. Good night, all."

"Be careful, John," I said, as he left the house.

On All Saints Day, October 31, 1863, I reminisced on how simple life was only three long years ago at the Love's party. Our close friend, James Monroe Love, lost an arm in battle in Fauquier County on October 11, 1863. I wondered whether Charlie was near his boyhood friend when that happened. Our army had recently sent James home to a grateful mother, and I set my mind to visit him, Rose, and his family soon. Since Robert Love's death over one year ago, Mrs. Love behaved differently, prone to depression and anxiety.

In the parlor, my mother read, while I wrote a letter to my beloved Major, regretting the bad roads separating us. I started my letter in the early evening, but decided to finish it using candlelight in the parlor, thus providing a suitable atmosphere for my innermost thoughts. I took a little break to peer out the window and I saw millions of stars in the cold, wintry sky. I stood, transfixed, then walked back to the writing table, sat down, and resumed writing.

"To whom are you writing, Antonia?"

"I am writing to my beloved, who thinks 'my writing is a feast.' Is it too forward for me to sign my letter to Major as 'yours faithfully, Antonia'?"

"It is ironic, is it not, that you may sign, 'yours faithfully', yet he cannot, due to his marital status."

"Oh, Mother. He is as good as divorced right now. He claims that there have been no marital relations between them for years."

"Do not put your cart before the horse, missy," she admonished.

"He's due for a visit soon. My heart beats too fast, just thinking of it. Did you experience similar emotions about Father?"

Mother smiled, put down her book and faced me saying, "People marry for various reasons—convenience, protection, social status, and monetary gain. I married for love, as I know you will. I only wish for you that your path was not so full of obstacles."

"Will you read some tea leaves with me tonight, Mother?"

"You know I do not believe in consorting with the Devil by doing that nonsense."

Pattie and Clanie came in, and we amused ourselves with some parlor games.

Major did not visit me as soon as he had anticipated. Not until three o'clock in the afternoon on Wednesday, November 11, did he knock on our door. The days and nights were getting chilly and we had a fire burning brightly in the parlor fireplace. I greeted Major at the door, Mathilde took his cloak, and we retired to the couch in front of the fire.

"What is the occasion of your visit, Major? You usually come on Saturdays."

"I planned on not telling you, but today is my birthday. I am forty-three years old. I am just an old soldier for a young lady," he said mournfully.

"You're as young as you feel, darling," I said. "This calls for a celebration, indeed. Pray let me go for a moment to ask Mathilde to fix us something special to eat."

I went into the kitchen and told Mathilde the news. "What am I to cook with? We have no flour."

"Be creative, Mathilde. I am counting on you," I said as I left the kitchen.

I brought some tea into the parlor. The tea floated loose in the wide-brimmed white cups with saucers underneath. I had a game in mind. Major looked a bit dejected.

"I know I did not write you on Monday, although I thought of you often and missed you. Is that why you are so dejected?"

"I have things on my mind, namely my impending resignation and divorce."

"Do you know that you have spoilt me? I look for the military orderly as regularly as the 'evening shades descended.' If you could see my disappointed face and impatient gesture when only a short note comes, you would always write an epistle."

"You know that I am a person of small words."

"Thank you for the papers that you sent. Father enjoys them also, but please do not think you have to buy us expensive gifts to win our love."

"Have I won your love?"

"You know you have. Will you read some tea leaves with me? Perhaps we can elevate your spirits and produce an enlivening effect on your melancholy."

"I reluctantly will do so to please you. I fear that it is not a Christian thing to do."

"Have you drunk all your tea? Make sure you leave a little bit of water with the loose tea leaves in the bottom of your cup. Now, take the cup in your left hand and swirl it around clockwise three times. I will do the same." I paused a moment. "Now, cover the top of your cup with your right hand. Swirl your leaves up and around the sides and rim of the cup."

"Now can we peek?"

"Yes. Let us interpret each other's, to keep it impartial. I see a bird in the bottom of your cup. The bird on the bottom of the cup is a significant sign for either good luck or good news, definitely a change coming."

Major said, "I see a ring symbol on the rim of your cup."

"See how amazing this can be! A ring on the rim indicates an upcoming marriage. The fact that it is on the rim says that it is a big, life-changing event! How lucky I am. Oh, silly me. Perhaps the prophecy is not even for me," I said coyly. "Do we know any young couples contemplating marriage?"

Major took my cup and set it down, along with his. He put his hands on either side of my face and gave me a tender kiss. He abruptly stopped when we heard footsteps approaching. Mathilde arrived with a tray in her hands. Mother and my brothers and sisters trailed in after her.

She set it down in front of us and said, "I hope this will taste good, Miss Antonia. It is all we had."

"I am sure it is delicious. What do you call it?"

"Molasses crabapple sticky cake. It is an original recipe. Happy Birthday, Major Willard."

We all wished him a Happy Birthday, and then after declaring the cake delicious and wishing us all good evening, he departed.

Chapter Forty-one

A Romance Like None Other, November 1863

We received a letter from Charlie stating that he was well, and had been promoted on November 10. I started writing letters to Major every day, and looked eagerly for the orderly to bring me his letters.

On November 12, I wrote:

> *If I were ever so much inclined my dearest friend, I could not forget you; your kind attentions are unremitting—one favor is not dim in my remembrance, ere another claims attention. I shall be compelled to search the vocabulary for language to express my indebtedness. You sadden me by your continued melancholy. I know you are in some respects unpleasantly situated; but life is not all dark. Remember Longfellow's lines in "A Psalm of Life":*
>
> > *Not enjoyment, and not sorrow,*
> > *Is our destined end or way;*
> > *But to act, that each to-morrow*
> > *Find us farther than to-day.*
>
> *If I don't write as often as you wish, remember I'm very busy: as you know my baggage is in the country, and I'm replenishing my wardrobe somewhat.*
>
> *Ma's kind regards and good wishes always understood if not expressed. I didn't receive a line from you yesterday. What was the matter? I felt uneasy—feared you were sick and dear knows what all.*
>
> *Do send a line on time every day. Can't you?*

Clanie saw me writing, in the parlor, and said, "Tell Major Willard I'm very much obliged for his kind regards, and hope he may be successful in every undertaking through life."

My goodness, I thought, Clanie is growing up. Please, God, let this war end before he has to go and fight.

Even Frank requested that I send quantities of love. During Major's last visit, he brought candy, a delicacy, for Frank to gobble. Frank had a decided sweet tooth!

I ended the letter with, "Write long letters to Yours Truly, Antonia."

Two days later, on Saturday, Major came to visit. We took a walk in order to talk privately.

"Major," I said, "do you know that your last letter to me was elegantly written? It replied to every part of mine—I think I'm a judge of letters, and I pronounce it, without exception, the most complete *answer* I ever read."

"You mean the answer to your question of is it possible to fall in love at first sight?"

"Yes, and I would love for you to expound upon that in your letters. You know how much I enjoy love letters. By the way, you never once said you missed me or wanted to see me—do you?" I asked.

"I think about you constantly and want to gaze upon you every day of my life. Perhaps you could teach me to write better letters?"

"Excuse the expression, but it is simply absurd for you to talk of my teaching you—anyone capable of replying as you have needs no instruction—in that area at least."

"You're a true literary master, Antonia. It gives me great pleasure to peruse your letters to me during my melancholy moments."

"Whatever you may say to the contrary, I'm satisfied that some portions of my last letter were not as agreeable as they might have been—for instance where I spoke of Pattie and her comments; especially the remark about my falling in love."

"Am I the first man you have ever loved?" he questioned.

"You know that is true, although I have fond feelings for some long-time friends."

Walking towards us on Fairfax Street was Eliza Gunnell, a neighbor.

"Good day, Mrs. Gunnell," I said pleasantly. Major tipped his blue officer's hat at her.

"Good day, Antonia," she replied curtly and dismissively.

She gave a disapproving look at Major, dressed in his clean blue uniform, and walked on.

"I've received an earful of advice about you Major, from my neighbors. They wonder at our relationship. I admit that I mentioned that you were seeking a divorce from your first wife at a recent quilting bee, and some friends cannot hold their tongues."

"Could it be possible that these dear villagers have such a miserable opinion of you, because of our love, and my duty to my country?"

"During these times, anything's possible, because divorce is a social stigma. Most of us have loved ones fighting against your compatriots. Anyway, how often have I told you that it is all a mistake—you were meant to be a Virginian?"

"Perhaps the less you say about us, my dear, the better."

"I'm sorry for that lapse of discretion; it was both impolite and unkind. I won't do so again—trust me."

"I will try to trust you, in that, and other things as well."

"By the way, in your last letter you merely mentioned the Alexandria railroad cars running off the track, without entering into particulars: *if not detrimental to the service*, I should like very much to hear all about it."

"There is not much to tell. I contrived some business to tend to at Fairfax Station, then planned on coming here to visit you. The cars that remained on the track continued on, with me aboard. I do not believe the Rebels, excuse me, I mean Confederates, caused the accident."

"How very glad I am you were not injured; if anything had happened to you I could not have forgiven myself, for though innocent, I would certainly have been the cause. You must take better care of yourself, for if you have an 'object in life,' and I think I've heard you say something of the kind more than once, you surely want to live for that 'object.'"

"My object in life is to find true happiness—with you. I have a gift for you."

He reached into his pocket and withdrew a small wrapped object. I excitedly unwrapped it. How I loved to receive gifts!

"How kind you are to anticipate my wants. You couldn't have picked out anything more acceptable than this beautiful pencil. You are just as good as you can be."

"Will you be as good to me and write to me more often?"

"I ought to write as often as you wish, so I will. I hope you know that I write to you twice as often as you write to me. You are as *unreasonable* about that as *some other things I could mention*."

"You are referring to the slowness of my obtaining a divorce?"

"Yes."

"As much as you might wish for me to pester my commanding officer, my wife, my lawyer, and the judge every day, it just is not possible. I have other responsibilities I have to attend to."

"I will try to be patient, my love."

By this time, we were back in front of my house. Major came inside, and we had tea and cakes together. He kissed me goodbye and promised to visit again soon.

Chapter Forty-two

Letters To and Fro, November 1863

More than once in my life, I felt glad that I graduated as a Mistress of English Literature. Writing came naturally to me, and it soothed my soul—the same way that quilting soothed Mother's soul. Truthfully, I would much rather trust an orderly with delivering letters to and fro than to risk Major's life by having him visit me too frequently. Our courtship in some ways embodied an affair of words.

Fairfax Courthouse, Friday night
My dear Major,

I was very much astonished to learn from your note this evening that my letters of Thursday have not reached you. Where can they be? I gave them to the orderly myself—there is something wrong. Perhaps you can investigate the matter; remember the orderly of Thursday received them. This is the sixth letter I've written you, and only two have gone safely—do you understand it?

Come at once if possible and we can discuss the affair at length. I don't know that this will reach you. Thanks for the papers. I am very much worried about the letters.

Yours very truly, Antonia
Ma's kindest regards. Frank says tell you, "He is Union now—that is the strong side." Come tomorrow.

Our letters back and forth carried codes that only the two of us understood. I enjoyed something secret and delicious about our correspondence. Although uncensored, I strove to use my best, well-mannered prose. Unlike conversation, the same sweet words from my love could be enjoyed repeatedly just by re-reading a letter.

I enjoyed sending Major remembrances of me—a lock of hair, dried leaf, or even tea leaves that seemed particularly insightful.

My dear Major,

As usual, I was too late for breakfast this morning so haven't time to write—take the bill for the deed this time. Am sorry to trouble you with enclosures.

Yours truly,

Antonia
Symbolically (there are some tea leaves enclosed)

On November 30, I opened a letter from Major, anticipating a warm, encouraging letter. Perhaps, he would write a poem, or words of love.

Sunday night, Washington City, November 29, 1863
My dear Antonia,

> *You are always in my thoughts, no matter where I am or what I am doing. Your sweet smile and gentle mannerisms make me feel so warm and safe that I never want to leave you. Our last visit was particularly enchanting. I yearn for your kisses and to caress you. Your womanly scent when we are close together drives me to distraction. Caroline used to give me pleasure, and I enjoyed her scent, but not as much as yours, Antonia. When I see her now, at the hotel, I feel no love whatsoever. I then think of you, and my heart beats rapidly and my attention strays from whatever task I am doing.*
> *My dearest, are you sure you want to be married to a divorced man? We could go somewhere where no one knows us, set up house, and live happily ever after, unmarried. I could liquidate my savings and start up a hotel in parts far away. Think about it. Until our next meeting,*

> *Yours truly,*
> *Joseph*

I ran, shrieking, from the parlor, upstairs, into my room, and threw myself on the bed. Pattie appeared in the doorway.

"What does Major have to say?"

"That miserable, skunk of a man! I cannot believe his insensitivity. First he mentions bodily functions, then he mentions his wife's name, and finally, he suggests that we live in sin, and not marry at all!"

"I don't believe it. Let me read that letter."

I passed it to Pattie, and she read it quickly, gasping at the parts too grotesque to believe.

"You should write him a reply letter, and let him know in no uncertain terms that you were very displeased. What offends you most about the letter?"

"I think mentioning her name and mine together in the same sentence is the most obnoxious part of the letter, but thinking I would live in sin with him is a close second."

I took out paper and pen, and wrote a letter back to him, clipping out and enclosing in the envelope the sentence that mentioned his wife's name.

Monday night 8 o'clock, Fairfax Courthouse, November, 30

Your letter was received at the usual time this evening. Major, and the shriek at reading one sentence was greater than you can conceive, (that obnoxious sentence I enclose, I cannot allow it to remain in my possession)—I not only never had such language addressed to me, but never in all my life heard of it being used to a <u>decent</u> girl much less a <u>lady</u>. Answer me one question, did you mean to insult me? Great God, what am I to think! Hasn't my suffering been sufficient! Is there a bitterer drop yet in my cup of anguish! Am I mistaken in <u>you</u>! Is it, can it be, possible <u>you</u> intend adding the deepest to the long list of degradations I suffered at the hands of Federalists?

Major, Major answer me in heaven's name what you meant, are you going to keep me in horrible suspense over your intentions? I close now, perplexed and wondering.

Yours truly,
Antonia.

Major redeemed himself on his next visit with a gift of a costly gold necklace containing a large topaz stone. He truly did not know what he had done that so disturbed me, and apologized profusely. I couldn't stay angry with him, but told him what *not* to write in future letters to me, and we came to an understanding about that.

Union officers used our house sporadically and I grew weary of entertaining them night after night. The homesick men looked undernourished and bedraggled. They didn't smell too good either, as men did not commonly take baths in the dead of winter. Some of them were ill, but not sick enough to go into a hospital. I would hear the officers hacking away, their coughs undiagnosed. Because tuberculosis was so contagious, I feared for possible transmission of illness to my own family.

Fairfax C.H.
December
My Dear Major,

I have only time to acknowledge the receipt of your letter of last evening. We have a general hospital here. I'm not enamored of those big shots. I'm very busy, notwithstanding, the numerous duties devolving upon me as housekeeper and overseer, but I cannot allow the little orderly to go without a few lines. He is here now.

Fondly yours truly and sincerely,
Antonia.

In between our frenzy of letter writing, I was secretly making Christmas slippers for Mother. The pattern of a vase and flowers came from the December 1860 *Peterson's Magazine*. I worked all the designs in colored silk, with colors to imitate nature. I stitched the fruit and flowers in bright gold, red, and yellow, and the vase in gold and green. The silk for the slippers and appliquéd designs consisted of scraps from worn-out dresses, as there was no chance of purchasing new quantities of silk anywhere.

Chapter Forty-three

Christmas, 1863

Mother decided that we should try to celebrate Christmas this year and I wholeheartedly agreed. After all, I was in love, and my future looked rosy, even if the South's did not. She said our primary focus should be on the Christ-child, enabling us to forget the war now and then. We had toned down the last two Christmases, so we wanted to make it special for six-year-old Frank, in particular. We decorated our home a week before Christmas with mistletoe, spruce, balsam, laurel, cedar, and ivy. Holly graced our tables, banisters, chandeliers, archways, columns, mantle, and woodwork. Mistletoe dangled from the ceiling of the entry hall. I even draped picture frames and mirrors with evergreen garlands. I made a pinecone and balsam wreath to decorate our front door.

A few days before Christmas, Father, Clanie, and Frank went into the woods and chopped down a balsam tree for the parlor. Pattie and I made chains from strips of paper to hang on the tree. We also made some paper cornucopias filled with dried berries and nuts. Paper fans with embroidery thread tassels hung from the boughs. Sweets for hanging on the tree were hard to come by, so we "made do" with what we had. Frank helped us string popped corn alternating with cranberries, which made a nice garland for the tree. We hung a tin whistle and one of Frank's toy soldiers on the tree. We carefully placed hand-dipped candles on each of the branches. A Christmas angel adorned the top of the tree. Mother set up a Nativity scene under the bottom boughs, with straw inside the stable.

Frank seemed enchanted—so happy and excited, with a spirit contagious to all of us. He was just full of questions, though.

"Can we keep the Christmas tree always?" he asked hopefully.

"Sweetie, no," Mother answered. "Even with the tree in a bucket of water, it will eventually die. We can do it again next year, though."

"Why do we have one?" he asked.

Mother replied, "The Christmas tree was introduced into England fifty years ago. Then, in 1841, the German Prince Albert, husband of Queen Victoria, decorated a large Christmas tree at Windsor Castle to remind him of his childhood celebrations in Germany. It became fashionable here in America to do the same."

Finally, Christmas Eve arrived. I arranged an impromptu caroling around the neighborhood. The Farrs, Murrays, Loves, and Thomases joined my family and we went house-to-house singing our favorites: "Adeste Fidelis," "The First Noel," "God Rest Ye Merry, Gentlemen," and "Joy to the World." There would be no church service this year, but Mother invited the carolers to our home afterwards to read the Bible together, pray, and then have hot beverages and meager delicacies. I tried my hand at cooking and made some flummery using the recipe from Mary Randolph's cookbook, *The Virginia Housewife*. We had a roaring fire going with pinecones in it to add a satisfying crack every now and then. Cinnamon, cranberry, and apple scented the air. I looked around at the happy faces, communing with one another, and thought sorrowfully of the boys we had lost amongst us. No young men graced our gathering—only middle-aged men, women, and children.

I awoke on Christmas Day at dawn, the air frigidly cold. Father already had a roaring fire blazing in the downstairs fireplaces and Mother was in the kitchen preparing a feast for breakfast. I anticipated an extra-special day because I expected Major to join us sometime today, even though it was a Friday, not his customary visiting day of Saturday.

I went up to Mother and hugged her.

"How can I help?" I asked.

"Set the table for me, please."

Frank came downstairs still dressed in his nightclothes. "Can I go in the parlor, Mother?" he asked.

"Not until after breakfast," she replied. "Go upstairs and get dressed. It is too cold for you to be running around like that. Especially with bare feet!"

We had a special treat of real coffee, although weaker than I normally liked it. I sipped it gratefully, and waited for my family to convene for breakfast.

After breakfast, we finally entered the parlor. Father and Clanie lit the candles on the tree, and we waited expectantly for the gift exchange to start.

Mother opened her present from me first. I had worked diligently and successfully to get her embroidered silk slippers finished in time.

"Antonia, sweetheart, thank you. Where did you get the lovely silk to make these slippers?" she asked excitedly.

"Do you remember the silk dress that Pattie outgrew last year? I cut that up and had more than enough for the slippers."

Most of our wrapped gifts utilized colorful scraps of cloth or old newspapers with ribbons of yarn tied around them. Paper was far too precious to waste on wrapping gifts.

Frank could hold his excitement no longer and delved into the pile of gifts, looking for presents with his name on them. When he had retrieved all of his, and had a nice pile in front of him, he started opening them. He was enthralled with a top, toy drum, cloth soldier, and a carved wooden horse.

Clanie asked, "Do you like the horse, Frank? I worked several weeks carving that and getting it just right."

He did not even answer, engrossed in the midst of a battle with his soldier sitting atop the horse charging an imaginary enemy.

Father opened the monogrammed tobacco pouch from me.

"Thank you, Antonia. Your embroidery is exquisite. I needed a new pouch."

Pattie, aged thirteen, enthused in the family tradition of quilting and received a sewing kit of her own. She was making her first quilt, a square within a square design, colored red, and blue.

"I have something I made for you, Sister," she said. She handed me a little gift. I opened it to find a needle case, embroidered in red with the initials AJF.

"I will treasure this. It is just what I needed."

I wrapped the knitted muffler that I made Clanie around his neck, tied it carefully and gave him a kiss, saying, "Keep warm, my tall, handsome brother, and don't you even think about joining up with the army!"

Mother handed Father a leather stamp box. In exchange, he presented her a rather large and lumpy unusually wrapped gift. The wrapping, a plain sack with a piece of twine closing it, caused her to hold it with a puzzled expression on her face. Inside she found bags of sugar, flour, coffee, tea, and little containers of nutmeg, cinnamon sticks, and ginger.

Mother, so happy, had tears in her eyes.

"Where did you get these things?" she asked.

Father only smiled back and did not answer.

No one made mention of Charlie, but he abided in our hearts and prayers. I hoped that wherever he was, he was warm, safe, and nourished.

I received a subscription to *Godey's Lady's Magazine*. My family knew how much I loved to read.

Mathilde, Octavia, and the other servants received gifts of clothing. Although they did not have the day off, their duties were minimal today.

We scheduled dinner for three o'clock, about the time when I expected Major to arrive.

At 2:45, I peeked out the parlor window to see Major dismounting from his horse. Our groom took the horse away to the stable and Major climbed the front steps and knocked. I ran to the door and opened it breathlessly, rapt with happiness.

"Merry Christmas, Antonia," he said in greeting.

"Happy Christmas, to you. Come in—it's cold out there."

Major entered and Octavia took his cloak and hat. I led him into the parlor to join the family festivities. He had a bag under his arm and stooped to put some gifts under the tree.

"Dinner's served," cried out Mathilde.

"You are just in time, Major," said Father.

Father sat at one end of the table; Mother at the other. Frank, Clanie, and Pattie sat on one side of the table, and Major and I opposite them. Mother had decorated the table with pine branches, pinecones, holly with bright red berries, and candles. She even brought out the silver candlesticks for this occasion. The menu consisted of turkey, potatoes, cheese, bread, and cranberry sauce. We had two desserts—plum pudding and Nesselrode pudding, an old family recipe, consisting of chestnuts, water, sugar, eggs, raisins, currants, cherries, and apricots. Father brought out the homemade wine.

"How is the morale amongst your men, Major?" asked Father.

"Sir, it is as well as can be expected. The North is assured of victory—it is only a matter of time now."

"Recent activity in Knoxville, Tennessee, reflected a Confederate victory," Father pointed out.

"Perhaps," Major rejoined. "However the price was too high on both sides with nine hundred Confederate and seven hundred Federal casualties."

We all solemnly nodded our heads in agreement.

"Is there something for me under the tree from you, Major?" asked Frank.

"Frank!" Mother exclaimed. "You know better than to ask for gifts!"

"But, but, Mother," Frank stuttered. "Major always brings me little gifts!"

I smiled at the naivety and innocence of my little brother.

"Perhaps we should go see," I said gently.

We all left the table and went into the parlor.

Major said, "Look for the most brightly wrapped gift, Frank. That's for you."

Frank pulled out a bright green package and unwrapped it to find a package of hard candies—his favorite delicacy.

"Thank you, oh, thank you!" he said, while stuffing his mouth.

"This is for you, Miss Ford," said Major formally, while retrieving my gift from under the tree. I unwrapped it slowly. A hymnal and prayer book, bound in black monkey-skin, with my monogram in silver gleamed before me.

"This is so fine," I murmured appreciatively. "My gift to you is not nearly so costly."

I handed him a gift and he opened it. I had to explain its significance.

"Major, this may look like any ordinary hemmed fine handkerchief but I have to tell you that I sacrificed some of my hair strands to embroider your monogram on it."

"Your hair is your glory, my dear," he said. "Your sacrifice is my treasure, and far more valuable than what I gave you. I will keep it close to my heart."

He knew exactly the right thing to say, I thought. We ended the visit looking longingly towards each other as we said goodbye.

Chapter Forty-four

New Year's Eve, December 31, 1863

What a wild night it is! The leafless trees lift their arms toward heaven, and the wind sobs and moans like a human being in agony. I like this; it gives me a sad pleasure to hear the sighing of the storm alternating with its bursts of grief. I suppose now the elements are uniting to sing dirges for the departing year, as it is December 31, 1863. Mother, Pattie, and I, seated in the parlor before the fire, are keeping the watch, and awaiting Major's knock upon the door. The three of us are piecing some squares for a new quilt. It is ten-thirty, later than normal for a suitor to call on me, but we want to shoo out "Father Time" and greet the "Young Fellow" together.

"You cannot possibly be thinking of marrying him without a respectable engagement period, Antonia," Mother stated in a stern voice. "The sooner he resigns his commission, the better, as it is simply disgraceful for any Southern woman to consort with a Federal soldier."

Pattie chimed in, "It's not that we don't think he is charming, Sister. It breaks my heart to think that acquaintances of the major could have been responsible for some of our brave soldier friends' deaths."

I wondered what aspect of the major was more disagreeable to them, as we avoided entirely the fact that he was married!

"I will see if I can persuade him to resign his commission as soon as possible," I said. "He previously agreed to do so when I took the Oath of Allegiance. It was only under this condition that I agreed to our courtship."

The door chimed, I answered the door, and my beloved stood there, hat in hand.

"Good evening, Miss Ford," he politely greeted me with his disarming smile. He was rather reserved when he thought that other ears were listening.

"Good evening, Major," I breathlessly replied. My heart was already beginning to beat more rapidly in response to my excitement at seeing him. It had been one week since our last rendezvous.

"Please come inside by the fire. It is bitterly cold out there."

As Mathilde and Octavia had already retired for the evening, I took his cloak and hat, and laid them aside. We proceeded into the parlor, so that Major could greet my mother and sister, then we retreated to the dining room so that we could have some privacy in our conversation. Our dining room is quite a cozy room; the quietness of the room contrasts pleasantly with the roar of the elements and the ruddy firelight with the darkness of the winter evening.

"I am so pleased that General Augur allowed you to make this trip tonight. I suppose you have also come to check out the bordering towns, receive reports, and find out what is going on in our small village of Fairfax Courthouse."

"My love, my main attraction is to see you; you know that. I am only here for three days, and then must return to Washington. You still look pale and thin, but as beautiful as ever in my eyes. Have you regained your strength?"

"I do tire easily, but am feeling better each day, thank you."

We had not sat down yet, and Major gestured for me to move towards the side of the room—nearer to the fireplace. I did so, knowing that he wanted to seek some privacy. He then devoured me with his eyes, took me in his arms, and embraced me fervently. His lips sought mine and we passionately kissed, his body pressed up against mine, heart to heart. His hands brushed against my breasts and a low moan escaped from his lips as I pulled away. I guided him to a chair and sat facing him.

"Antonia, how long must I wait for us to marry? Can we not have a private marriage?"

"Dearest, you have placed me under so many obligations, I shall never be able to extricate myself, but I must be obliged to sway you from a speedy wedding. You know I love you, but Major, I can never consent to a private marriage; there are numbers of reasons why I refuse."

"Give me one good one."

I heatedly and passionately continued, "My parents and relatives would be mortified and distressed to death; acquaintances would disown me; it would be illegal as you are not yet divorced, and above all, it would be wrong." At this point, tears of frustration fell down my face.

"I'm being selfish, darling. Of course, you want a wedding day fit for a princess. I have already been through it once, so it is old hat to me. The religious aspect for a wedding cannot be denied you."

"I cannot claim to be a Christian, unfortunately, but I have a conscience, and am governed by it, at least to some extent, and I fear to do anything so diametrically offensive to its teachings. I dislike saying no to one so dear, but there is no alternative in this case; I will grant any request which is right and proper, and would make you 'the happiest man in the world' if I could without compromising myself."

"You told me once that you cared nothing for what society thinks."

"When I said I cared nothing for society I meant I never would enjoy a fashionable life: but I wouldn't place a barrier between myself and all friends—it is very different being given up by the world, and voluntarily giving it up. I have considered the matter well, dearest, as it would be wrong for you as well as me; neither of us could be happy, for the curse God would cast upon us."

"Antonia, I long for the consummation of our love. My heart aches for your love and companionship. My desires and thoughts of you are all consuming—I can think of nothing else."

"Although I know it improper for us to speak to each other in this way, I also have come to think of you with longing for the forbidden. You ask for my heart and hand, the heart is yours already; when your hand is free and you can claim mine before the world, then that also is yours. Surely you are now satisfied. I have promised to marry you when you are at liberty to marry. Can you ask more?"

"You talk as if I have not been trying to get Caroline to sign the divorce papers," he countered wearily. "I only ask that our chaste love be chaste no longer. I've waited since the day we met to feel your touch, caress your smooth skin, and be a man to you in every sense of the word."

"Ought you to be willing to wait if *I* am? You are the Christian, as you have told me before. Remember, Major, the obstacle is with you, not me; as I told you on your last visit, my hand is unfettered."

"My darling, it is difficult for me to wait for complete fulfillment, as I believe a man's needs in that respect to be more urgent than a woman's. Believe me; it is hard for me not to sin in this world of hatred and inhumanity towards one another."

"Major, loving you as I do, we must not do what I know to be wrong in the eyes of God, so be generous and don't insist upon this. I am not afraid of keeping to my decision, but it grieves me very much to utter words which pain you."

"I don't feel friendly to fate. The life of a soldier in this 'broken dream of a war' is unpredictable. I curse the cruel fate which has separated us in the past, and fear a separation yet again."

"Time or distance could never separate us, truly. Our lives are in the hands of fate. I think fate has had a good deal to do with us and how we met unexpectedly in General Heintzelman's office. My case was put in your hands, and after arranging my release, you were authorized to bring me home. It seems I was literally thrown in your way by a power above us— call it Destiny; I think that a prettier word than fate."

"I would rather hope that it was God who has been looking over us."

"Now, my love, let's be hopeful, and expect Destiny, as she had taken our fate in her hands, to work out something joyful for us. I am very superstitious about my dreams and in 'a vision by night', it was told me, in ten months, it would all be arranged as you wish. Wait patiently until that time has elapsed. I certainly put confidence in the prediction, for I never had a dream in my life about rumors that did not come true. At school I was called the dreamer; and would tell the girls regularly what they would get at examinations and I rarely proved a false prophet. Let's try our fortunes tonight. Two years ago, I tried it and the initials of my intended came J.C. I supposed it had reference to Mr. John Cooke who was visiting me regularly, and would not pick a third letter. I considered the coincidence singular *then*, think it more so *now*. What do you say to it? I had never heard of J.C.W. then."

"What an odd occurrence. Yes, let's try our fortunes. You are referring to apple peelings, I presume?"

"I'll go get an apple and a knife."

I returned with them, and we each peeled a small strip from the apple. We each had to think of a question that required a "yes" or "no" answer.

I asked, "Will I be married within six months time?"

I stood up, threw the peel over my left shoulder, and turned around to look.

"I have a straight line," I said with a smile. "That means yes."

Major asked, "Will I have a long, happy life with you?"

He threw his peel and said, "Mine looks like a 'U' to me."

"What nonsense we are doing." I did not tell him that a "U" or "O" meant the answer is no. "Pattie and Mother are in the kitchen. Let's go join them to welcome the New Year."

Mother said, "We missed you over the past week."

I said fondly, "He should be ashamed of himself for neglecting the border for such a long time. He really needs to know what is going on out here. Don't you think it is his duty to come and see, and receive reports? How could he keep track otherwise of what suitors are knocking at the Ford door?"

Pattie and Mother laughed at that.

Major said, "Maybe you can clear up a botanical question, Mrs. Ford. I think the meaning of the rose geranium is love, but Antonia claims it is preference."

Mother answered, "Well, let me see, I think it might be fidelity."

An awkward silence filled the room until Pattie exclaimed, "The clock, the clock!"

Indeed, the clock chimed midnight. Eighteen sixty-four had arrived.

After more chitchat, I retrieved Major's cloak and walked him to the door.

"Do you love me any less for refusing to accede to your proposition of a private marriage?"

"Never, my dear. Forget I ever said it."

"The withdrawal of your affection would be a real trouble to me. What should I do when sad and gloomy, without your affection, the one who loves me more than all others, in whose heart I reign supreme?"

"I love you dearly, and will love you as long as I live. I know you believe that," Major replied.

"I do, and I feel the same. Be satisfied for us to remain as we are; I'll comfort you when sad, you can hear from me daily, and need not love me less because fate has decided we shall be separated for a period. I hope to hear good news about your resignation soon."

"Good night my dearest," Major said.

"I wish you a very happy New Year, so happy that all your preceding life may seem darker than ever by contrast. Good night."

Chapter Forty-five

Trouble, January 1864

My entire family took a trip to Sangster's Station the first week of January to visit with relatives. Confusion reigned in trying to keep the genealogy straight, because my mother's maiden name was also Ford. Children of my maternal grandmother, Jane Ford, lived there, as well as descendants of my paternal Grandfather, Charles Fleming Ford. Cousin Fred lived nearby, and helped Uncle William with the farm. My aunt, Mary Randolph, married to Dr. Robert F. Simpson, had the most room for all of us, so we would be staying with them. We rode by a low hill past Fontainville, Grandfather's estate, where we passed a small frozen spring, with its clean water barely trickling through the ice. The springhouse stood there and served as an icehouse. The big wooden house, crowning the summit of the hill, displayed a porch, which ran the length of the front of the house. Locust trees shaded the large front yard. I felt sad to bypass this house, as I had stayed there during many happy girlhood days. We soon arrived at Aunt Mary's stone and brick home, made to last for centuries. Smoke spiraled from one of the three chimneys. We alighted from the carriage and went inside where Mary and her husband, Robert, greeted us. The last time I had seen Mary was on the day that I was first arrested.

As Mary hugged me she whispered, "What have they done to you? Are you well?"

"I am regaining my strength, be assured of that. I have wonderful news. I have a beau, and love him so much! He said he would come here to visit."

My family made the rounds of visiting relatives and generally had a good time catching up with them on family news.

The next time I saw Major was on Saturday, January 9. He arrived at Sangster's Junction in the early evening when it was lightly snowing outside. After introductions, dinner, and card games with everyone, we settled on the couch in Aunt Mary's parlor, watching the ever-changing flames and reveling in the comfort of each other's presence. Chaperones were nearby, but gave us some privacy.

"Do you think your relatives like me?" asked Major.

"It is difficult to know for sure. My aunt and uncle treated you civilly enough, don't you think?"

"Have they taken the oath?"

I knew they were secessionists and doubted that they had taken the oath, but answered, "I'm quite confident they have."

I enjoyed the warm security of his arm around my shoulders as we talked companionably about anything that struck our fancy.

We heard the stealthy clip-clop of horse hooves that stopped outside the house. We could see the outline of a lone figure who came to the front door and knocked. Father and Dr. Simpson came from the kitchen, carrying a lantern, to answer the door. We could dimly see a man dressed in a Confederate uniform who handed Father something, murmured softly for several minutes, then walked quickly away, mounted his horse, and rode off.

"He is putting himself in jeopardy coming to this town," muttered Major. "I could arrest him. I wonder what business he has with your father. After all, your entire family has taken the Oath of Allegiance, which prohibits aiding the enemy."

"I assure you, that my family takes its oaths seriously," I said with all the indignation that I could muster. I continued spitefully, "Unlike you who promised to love and cherish your wife."

There was a strained silence. He removed his arm from my shoulders.

"Do you also receive papers from and meet with Confederate soldiers, Antonia?"

"My father conducts his business with integrity. I assure you, I know nothing of his affairs other than that, and no, I have not met with any Confederate soldiers recently. Of course I love one—my brother."

"This could look very bad for me if other Federal officers knew what was going on here. I want to trust you, though."

"You say you do not mistrust me, but your continued attention to it seems very like trying to persuade yourself you do not, while all the time suspicion is leaving a poisoned trail in your heart."

"Why don't you clear up things with your father concerning his interpretation of the Oath of Allegiance, and we will talk again soon. I must get back to headquarters now. Good evening, Miss Ford," he said formally, and left without a backward glance.

Thus ended our first lover's spat.

I spoke to my father after Major left.

"Who came to the door, Father," I casually asked, as if I did not see the uniform.

"Oh, just a neighbor, asking the doctor for medical advice concerning a sick patient," he lied. "Did Major leave without saying goodbye to the rest of us?"

"Yes. We had some angry words between us."

The next day, Father and Clanie returned home. Father still felt uneasy as to my presence in Fairfax Courthouse, and promised that he would come back for the rest of us in two weeks.

I asked Father to carry a message home to convey to Major. I contemplated what to write, and childishly decided to test him. Brief, and to the point, as I was still angry with him, I wrote:

January 10, 1864
Dear Major Willard,

> *If you doubt my loyalty to the Union, that is your choice. I will assume by your mistrust of my family and me, and your abrupt departure yesterday, that you wish for our engagement to be broken. By the way, you had better burn my letters, for God forbid if someone should read them and think you were collaborating with a known spy! On the other hand, if you wish to apologize to me for your suspicions, please do so.*

Antonia Ford of Fairfax

I did not hear from Major. I tried writing a different kind of letter, as my ploy had not worked, and I was frantic now:

January 11, 1864
Dear Major Willard,

> *I have missed hearing from you, my love, these last few days. My young heart is breaking over you, and I think that would move you if anything would.*
> *Major, I'm tormented constantly by a verse of my saddest song; day and night. Since your last letter came, it has rung through my brain—*

> *"I've loved thee too deeply, the dream shall pass by.*
> *The cistern is broken the fountain is dry,*
> *And the angel that sent o'er the brink of the mass,*
> *Now weeps in the star light of love's early grave."*

> *I ask myself is this ominous, does it predict my fate! Heaven forbid! Surely, our love is strong enough to stand one shock. After what we've written and said, "shall a light word part us soon?" What say you?*
> *My dear Major, how dear you are to me. You can't imagine, and would hardly believe if I was to tell you. My <u>darling</u> (oh! Just see what I've said, but is it any worse to feel it than write?) how can I give you up! I would not write this if I did not know <u>we are</u> both unhappy at this estrangement. I admit I am for <u>I love you</u>. And Major this moment <u>you love</u> me and as you read these lines your heart <u>thrills</u> to every word. You*

can't gainsay it. I repeat it exultantly <u>you love me</u>, and you love me devotedly too: that is my only comfort in these unhappy moments.

Did you think poor fellow that you were the only sufferer? <u>Another</u> would find the sunshine of life unmoved and darkness in its place beside yourself—that ought to cheer you; the old adage says, "Misery loves company."

I will send everything except the letters and pictures; if you wish those come after them, and I give them up directly. If after reading this, you still wish the engagement broken, I'll be <u>dead</u> to <u>you</u> henceforth; if you wish it to stand I am now and forever your own and yours only.

Antonia.

I waited patiently all the next day for the little orderly to bring me a reply, but went to bed with nothing but a heavy heart. Not until two restless days later, Wednesday evening, did I receive a letter via the orderly. I opened it anticipating a sweet apology, and tender words of love:

Washington City, D.C.
January 12, 1864
Tuesday Eve, 11:30

Miss Ford,

Please burn my letters to you, and therewith let the "dead facts" be consumed.

J. C. Willard.

In the parlor, Pattie had been observing my expression as I read, and my alarm must have been evident as she exclaimed, "Pray tell, what has happened!"

"It is over between us. He wants me to burn his letters to me," I sobbed.

I buried my head into the corner of the couch and started crying in earnest. Pattie ran to get Mother and Aunt Mary.

"Antonia, dear, it is not the end of the world. It is just a little misunderstanding. You can put things right can't you?" Aunt Mary asked in a reassuring way.

"I do not know. What should I do?"

"Do nothing, if you do not love him. If you truly love him, bury your stubbornness and write him another note."

I did write as Aunt Mary suggested, but two days went by with no word from him. I had been suffering throughout my self-imposed ordeal with a migraine, and could not eat. My usual remedies for migraine did not mitigate the pain at all. I alternated crying with fitful sleeping. Finally, Mother took the matter in her own hands and wrote a letter to Major. I only found out after the fact what she had done:

Jan 15, 1864   Friday Morning

Oh Major for mercy's sake come up tomorrow or Sunday if but for an hour. The wildness of my poor child's anguish is alarming since the reading of your last letter. It has really made her ill. She has neither ate nor slept since you left. Her prudishness has been the cause of her present distraction. I beseech you come if possible. Mr. Ford knows nothing of her last letter—he is very much disturbed. Pardon me for interfering.

Your friend, Julia F.F.
I am not deceiving you when I say she is ill. Please write you will come.

The next day, the orderly came and simply told Mother that the major would visit as soon as he could get away, but would certainly write in the meantime.

Chapter Forty-six

Reconciliation, January 1864

The war went on, as tumultuous as my inner emotions. While still at Sangsters, we received a letter from Father relating how on January 18, Clanie disobeyed him, and rode to the nearby town of Flint Hill to visit a friend. The fact that the friend had a sister whom Clanie admired had a lot to do with it. After only a few hours, sooner than expected, Clanie arrived home. Father wrote an account:

I started going to the stable to have words with my wayward son when he cautiously entered the house. One look at his face, and I knew something had happened. I asked him what the meaning of his disobedience was. He replied, "You were right, Father. I should not have been out. I witnessed twenty of our men attack the picket at Flint Hill. The picket fell down, injured, or worse."

Clanie was lucky that he, himself, was not shot.

Clanie continued, "Our men were driven off after a single volley, which surprised me—being scared off so easily. That was my cue to turn around and come home."

Angry with Clanie, but relieved, I punished him by sending him to the woodpile to tame his restless energy by chopping until he exhausted himself.

Father also mentioned that New York troops were recuperating in makeshift hospitals in Blenheim and the Gunnell's house.

Major had resumed writing to me, thank God. After what Clanie witnessed, I warned Major in my next letter: *Bring an escort. We don't know when those awful rebels will make a raid. I should want to behead Mosby if he should capture you.*

Although John Mosby was a dear friend, I did not always approve of his tactics.

Dr. Simpson drove us home on January 30, to save Father the trip. Our cold carriage ride home was bearable because we kept warm by covering ourselves with wool blankets. That night, I wrote to Major:

Fairfax Courthouse, January 30, 1864
My dearest Major,
    I am at home again as you'll perceive by this, and right glad to get here: glad simply because <u>you</u> wished one to return, and that I can

receive and send letters to you <u>regularly</u>. It was so provoking at Sangsters. I wrote four times and don't know yet that one was received. Your orderly told Pa today he had a letter for me, and Pa said better not send it down as I was expected home; but he found a good opportunity and started it. I feel disappointed about it, for I anticipated a treat in reading it. Never mind, it will be sweet when it comes; and I hope to have a long one to relish.

You wish to know my birthday—it is the 23rd of July, and my birth room, the one you occupied at Fontainville. <u>No</u>, <u>I don't</u> think you are "an <u>old</u> soldier for a young lady"; I think you are very suitable for the young lady, she wouldn't have you changed a particle, as regards age or anything else.

I found the bundle awaiting me, am very, very much obliged; the matchbox is very pretty. Ma will write to you very soon, she said today coming home, "I wish the major would come by tonight." I fully echoed the wish, I assure you. Do come next week, will you not dearest?

Captain LaMotte knocked on our door this evening. Father and Mother declined to entertain him. I emphatically declined to make my appearance. Stars have no attraction for me. I much prefer the leaf. Capt. LaMotte is housed with the General nearby.

Good night, write every day.

Yours affectionately,
Antonia.

A few days later, Major came for a visit. We embraced on greeting each other, and headed to the parlor, our customary trysting place. We spoke the inane chatter of young lovers. My hair, long and flowing, felt majestic around my shoulders, and I rejoiced in being a woman at that moment.

"I love your hair," he said to me while stroking it. "May I have a lock to hold dear to my heart?"

I picked up my embroidery scissors lying on a table and cut off a lock.

"'Tis the 'Simon pure' and no deception," I said as I held it aloft. "I've charmed it, it's a talisman to send the sunshine to you,—you must never feel sad or doubtful in the slightest degree with that about you."

"You do have a way with words, my sweet."

"Remember I've pronounced an incantation over it, and its power will remain while your affection is undiminished."

"You have 'a heart whose love is innocent,'" he said with utmost sincerity.

"He quotes Lord Byron!" I exclaimed. "Oh, Joseph, I regret everything unkind I've said to you in past weeks. Believe my promises of loyalty and devotion to you. Can you doubt my attachment?"

He would have replied, but Mother and Father came into the room at that moment and sat down.

"How are divorce proceedings coming along, Major?" asked Mother, not mincing her words.

"Slowly, ma'am. I have Major Bradley intervening on my behalf, but it is just a matter of time now."

Father said, "We look forward to welcoming you as a son-in-law."

"Thank you, sir," he replied stiffly.

"Do your people know the situation here?" Mother asked.

"Yes. Of course, Henry knows. I have written a letter home to Vermont explaining my course of action. There has been no reply, I'm afraid."

"When do you think we will be able to marry?" I asked.

"First of all, I have decided to resign my commission. I expect sometime in March we will be free to marry."

"No one here in Fairfax Courthouse can issue a marriage license, Major," I said.

"We'll just have to get married without one," he said.

I said, "I cannot do that. Check in Washington City. You should probably not come here again, Major. I fear that you will be apprehended by Mosby."

Father stated, "In order to avoid a possible interruption of the ceremony by raiding bands, the wedding should be in Washington."

Major stammered a bit, and then said, "I would offer my hotel as the ceremonial place, but the hotel is full of Federals, and is in a bit of disrepair. All of my fellow hotelkeepers in town offer one another a 'professional courtesy' to use their hotels for events. My brother Caleb runs the Ebbitt House now, and I'm sure he would acquiesce to a ceremony there. On second thought, I recommend the Metropolitan Hotel, formerly known as Brown's Hotel, as it is more elegant and suitable for our joyous event."

I wondered just how embarrassed the major felt at marrying a Rebel, that he would not want it widely publicized at his own hotel!

"I know the Metropolitan Hotel is nice. There should not be as many Federals milling about in that hotel as in yours," said Mother knowingly.

"Does that mean that you and your family will transport yourselves to the Metropolitan Hotel on our wedding day?"

"Absolutely not!" exclaimed Father. "I suspect that we are more in danger from your men, than from Mosby, and with you in the conveyance we are assured safe passage."

Major stood up abruptly and said, "I'm due back at headquarters and must leave now. Seeing you was pleasant, as always; I will return next week."

After he left, my parents and I stared at each other.

"Was it something I said?" asked Mother.

"He is a moody man. He has a lot on his mind right now. Must you be so abrupt and nosy about his affairs, Mother?"

"I am only showing motherly concern for a daughter whom I love."

The next day, I wrote a letter to Major:

> *I suffered very much with the headache yesterday evening; and when the intense pain came on, my thought reverted to you and all your kind sympathy. Your gentle attention lived again in my memory, intensified by the thought that we are now parted—that sixteen cruel miles stretch their length between us. The fact is Major, I <u>miss you</u>. I <u>want</u> to <u>see</u> you. I can't get accustomed to your absence; when a bell rings I jump as if to meet you, but alas, "he comes not!"*
>
> *Ma was <u>very</u> much worried and disappointed yesterday at your reserved manners, she thought you were displeased at something—what was the matter? I felt your altered behavior very sensibly; I think and hope however, I could have brought a smile by less animated talk. Am I mistaken?*
>
> *Come whenever you can, and write as often as you feel like it. <u>Don't forget</u> me and stay away from pretty young girls especially Blanche Helm.*

> *Yours faithfully,*
> *Antonia.*
>
> *They say a lady's postscript is invariably the most important part of her letter, I leave you to judge of it's correctness in this case, the pith of mine being—have you seen Major Bradley, and what does he say?*

I expressed in my letters what I could not say to Major in person. Writing provided a catharsis for me to be able to write my innermost feelings:

> *Tuesday, February 2, 1864*
>
> *I miss you, and wish you were with me right now. I am pleased to hear that your wife is being cooperative. Is it not remarkable that "<u>that person</u>" won't be accommodating enough to march out of the world, when <u>we</u> wish it so earnestly? I hope she may prove like our old cook, who deliberately and firmly made up her mind to die, whether she had disease enough to kill her or not. Now Major, "isn't it a consummation devoutly to be wished for"—that she may follow Aunt Margaret's worthy example? Another solution of the difficulty would be to bring about a match between her and Major Bradley (is he single?); if she should wish to marry of course, she'd want her freedom and in that case could liberate you. Suggest it to Maj. B. Above all, don't let her hear <u>my</u> name. I think if in addition to my other troubles, an infuriated female was to start*

in pursuit; I should show the white feather and take refuge in inglorious flight. If you have reason to mention me where it will reach her, call me Miss Smith (cousin of <u>Colonel Smith</u> of last Sunday's notoriety.)

Don't be surprised at my flow of spirits. You must remember I have no Major Bradley to depress me by long prosy law talks, but instead of that the pleasant countenance and agreeable conversation of Lieutenant Henry Gawthrop. Sad to relate he expects to leave tomorrow; can't you use your influence for the 4th Delaware to remain longer?

Am I not a good girl to more than fulfill a promise? I said I'd write half a dozen lines a day; this is only Tuesday, and see how many half dozens are on this sheet. I hope you appreciate the magnanimity of such conduct. I charge you eight full pages for it. Let me know which style you prefer—the <u>sentimental</u> or <u>comic</u>, neither is exhausted, and I can enlarge indefinitely on both: just specify your choice.

Write immediately, if not sooner.

Yours faithfully,
Antonia

Our love affair progressed to the point that we were both "all consumed" with thoughts of each other. I never knew I had so much passion stored up in me.

Chapter Forty-seven

Planning the Wedding, February-March 1864

I felt reassured to know that a wedding was in my imminent future. We planned to marry as soon as possible after a Washington City judge granted the divorce, even if it meant last minute scurrying. For that reason, Mother and I did as much as possible now. My cedar hope chest bulged with exquisitely embroidered items—table, bath, bed, and personal. Most young women started working on their hope chest items at a young age, and I was no exception. Any work that I could do by hand, such as quilted and knitted items, was a part of my dowry. Our local seamstress made me two velvet dresses, a black silk traveling dress, and a visiting and reception dress of maroon velvet. Mother made me lace flounces, an evening robe, and two fine cotton nightdresses. Jewelry and toiletries rounded out the collection. We had Major to thank for the supplies, which he obtained through his contacts in the North.

Major wrote me news that he resigned his commission on February 12, and awaited its acceptance. I wrote my beloved a letter on February 22, inquiring about his safety using a Falls Church route to get here from Alexandria. Mother reminded me to ask him about the marriage license.

"It would be just like a man to forget that most important of documents," she said with a smile.

I could not help but to add a witticism referring to his soon to be status as a civilian: "Your successor, Mr. Willard, will be as dear to me as the major."

One of our neighbors came over and congratulated me on my "recent marriage" to the newly decommissioned Joseph Willard. I included that erroneous remark in the same letter. Rumors flew around Fairfax Courthouse!

On a rainy March 1, Mother came into Pattie's and my room to join in the wedding planning conversation.

"I can tell he loves you, Antonia. Whenever a man smiles continuously at a woman, it is a sure sign," said Pattie.

"The experienced woman speaks," said Mother laughingly. She looked at me, "I have to admit, though, that you reciprocate your smiles equally, and I can also see abounding love between the two of you."

Pattie said, "I know you are superstitious, Antonia. Do you know this rhyme?"

She chanted:

Monday for health, Tuesday for wealth, Wednesday the best day of all;
Thursday for losses, Friday for crosses, And Saturday no luck at all.

I hugged Pattie for being the concerned younger sister. She would be my maid of honor with Rose Love as bridesmaid.

"I would not hesitate to get married on a Saturday! Although, God knows, our union needs all the luck it can get. Have any villagers made cruel remarks lately?" I asked Mother.

"They would not dare say anything to my face," Mother replied.

Pattie said, "You are so highly regarded in this village, Mother. Everyone likes you."

Mother and I had made a trip to Alexandria last month and commissioned a seamstress who owned her own shop to create my wedding gown. We gazed at the magnificent one-piece, silk frock; colored a brilliant burnt umber and green floral. The lined bodice, with stays, had a classic V-back construction with a modestly rounded jewel neckline and dropped shoulders. A pleated waistband, lined, trained skirt, full sleeves, and shallow cuffs showed the attention to details that the seamstress utilized.

My beige, kid leather shoes were trimmed with pale green ruffles.

Pattie and Rose wore similar gowns of a pale creamy tan, but the material was not as fine.

Some brides were choosing white dresses as it symbolized joy, but I liked the way that the pale tan color, known as umber, made my complexion glow. Other brides chose a purple dress, which represented the honor and courage of our fallen soldier boys, but that color did not flatter me.

I would wear short off-white lace gloves, even though the wedding location was a hotel instead of a church. I had a long lace veil that lay flat on my head, held in place by combs, which Mother wore at her wedding.

Pattie sang, "Something old, something new, something borrowed, something blue, and a silver sixpence in her shoe."

"All right," I laughed. Mother's pearl necklace is old, my dress is new, I am borrowing Mother's wedding veil, and my dress has a navy blue silk band around the bottom. Do you have a silver sixpence I can put in my shoe?"

I knew Pattie had no money at all, and she looked at me curiously.

"I bet Major does. He is richer than God," she said.

"Pattie!" reproached Mother.

"Well, it is true," she retorted.

Mother changed the subject, "The wearing of blue dates back to biblical times when the color blue represented purity and fidelity."

"Appropriate for me," I said, smiling. "Mother, I am so worried that Major will be stopped by a Confederate raiding party on the way to escort us to the hotel for the wedding. Can't we meet him there? Besides, I thought the groom should not see the bride until the ceremony."

"In these times, customs have to be put aside. Don't you think that Father and I are worried about being stopped by Federals and told to go back home? With Major in the carriage with us, we will have some protection."

"So, the four of us will be in one carriage, and Pattie, Clanie and Rose Love in the one following?"

"Yes. Mathilde and Octavia will watch Frank here at home."

That evening, a telegram arrived for us from a lieutenant in Stuart's horse artillery, regretting to inform us that Charlie had been killed in a skirmish.

Our pain was no different from the thousands of other families who had lost a loved one, although I never realized just how painful that could be. I felt helpless because there was nothing I could do. We didn't know when we would be able to bury his body, or even if we would get it back. We all went to bed brokenhearted.

The next morning, Jeb Stuart sent a personal note of apology. He explained that there had been a misidentification of the dead soldier, and that Charlie was fine. Under these circumstances of extreme mood changes in our household, Major drew up his galloping horse in front of the house, ran up the front path, and knocked rapidly on the front door.

Mathilde opened it and let him in.

"Where is Antonia?" I heard him ask Mathilde with great excitement.

"She is in the parlor," she replied.

"Major, what brings you here so unexpectedly in the middle of the week?" I asked as I came to the door.

"I have news. May we talk privately?"

We went into the parlor and sat down.

After informing him what was transpiring in our household and our terrible scare, I asked, "Did you see any pickets along the road on the way?"

"Not a soldier in sight. My big news—my resignation was accepted yesterday."

I kissed his cheek and smiled. "Tomorrow you go before the judge about the divorce. I hope I can give you congratulations on a more delightful release than from the army."

Father entered the parlor and said, "I guess Antonia told you about our grief, followed by pure relief that we all experienced over the last twelve hours."

"Yes sir. I am a civilian now, sir, and hope to befriend myself to you, your family, and your entire village."

"You became a friend when you helped Antonia," Father said.

"Mrs. Love just spoke of you fondly the other day, and the other neighbors do not consider you an enemy," I said.

Major said, "I am still loyal to the government, however. Just as all who take the Oath of Allegiance are loyal . . ."

I interrupted, "My dear Major, no one has ever accused you of being anything but the most decided unionist and I love you none the less for it. With all my heart I do believe in one union—do you know what it is?"

Everyone laughed at that and we continued to work out the details of the wedding. Unfortunately, Major's family from Vermont would not be able to attend, but he expected Henry and his family, and Caleb to be there.

I murmured to Major, "Edwin will be with us in spirit. I'm sure he will smile down on us from heaven."

Major nodded stoically, and our visit ended with high expectations for our joyful occasion.

My next letter from Major described his divorce proceedings:

> *On March 2, Caroline and I were required to go before a judge at the courthouse, sitting in equity. I described to the judge the sad circumstances of our marriage and life together. My wife was calm and agreeable to the financial settlement that the lawyers had worked out. The judge, as respondent, stated that he believed it better that the marriage should be severed and joined Caroline in her petition. He felt that divorce would promote "Happiness of both."*

I felt so relieved that the last barrier to our marriage was eliminated that I wore a smile on my face all day.

We received a letter on March 3 from Charlie, bivouacked in Albemarle County, six miles north of Charlottesville. He told us about the Battle of Rio Hill that he fought on February 26, 1864. The famed Union General, George Armstrong Custer, led a cavalry detachment to burn a railroad bridge across the beautiful Rivanna River—the river that had so struck me on my voyages to and from college. Custer's only opposition came from Confederate General Jeb Stuart's Horse Company. Charlie said that he and fellow infantrymen chased Custer out of Albemarle, but not before he burned the covered bridge and gristmill at Rio Mills.

On March 7, Major sent a note saying: "I shall come for Antonia on the morning of the tenth."

Chapter Forty-eight

Our Wedding Day, March 10, 1864

My wedding day had finally arrived. Pattie and Mother, more nervous than I, fluttered about aimlessly. So many young women whom I knew married for convenience or money. I was ecstatic that I could marry the man I loved. I also felt fortunate that my circumstances allowed me my choice of husband.

My family had arisen early, and we ate a very light snack, as we would be dining on a wedding breakfast following the ceremony. I packed my luggage for my wedding trip to Philadelphia.

Mother handed me a package that had just arrived. I opened it to find a quilt—the same one that I had worked on in Warrenton. The central medallion quilt, with a row of nine-patch squares around it, was beautifully finished with embroidered names of the quilters and the date forever stitched as part of it.

Mother examined the quilt, and then said, "You and your friends did fine handwork on this. You should be pleased."

Pattie said, "If you sleep under a new quilt, your dreams will come true."

"It will be a family heirloom, I'm sure." I put the quilt down and started pacing the room, in a fretful state. "I hope nothing has happened to Major. I wish he would get here."

Pattie and Rose, in my bedroom, assisted me with my toilette. Pattie brushed my hair until it gleamed, then we piled it on top of my head. Rose advised me on how much rouge to use and used my kohl pencil to line my eyes and eyebrows.

Rose laughed at my primping and said seriously, "You better consult your mirror as often as you please now, because once your toilette is complete, you may not look again or it will be 'dreadful unlucky.'"

"I have had all the dreadful luck that I am entitled to in this life!" I said lightly.

The time had come to get dressed. First, I put on my short-sleeved chemise, followed by my pantalettes. I wore a corset on top of the chemise. My caged crinoline was composed of a series of hoops of varying sizes suspended from strips of tape that descended from my waist. Pattie pinned a small pouch to my wedding petticoat.

"This pouch contains a small piece of bread, cloth, wood, and a single one-dollar bill," she said.

This ensured that there would be enough food, clothes, shelter, and money for Major and me.

She and Rose assisted me with arranging all my garments and in fastening my dress. My attendants dressed in their new outfits with white crocuses in their hair. Mother came into the room and placed the veil that she had worn at her wedding on my head.

"Thank you, Mother. This will protect me from evil spirits floating around me during my wedding day." My lacy veil stopped about twelve inches from the floor.

"Nonsense, child," she retorted.

To my dismay, I saw tears trickling down her cheeks. I hugged her and wiped away her tears.

"I hope it is true that I am not losing a daughter, but gaining a son-in-law," she said.

"We will visit often. Just think of the fun that you, Pattie, and I will have in Washington City when you visit me! Mother, really, save your tears for the ceremony!"

Rose handed me my bouquet, symbolizing a woman in bloom, which consisted of lavender crocuses and snowdrops, tied together with a lace bow. Snowdrops had the traditional meaning of "hope." The bouquet enhanced my burnt umber dress. We went downstairs, at last.

Father said, "We are hoodwinking the villagers, aren't we?'

"This is not the secret you might think," I replied with a laugh.

Major arrived and gazed speechlessly at me. "You are the loveliest woman I have ever seen," he finally said. He handed me a small package. I opened it and found a solid gold pendant watch, engraved with both our initials and the date.

"Thank you, Major. I will treasure it. Turn around please, so I can admire your attire," I said. "I have never seen you dressed in clothes other than a uniform."

He had chosen a shirt with a separate collar, cuff, and removable bib front with a black wide-cut cravat. He wore an extremely fancy silver silk vest under a black, single-breasted tailcoat. The tailcoat, with knee length skirt in the back, had a short pointed front with only the top button fastened, thereby allowing more of his vest to be seen. His black trousers were gray-striped. A pocket watch and fob prominently hung from his front vest pocket. He wore white gloves and carried a walking stick.

"I am astonished, Major, at your transformation. How distinguished you look! You even got a hair cut!"

"Thank you. Does that mean my appearance was undistinguished before?"

"You know what I mean. It is a different kind of distinguished."

"My brother, Henry, and his wife will meet us at the hotel. We should go now."

Father had arranged for our carriage and one other from the livery stable to be brought to the front of our house. As planned, Clanie, Pattie, and Rose rode in the first carriage, with Father, Mother, Joseph, and I following. We sent the other carriage on ahead of us, to avoid being too conspicuous. Octavia and Mathilde stood at the door with little Frank. As our carriage pulled away from the house, Frank waved goodbye. At the corner of Fairfax Street, we overheard the conversation of two soldiers talking in front of the Willcoxon Tavern.

"Levi McCormick, you think you know it all," said a young private.

"I'm telling you, Jim. One of our Majors is marrying a Rebel here at the Courthouse."

Major looked at me bashfully, and we all pretended that we had not heard it. Certainly, we were the talk of the Union camps.

Major pulled from his pocket the pass that J. A. Slippen, A.A.G. had written for him:

Headquarters Department of Washington
Washington, March 8, 1864

Pass: Mr. J. C. Willard and two friends with conveyance and driver over any bridge to Fairfax Court House, Va. and return. This pass will expire March 13, 1864.

By command of Major General Augur.

"I feel comforted knowing that we have this pass," I said.

We traveled on the pike to Alexandria, and then planned to ride a train into Washington. We had not gone far out of Fairfax when a Rebel soldier stepped from behind some roadside bushes and halted us. I recognized him as one of Mosby's men.

"Who goes there?" he asked.

"Ford of Fairfax," said Father. "I am taking my daughter to Washington to see a doctor."

The sentry did not look into the carriage to verify the statement, and let us pass.

I leaned close to Major and closed my eyes.

"You're shivering," Major said. He wrapped a wool blanket around me.

"Do you have the license?" I asked.

"Yes. My minister, the Reverend Phineas Gurley, issued one to us. He is the pastor of Lincoln's New York Avenue Presbyterian Church. You will like him. He is a fine pastor and a good public speaker."

We arrived at the train station and my entire party boarded the train for the short ride to Washington City.

We took a carriage from the train station to the Metropolitan Hotel and walked through the entrance. I had been there many times before the war, and admired the wood paneling on the walls. Ornate, carved wooden pillars and moldings festooned each entranceway. Lush velvet draperies hung from the windows and gilt framed pictures decorated the walls. I saw an oval mirror sitting on an end table and prevented myself from looking just in time to avoid terrible bad luck! The worn Oriental carpets appeared to have been just recently cleaned.

A porter took my luggage to a room reserved for me, and then we all went to the private dining room designated as the venue for our ceremony.

Pattie, Clanie, Rose, and the Reverend Phineas Gurley awaited us, happy to see that we had arrived. Caleb Willard looked dashing. Henry, Sarah, and little Henry arrived from New York yesterday on the train. Sarah had the kindest face I had ever seen. I greeted her with a hug and said, "This must bring back memories of your own wedding."

"It does, but we married at Willard's. Circumstances have changed, haven't they? This hotel is much more appropriate for you two. I'm so happy that we will be sisters. Meet your almost nephew, Henry."

I reached down and solemnly shook little Henry's hand. "You look so grown-up in your little suit. I hope I get to see you more often."

Major introduced the clergyman to me.

"I am so pleased to meet you, Reverend Gurley," I said.

"Likewise. Are you ready? Let's get started then."

We took our places at the area set aside for us at the front of the room. Flowers adorned the room, with candles burning softly. My two bridesmaids stood at my left side, with Pattie holding my bouquet and gloves.

Henry and Caleb stood to Joseph's right. Our few other seated guests watched as we exchanged traditional wedding vows and Reverend Gurley pronounced us "man and wife." I would have preferred the phrase "husband and wife," but Reverend Gurley refused to alter the service.

Although rare, I insisted on a double ring ceremony, telling Major that a visual reminder to the world of our union was a good thing. We slipped each ring on the third finger on the other's left hand. We had our plain gold bands engraved with our initials and the date. Joseph lifted my veil and gave me a long kiss on the lips. A photographer took a few wedding photos and then discreetly left.

With only twelve of us, the wedding breakfast was set up in that same room. We all sat around one big rectangular table, draped with fine white linen. Candles lit the room, and a violinist played music. Major and I sat side-by-side at the midpoint of the table, and my father and mother took the head and foot seats, showing honor to our guests. Servants gave us lavish quantities of eggs, cured ham, bacon, cinnamon buns, hash brown potatoes, and coffee.

Our two-tiered wedding cake had plenty of white icing. I planned the tradition of ribbon pulling even though I only had two bridesmaids to participate. The baker had embedded charms in the frosting of the cake, attached to ribbons. Each bridesmaid pulled one ribbon and received a special souvenir of our big event.

"I received a pansy emblem," said Pattie.

"That is the symbol for blooming love," I said.

Rose pulled her ribbon and withdrew a church charm. "I hope I am indeed the next to be married," said Rose with a smile.

Just for fun, I tugged on a ribbon, but it broke before the charm came fully out of the cake. A heart in hand meant a life filled with love. I looked at Major and pecked him on the lips. "Our lives together will be overflowing with love!" I exclaimed.

Joseph and I cut the cake together, his hand over mine, and then we shared portions by feeding each other. It was then time for toasting with fine wines.

Henry stood up, raised his glass, and said, "Although I am called the best man, it is truly Joseph who is the best man I know. Love and cherish your wife, Brother, and welcome to our family, Antonia. Here is to the health and happiness of both of you."

We raised our glasses and drank. More toasts and well wishes were duly proffered and acknowledged.

After our breakfast, Pattie, Rose, and I slipped out so that I could change into my going-away outfit. We went to my hotel room, and I flung myself on the bed, stretching my arms overhead.

"Careful, Sister. You'll rip your dress."

"I'm so happy to be married to Major, that it would not matter."

"Are you always going to call him Major?" asked Rose.

"It suits him. I like it better than Joseph. Joseph sounds too stuffy."

Rose timidly asked me, "You'll tell me all about your wedding trip afterward, won't you?"

I knew what information she wanted. "Don't you worry, Rose, I promise to 'tell all.' Do you think you might need some carnal knowledge soon?"

Rose blushed and replied, "Not too soon."

I gave each bridesmaid a flower from my bouquet.

I put on my gray silk traveling dress and bonnet. Out of respect to the sensitivity of Joseph, I chose not to wear something too conspicuous, as he said he did not want people to know that he was newly married.

We rejoined the rest of the wedding party to say our farewells. It was two o'clock and we needed to catch the train to Philadelphia. Henry preceded us to the station to look after our luggage.

I kissed Mother and Father goodbye, and we set off in a carriage drawn by four white horses, amidst a shower of rice, as the new Mr. and Mrs. Willard. The wedding guests threw satin slippers after us, and one landed in the carriage.

"We will have good luck forever, Husband," I said dreamily.

"It is a left slipper, so all the better, Mrs. Willard," he replied.

Chapter Forty-nine

Our Wedding Trip, March 1864

Now we had two weeks before us to really get to know each other, without the constant pressure of family and friends. The 134-mile train ride from Washington City to Philadelphia via Baltimore took six hours. I recalled my travels to Baltimore only the previous year on the B & O and rejoiced in my improved circumstances.

The railroad depot on Market Street was across the street from the La Pierre House, located on the West side of Broad Street at Samsom Street. Gas street lamps and trees spaced evenly along the cobblestone street. A police officer stood at attention on a street corner. I noticed the sculpture of an eagle on the roof and the ornately decorated cornice as we approached the massive six-story building. To the right of the hotel we saw a Real Estate Broker and Conveyancer business, and a paper company to the left. Our carriage stopped at the front door. The driver unloaded our luggage and a bellman whisked it away into the hotel. A door attendant greeted us with, "Welcome to America's most luxurious hotel—La Pierre House."

Major informed me, "This building, built in 1853, was designed by John McArthur, Jr. It is the grandest hotel in Philadelphia—I only want the best for you, my dear."

Being so awestruck at the sophistication of Philadelphia, I only smiled back gratefully.

I waited in the reception room while Major went to the office to register us. The room struck me very forcibly; the carpet was very light, the chairs and sofas covered with white, the curtains white, and a great deal of marble in the room. Major rejoined me and I laughingly said to him, "This is bride-like indeed!"

"Wait until you see our room," he replied. "It is the bridal suite, and should be magnificent."

A bellhop showed us to our room. We stopped at the door to our room and Major suddenly lifted me up and carried me over the threshold.

"This is to protect you from evil spirits," he said.

"I thought you didn't believe in superstitions," I replied.

"Better to be safe than sorry."

I suspected he just wanted to touch me.

He tipped the bellhop, who thanked him and said, "Supper is downstairs in the dining hall at seven o'clock."

I looked around at the spacious suite that we would call home for a while. The décor, similar to the reception room downstairs, had plenty of white marble, white carpeting, and white and gold decorations. Gas lamps lit the room. The sitting room appeared comfortable and I walked through it to peer into the bedroom. A large bed stood in the center of the room with a white canopy and eyelet lace hanging down from the sides. A white satin coverlet covered the bed.

I saw indoor plumbing and thankfully headed toward the water faucet to freshen up after my journey. I had to admit I felt weak, and not a bit hungry, but I didn't want Major to know that. He distractedly glanced through *The Daily Age* newspaper.

"Would you like to take in a show at the Chestnut Theatre?" he asked me as he looked up from the newspaper.

"What is playing there?"

"*Romeo and Juliet*."

"How appropriate; I would love to see it!"

"Shall we go down to supper now, darling?" Major asked me.

"Would you mind terribly if I had something sent up? Please go without me. I just feel the need to rest some more."

"Very well. I will tell a servant to come and take your order—whatever you want, and I'll be back soon," he said as he left.

Shortly, I answered the knock on the door, and a servant showed me a menu.

"Just tea and crackers, please, in one-half hour."

"But ma'am, look at all the wonderful delicacies we have. Surely you want more than tea and crackers?"

"Not now," I replied.

I went back to the bed and pulled back the covers to find fine, tightly woven cotton sheets. I plumped two pillows behind my back and took some deep breaths. I felt better already. Was I experiencing nervousness because it was my wedding night? I wanted so much to please my husband, and I hoped that my very first sexual experience would be satisfying to me as well.

A knock on the door told me that my tea had arrived. The servant brought the tray into the sitting room and set the table nicely for me. I noticed that he brought me a basket of bread, with jam and butter, as well as crackers. I thanked and tipped him, as he left. I poured from the teapot and thankfully sipped at my tea. I even managed to eat the delicious bread.

Major soon returned, and paced restlessly around the room, looking at me frequently to see if I had finished drinking. He sat next to me and playfully ran his hands through my hair. After another ten minutes went by and I still sipped my beverage, he said, "Are you still fooling over your tea?"

"Yes, I know it's ridiculous, dear. I'm through. Have you seen the bedroom?"

We walked together into the room, lit only by candles, and before I could comment on anything, Major started undressing before me as if I were a statue.

"I am being so free on purpose, darling, as I am determined to break down all restraints between us and to put you at your ease." By this time, he was in his underwear.

"Great God—you think this puts me at my ease?" I queried.

"This is me, who I am. Do you desire me?" he asked as he stripped nude.

"You know I desire you." I came close to him. We put our arms around each other and kissed passionately. He unhooked my dress in the back, and I struggled to wriggle out, but it caught on the crinoline before it fell to the floor. Next, he stripped my crinoline from me, leaving my chemise and pantalettes. Soon they joined the pile on the floor. He removed the pins from my hair, and it fell loose and flowing, over my bare breasts. We fell on the bed together, skin against skin.

I had never seen a naked man, except for anatomical pictures in textbooks. I shyly and furtively glanced down and then back up again. He must have seen a look of amazement on my face, as he said,

"You excite me so much, and we have waited so long for this final consummation of our love. Touch me."

I did as he asked. He then touched me in places that had never been touched before. We explored each other's bodies, reveling in the uniqueness and contrast in each other's textures and scents. When our consummative moment occurred, he moved gently, and I was so beside myself with passion at that time that I only experienced pleasure, as we became one through our union. Afterwards, as we lay entwined side by side, I said with a deep, contented sigh, "You succeeded in putting me at my ease much better than I supposed could be the case."

Epilogue

Antonia and Joseph Willard had three children together: Joseph Edward, May 1, 1865 to April 4, 1924; Charles F., April 13, 1867 to September 2, 1867; Archie F., February 9, 1871 to February 9, 1871. Antonia died on February 14, 1871, due to childbirth complications, at the age of thirty-two, after only seven years of marriage.

E.R. Ford died suddenly, of paralysis, on November 26, 1871, aged fifty-eight. *The Alexandria Gazette* stated, "He had acquired a character for justice and integrity rarely equaled."

Charlie Ford died on May 25, 1864, aged twenty-four, after the Battle of Hanover Court House, also known as North Anna. He was in Company 2nd, Stuart's Light Horse Artillery.

Clanie Ford married Mary McBride at the close of the war, and they had one son. Clanie died in 1889, aged forty-four.

Pattie Ford married Lieutenant McKim Holliday Wells on February 25, 1874. They had four children. She died in 1888, at the age of thirty-eight.

Frank R. Ford went to VMI in 1873. He was a medical student in June 1880. He married Barbara Bingham and they had five children. He died on February 17, 1904, aged forty-seven.

Joseph Clapp Willard never remarried. He spent the rest of his life mourning his beloved Antonia. In 1892, he became the sole owner of Willard's after purchasing Henry A. Willard's interest. He died on January 17, 1897, aged seventy-seven.

James Ewell Brown (Jeb) Stuart was probably the most famous cavalryman of the Civil War. On May 11, 1864, during Grant's drive on Richmond, he halted Sheridan's cavalry at Yellow Tavern on the outskirts of Richmond. In the fight, he was mortally wounded and died the next day in Richmond at the age of thirty-one. He left behind a wife, Flora, and four children. One of his true friends, John Esten Cooke, described his last moments:

> *As his life had been one of earnest devotion to the cause in which he believed, so his last hours were tranquil, his confidence in the mercy of heaven unfailing. When he was asked how he felt, he said, "Easy, but willing to die, if God and my country think I have done my duty." His last words were, "I am going fast now; I am resigned.*

God's will be done." As he uttered these words, he expired.

John Mosby was promoted to Colonel, Mosby's Rangers, or the 43rd Battalion of Virginia Cavalry, on December 7, 1864. He and his wife, Pauline, had four sons and four daughters. A son, George, died in 1873, and Pauline and an infant son, Alfred, died in 1876. John Mosby died in 1916, aged eighty-three.

John Gunnell, the Ford's bookkeeper, was wounded at the Battle of Gravelly Run on March 31, 1865 and became disabled from a gunshot wound. He died in May 1905, at age eighty-one.

John Esten Cooke married Mary Francis Page on September 18, 1867. He wrote a number of Civil War novels after the war, based on his experiences. He died in 1886, aged fifty-six.

Robert T. Love, a private in Company "K," 17th Virginia Infantry, died at age twenty-one from wounds received at the Battle of Seven Pines on May 31, 1862.

James Monroe Love, a private, Company "H," "Black Horse Troop," 4th Virginia Cavalry, joined the Black Horse when it was first organized and "became conspicuous in the Troop for gallant conduct." Jeb Stuart cited him for gallantry. On October 11, 1863, in Stephensburg, he wounded his arm, causing it to be amputated. He became a lawyer and judge in Fairfax Courthouse, and died on June 12, 1933, at the age of ninety.

Lewis C. Helm was a private in the Ordnance Department, a non-regimental group. He pined over Antonia for seven years while farming, until January 26, 1871, when he married Mary A. Clarke.

Family Tree of Antonia Ford

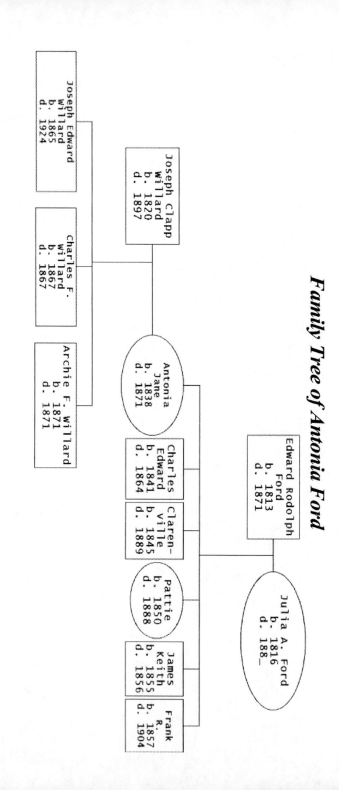

Joseph Clapp Willard
b. 1820
d. 1897

Antonia Jane
b. 1838
d. 1871

Edward Rodolph Ford
b. 1813
d. 1871

Julia A. Ford
b. 1816
d. 188_

Joseph Edward Willard
b. 1865
d. 1924

Charles F. Willard
b. 1867
d. 1867

Archie F. Willard
b. 1871
d. 1871

Charles Edward
b. 1841
d. 1864

Claren-ville
b. 1845
d. 1889

Pattie
b. 1850
d. 1888

James Keith
b. 1855
d. 1856

Frank R.
b. 1857
d. 1904

Sources

Manuscripts

City of Fairfax Historic Collections, Various letters and documents (11/12/63, 11/30/63, 12/63, 1/11/64, 1/12/64, 1/15/64, 1/30/64, 2/1/64, 2/2/64).

Ford, Antonia. Letters (4/21/61, 10/7/61, 11/25/61, 4/13/63, 4/63, 6/18/63, 6/26/63, 9/18/63, 12/31/63), Library of Congress, Manuscript Division, Willard Papers, Boxes 1, 198, 201, 202, 203, 204.

Harris, Rose R. *Rightly To Know A Man You Should Have Known His Ancestors.* Library of Congress, Manuscript Division, Willard Papers.

Published Firsthand Sources

Holy Bible. Revised Standard Version, Dallas, Texas: The Melton Book Company, 1952.

Hopkins, G.M. *Atlas of Fifteen Miles around Washington including Fairfax and Alexandria Counties,* C.E., Philadelphia, 1879.

Sansone, Cordelia Grantham. *Journey to Bloomfield,* self-published, 2004. Letters to and from Antonia Ford.

Secondary Sources

Bakeless, John. *Spies of the Confederacy,* New York: Dover Publications, Inc., 1970.

Brackman, Barbara. *Quilts from the Civil War,* California: C&T Publications, 1997.

City of Fairfax Public Information Office. *City of Fairfax Historic Sites,* Fairfax City, Virginia: MasterPrint, 1988.

Cooke, John Esten. *Surry of Eagle's Nest,* New York: G.W. Dillingham Co., 1894.

Coulling, Mary P. *The Lee Girls,* Winston Salem, North Carolina: J.F. Blair, 1987.

Detzer, David. *Donnybrook: the Battle of Bull Run,* New York: Harcourt Books, 2004.

Eskew, Garnett Laidlaw. *Willard's of Washington,* New York: Coward-McCann, Inc., 1954.

Evans, D'Anne. *The History of the Jerusalem Baptist Church 1840-1990,* Jerusalem Baptist Church, 1990.

Furgurson, Ernest, B. *Freedom Rising: Washington in the Civil War,* New York: Alfred A. Knopf, 2004.

Jensen, Oliver. *American Heritage History of Railroads in America,* New York: Random House, 1975.

Jones, Virgil Carrington. *Gray Ghosts and Rebel Raiders,* Atlanta: Mockingbird Books, 1956.

Kane, Harnett. *Spies for the Blue and Gray,* Garden City, New York: Doubleday, 1954.

Larson, Rebecca D. *Blue and Gray Roses of Intrigue,* Gettysburg, Pennsylvania: Thomas Publications, 1993.

Leech, Margaret. *Reveille in Washington 1860-1865,* New York: Harper & Brothers, 1941.

Leisch, Juanita. *An Introduction to Civil War Civilians,* Gettysburg, Pennsylvania: Thomas Publications, 1994.

Leisch, Juanita. *Who Wore What?: Women's Wear, 1861-1865*, Gettysburg, Pennsylvania: Thomas Publications, 1995.

Leonard, Elizabeth D. *All the Daring of a Soldier. Women of the Civil War Armies,* New York: W.W. Norton & Co., 1999.

Lossing, Benson J., LL.D. *Mathew Brady's Illustrated History of the Civil War,* New York: Portland House, 1988.

Markle, Donald E. *Spies & Spymasters of the Civil War*, New York: Hippocrene Books, 1994.

Martine, Arthur and R.L. Shep. *Civil War Era Etiquette,* Mendocino, California, 1988.

Massey, Mary E. *Women in the Civil War,* Lincoln, Nebraska: University of Nebraska Press, 1966, 1994.

Matusky, Gregory. *United States Secret Service,* New York: Chelsea House, 1988.

Montez, Lola. *Timeless Beauty: Advice to Ladies & Gentlemen,* Gettysburg, Pennsylvania.: Thomas Publications, 1998.

Netherton, Nan. *Fairfax, Virginia: A City Traveling Through Time,* Fairfax, Virginia: History of the City of Fairfax Round Table, Fairfax, 1997.

Oates, Stephen B. *A Woman of Valor. Clara Barton and the Civil War.* New York: Free Press, 1994.

Shepard, William. "Buckingham Female Collegiate Institute," *William and Mary College Quarterly Historical Magazine*, 2nd Serial Vol. 20, No. 2 (April 1940), 167-193, and No. 3 (July 1940), 345-368.

Simmons, Linda J. "The Antonia Ford Mystery," *Northern Virginia Heritage,* October 1985, 3-6, 20.

Sweig, Donald M., PhD. *Fairfax County and the War Between the States,* Official Publication of the Fairfax County Civil War Centennial Commission, First Edition, 1961. Reprinted 1987 by the Office of Comprehensive Planning, Fairfax County, Virginia.

Volo, Dorothy Denneen and Volo, James M. *Daily Life in Civil War America,* Westport, Connecticut: Greenwood Press, 1998.

Wert, Jeffery D. *Mosby's Rangers,* New York: Simon & Schuster, 1990.

Wise, Daniel. *Young Lady's Counselor*, New York: Carlton & Phillips, 1852.

Newspapers
Washington, D. C. - *The Alexandria Gazette, The Local News, Washington Star*
New York, N. Y. - *New York Times*
Nebraska - *Omaha Herald*, "Hints for Plains Travelers," 1877

Internet Sites
(All sites were re-accessed on 11/1/05 to verify existence.)

Adventures of Wells Fargo—Aboard the Stage, from Hints for Plains Travelers, 2005,
    http://www.wellsfargo.com/about/stories/ch1.jhtml
America's Civil War Links, 10/2005, http://home.ptd.net/~nikki/cwlinks.htm
Annie Jones, Custer's Cape Cod Mistress by Evan J. Albright, 12/01,
    http://www.capecodconfidential.com/cccanniejones011230.shtml
Antonia Ford by John T. Marck, http://www.aboutfamouspeople.com/article1037.html
Antonia Ford, About, J. Lewis, 2004,
    http://womenshistory.about.com/library/bio/blbio_antonia_ford.htm
Antonia Ford, Who Was, http://users.erols.com/kfraser/fairfax/antonia.html
Antonio Ford, http://home.att.net/~mysmerelda/antonio-spy.html
Antonia Willard (Memory) American Treasures of the Library of Congress,
    http://www.loc.gov/exhibits/treasures/trm160.html
Battalion Rosters, http://www.bonnieblue.net/battalion_rosters.htm
Battle of Groveton, Chapter 8 of *The Army Under Pope* by John Codman Ropes, 2/02,
    http://www.civilwarhome.com/groveton.htm
Black Horse Cavalry, by Lynn Hopewell, 2002,
    http://blackhorsecavalry.org/files/ROSTER%20August%202002%20special.pdf
Brentsville, Virginia, The Friends of Brentsville Historic Centre, 11/05,
    http://brentsville.org/heritage.htm
Brief Timeline of American Literature and Events 1860-1869, 6/05,
    http://www.wsu.edu/~campbelld/amlit/1860.htm
Centreville, Virginia, Celebrating Our Heritage by Cheryl Repetti, 2005,
    http://www.centrevilleva.org/index.cfm?action=a26&id=292,4097,48100001
City Point, Diary, Civil War 1864-1865 Diary of George Taylor Granger, 1827-1912,
    http://users.htcomp.net/dogpatch/grangerdiary.html
City Point, Virginia, http://www.craterroad.com/citypoint.html
Civil War Calendar, This Week in the Civil War, 11/99,
    http://www.civilweek.com/calendar/cal61.htm
Civil War Etiquette, The Washington Artillery - 5th Company / 6th Massachusetts Light
    Artillery Home Page, http://www.geocities.com/Heartland/Woods/3501/index.html
Civil War Hospitals, Surgeons, and Nurses, from Henry Steele Commager's "The Blue and
    The Gray," Volume II, Chapter XXII, 2/02,
    http://www.civilwarhome.com/hospitalssurgeonsnurses.htm
Civil War in America Timeline of Battles, http://www.americancivilwar.com/tl/timeline.html
Civil War in the Shenandoah Valley,
    http://www.angelfire.com/va3/valleywar/people/mosby.html
Civil War in Virginia, http://www.virginiaplaces.com/military/civwar.html
Civil War Soldiers and Sailors System, National Park Service,
    http://www.itd.nps.gov/cwss/soldiers.htm
Civil War Terminology, 21st Missouri Volunteer Infantry Regiment by Brenda Schnurrer,
    2001, http://www.geocities.com/mo21infantry/cwterms.htm
Civil War Traveler, Northern Va.: Timeline of Civil War Events, 2/05,
    http://www.civilwar-va.com/virginia/north/no-timeline.html

Civil War—Uniforms, by Christopher Wagner, 10/02,
 http://www.histclo.hispeed.com/essay/war/cwa/cwa-uni.html
Civil War, Early Weather Events, from *Washington Weather*,
 http://www.weatherbook.com/early.html
Confederate Officers, CS Officers, 1999, http://members.aol.com/awill84810/csofficers.htm
Cooke, Biography, U. of Va. Library,
 http://hatbox.lib.virginia.edu/servlet/SaxonServlet?source=http://etext.lib.virginia.edu/eaf
 /bios/eafAlli.xml&style=http://etext.lib.virginia.edu/eaf/bios/biostyle.xsl&clear-
 stylesheet-cache=yes&id=jec
Cooke, Genealogy, Pendleton Family, http://www.geocities.com/janet_ariciu/Pendleton.html
Cooke, John Esten, U. of Va. Library, http://etext.lib.virginia.edu/eaf/authors/jec.htm
Duties of Army Personnel, Organization and Duties of the Staff by Captain W.D. Connor,
 1904, http://www-cgsc.army.mil/carl/download/lectures/Connor.pdf
Drewry's Bluff—Ft. Darling, http://www.nps.gov/rich/ri_drew.htm
Fairfax County Civil War Sites Inventory,
 http://www.co.fairfax.va.us/parks/resources/civilwarinventory.pdf
Fairfax Court House, Skirmish at, June 1, 1861, Living History Society, 2005,
 http://www.fairfaxrifles.org/marr.html
General Irvin McDowell's Report of 1st Manassas (1st Bull Run), The American Civil War,
 http://www.swcivilwar.com/McDowellReport1stManassas.html
Harland, Marion Autobiography; "The Story of a Long Life,"
 http://docsouth.unc.edu/harland/harland.html#harland363
History of Sewing Machines, Stitches—The History of Sewing Machines by Mary Bellis,
 http://inventors.about.com/library/inventors/blsewing_machine.htm
Homespun Clubs, Southern Homespun: Articles in Civil War Era Newspapers,
 http://www.uttyl.edu/vbetts/homespun.htm
Innocence Lost: The Sad Side of 19th Century Childhood, 3/04,
 http://www.geocities.com/victorianlace10/home.html
Inventions: 1850-1900, http://www.krysstal.com/inventions_12.html
Inventors and Inventions from 1851-1900, 2005,
 http://www.zoomschool.com/inventors/1800b.shtml
James Ewell Brown Stuart Biography, Source: "Who Was Who In The Civil War" by
 Stewart Sifakis, http://www.civilwarhome.com/stuartbi.htm
Jeb Stuart's Children, http://genforum.genealogy.com/cgi-
 bin/pageload.cgi?jeb::stuart::1701.html
Jeb Stuart at the Battle of Gettysburg, from "The Life and Campaigns of Major-General JEB
 Stuart" by H. B. McClellan, A.M., http://www.civilwarhome.com/stuartatgettysburg.htm
Lafayette Baker, http://www.spartacus.schoolnet.co.uk/USAbakerLaf.htm
Library Historical Newspaper Index Search, Fairfax County, Virginia,
 http://www.fairfaxcounty.gov/library/newsindex/default.asp
Love, James Monroe, Virginia Military Institute Archives,
 http://www.vmi.edu/archives/records/smith/59aug001.html
Love, James Monroe, Virginia Military Institute Archives,
 http://www.vmi.edu/archives/archiverosters/Details.asp?ID=1400&rform=search
Military Etiquette, Dan and Nathan Lee,
 http://www.geocities.com/Heartland/Woods/3501/favorite.htm
Military Map of Philadelphia, 1861, http://memory.loc.gov/cgi-
 bin/map_item.pl?data=/home/www/data/gmd/gmd382/g3824/g3824p/cw0358100.sid&ite
 mLink=r?ammem/gmd:@filreq((@field(NUMBER+@band(g3824p+cw0358100))+@fiel
 d(COLLID+milmap))&title=Military+map+of+Philadelphia+1861-1865+Mosby Raid
Mosby in the Shenandoah Valley, The Civil War in the Shenandoah Valley, 9/01,
 http://www.angelfire.com/va3/valleywar/people/mosby.html

Mosby, John Singleton Biography, Source: "Who Was Who in the Civil War" by Stewart Sifakis, http://www.civilwarhome.com/mosbybio.htm

Mosby, Memoirs of Colonel John S. Mosby, http://docsouth.unc.edu/mosby/mosby.html

Mosby, Reports of Capt. John S. Mosby, Virginia Cavalry, http://www.civilwarhome.com/mosby.htm

Norfolk Highlights 1584-1881, by George Holbert Tucker, Norfolk Historical Society, http://www.norfolkhistorical.org/highlights/47.html

"Old Capitol and Its Inmates. By a Lady, Who Enjoyed the Hospitalities of the Government for a Season." by Virginia Lomax, http://docsouth.unc.edu/lomax/lomax.html

Old Capitol Prison (1862 description), source: New York Times, 19 April 1862, page 2, 8/05, http://freepages.military.rootsweb.com/~pa91/cmocp1.html

Ox Hill Battlefield, Historical Analysis by Mario Espinola, http://www.espd.com/salute/historicalanalysis.htm#9

Prisoner Exchange System, Source: Atlas Editions; Civil War Cards, http://www.wtv-zone.com/civilwar/exchange.html

Quilts and Quilters—Yesterday and Today, Womenfolk, http://www.womenfolk.com/

Quilts for Fundraising and Soldiers, America's Quilting History, http://www.womenfolk.com/quilting_history/civilwar.htm

Quilts, Civil War Era, by Vickie Rumble, http://www.geocities.com/BourbonStreet/Quarter/2926/Civil_War_Era_Quilts.html

Quilts-dating, Quilt History by Kris Driessen, http://www.quilthistory.com/dating_quilts.htm

Smith, William, "No Limit to Achievements of 'Extra Billy'," by John E. Carey, Washington Times, September 6, 2003, http://www.washingtontimes.com/civilwar/20030905-082356-8824r.htm

Stagecoach Travel and Etiquette, RomanceEverAfter, http://www.romanceeverafter.com/stagecoach_etiquette.htm

Stagecoach, The Columbia Encyclopedia, Sixth Edition. 2001-05, http://www.bartleby.com/65/st/stagecoa.html

Tea Leaves, http://www.soyouwanna.com/site/syws/tealeaves/tealeaves2.html

This Day in History, The History Channel, http://www.historychannel.com/tdih/tdih.jsp?month=10272954&day=10272994&cat=10272941

Victorian Dance, W.R. Donaldson, 2004, http://www.company-q.com/coq_dances.htm#jennylind

Victorian Era Names, G.M. Atwater, 12/04, http://freepages.genealogy.rootsweb.com/~poindexterfamily/OldNames.html

Victorian Holiday Traditions, Linda Ashley Leamer, http://www.teatimeworldwide.com/Tea_and_Women/victorian-traditions.html

Victorian Halloween, Halloween in Victorian America by Lesley Bannatyne, http://www.people.fas.harvard.edu/~bannatyn/articles.html#victorian

Victorian Halloween: Halloween stories, games, etc., http://www.victorianhalloween.com/

Victorian Parlour Games by Tamera Bastiaans, http://www.oldfashionedliving.com/parlour-games.html

Victorian Wedding Day, Welcome to Victoria's Wedding Day, 2/04, http://www.victoriaspast.com/VictorianWedding3/blushing.htm#breakfast

Victorian Wedding Traditions, "Bride and Groom Magazine, Inc.," 2004, http://www.brideandgroom.com/tradition.htm

Virginia Directory and Business Register, 1852, Elliott and Nye's, http://www.ls.net/~newriver/va/enve1852.htm

Vivandières, Civil War Vivandières and Daughters of the Regiment, Elizabeth Atkins, 2000, http://www.vivandiere.net/

Walt Whitman Notebook, The Library of Congress,
http://memory.loc.gov/cgibin/ampage?collId=whitman&fileName=wwhit094.data&recNum=149

Warrenton, March to Warrenton, Virginia, from *My Life in the Irish Brigade* by Private William McCarter, http://www.pasorobles-usa.com/warrenton.htm

Wide Awakes, 2002, http://lincoln.lib.niu.edu/gal/wideawak.html

Willard Family, A Register of Its Papers in the Library of Congress, http://www.loc.gov/rr/mss/text/willardf.html

About the Author

Karla Tysdal Vernon graduated from the Medical College of Virginia with a bachelor of science degree, and has worked as a medical technologist, software engineer, and textile artist. She lives in Vienna, Virginia, with her husband, two children, and two dogs. This is her first novel.